INTERNATIONAL ACCLAIM FOR
Brooklyn

"A novel that offers the reader serious pleasure. . . . A lovely, thoughtful book. I don't know of any contemporary writer of English prose who can outdo Tóibín for clarity, simplicity and elegance." — *The Telegraph*

"A small masterpiece." — *The Guardian*

"In spare yet delicate prose, Tóibín delineates characters desperately hiding their deepest emotions from each other and from themselves." — Montreal *Gazette*

"[Tóibín is] his generation's most gifted writer of love's complicated, contradictory power." — *Los Angeles Times*

"[A] masterly tale. . . . There is not a sentence or a thought out of place." — *Irish Times*

"A beautifully rendered portrait of Brooklyn and provincial Ireland in the 1950s. . . . Tóibín writes about women more convincingly, I think, than any other living, male novelist." — Zoe Heller, author of *The Believers*

"Tóibín's prose is as elegant in its simplicity as it is complex in the emotions it evokes." — *New York Times Magazine*

"A compelling characterization of a woman caught between two worlds. . . . A fine and touching novel, persuasive proof of Tóibín's ever-increasing skills and range." — *Booklist* (starred review)

Also by Colm Tóibín

Brooklyn

A NOVEL

Colm Tóibín

EMBLEM

McClelland & Stewart

Copyright © 2009 by Colm Tóibín

Cloth edition published 2009
Emblem edition published 2010

Emblem is an imprint of McClelland & Stewart Ltd.
Emblem and colophon are registered trademarks of McClelland & Stewart Ltd.

Library and Archives Canada Cataloguing in Publication

Tóibín, Colm, 1955–
Brooklyn / Colm Tóibín.

ISBN 978-0-7710-8432-4

I. Title.

PR6070.O44B76 2010   823.'914   C2009-906540-1

We acknowledge the financial support of the Government of Canada through the
Book Publishing Industry Development Program and that of the Government of
Ontario through the Ontario Media Development Corporation's Ontario Book
Initiative. We further acknowledge the support of the Canada Council for the Arts
and the Ontario Arts Council for our publishing program.

Printed and bound in the United States of America

This book was printed on paper that is 20% recycled.

McClelland & Stewart Ltd.
75 Sherbourne Street
Toronto, Ontario
M5A 2P9
www.mcclelland.com

1 2 3 4 5   14 13 12 11 10

For Peter Straus

Part One

Eilis Lacey, sitting at the window of the upstairs living room in the house on Friary Street, noticed her sister walking briskly from work. She watched Rose crossing the street from sunlight into shade, carrying the new leather handbag that she had bought in Clerys in Dublin in the sale. Rose was wearing a cream-coloured cardigan over her shoulders. Her golf clubs were in the hall; in a few minutes, Eilis knew, someone would call for her and her sister would not return until the summer evening had faded.

Eilis's bookkeeping classes were almost ended now; she had a manual on her lap about systems of accounting, and on the table behind her was a ledger where she had entered, as her homework, on the debit and credit sides, the daily business of a company whose details she had taken down in notes in the Vocational School the week before.

As soon as she heard the front door open, Eilis went downstairs. Rose, in the hall, was holding her pocket mirror in front of her face. She was studying herself closely as she applied lipstick and eye make-up before glancing at her overall appearance in the large hall mirror, settling her hair. Eilis looked on silently as her sister moistened her lips and then checked herself one more time in the pocket mirror before putting it away.

Their mother came from the kitchen to the hall.

"You look lovely, Rose," she said. "You'll be the belle of the golf club."

"I'm starving," Rose said, "but I've no time to eat."

3

"I'll make a special tea for you later," her mother said. "Eilis and myself are going to have our tea now."

Rose reached into her handbag and took out her purse. She placed a one-shilling piece on the hallstand. "That's in case you want to go to the pictures," she said to Eilis.

"And what about me?" her mother asked.

"She'll tell you the story when she gets home," Rose replied.

"That's a nice thing to say!" her mother said.

All three laughed as they heard a car stop outside the door and beep its horn. Rose picked up her golf clubs and was gone.

Later, as her mother washed the dishes and Eilis dried them, another knock came to the door. When Eilis answered it, she found a girl whom she recognized from Kelly's grocery shop beside the cathedral.

"Miss Kelly sent me with a message for you," the girl said. "She wants to see you."

"Does she?" Eilis asked. "And did she say what it was about?"

"No. You're just to call up there tonight."

"But why does she want to see me?"

"God, I don't know, miss. I didn't ask her. Do you want me to go back and ask her?"

"No, it's all right. But are you sure the message is for me?"

"I am, miss. She says you are to call in on her."

Since she had decided in any case to go to the pictures some other evening, and being tired of her ledger, Eilis changed her dress and put on a cardigan and left the house. She walked along Friary Street and Rafter Street into the Market Square and then up the hill to the cathedral. Miss Kelly's shop was closed, so Eilis knocked on the side door, which led to the upstairs part where she knew Miss Kelly lived. The door was answered by the young girl who had come to the house earlier, who told her to wait in the hall.

Eilis could hear voices and movement on the floor above and

then the young girl came down and said that Miss Kelly would be with her before long.

She knew Miss Kelly by sight, but her mother did not deal in her shop as it was too expensive. Also, she believed that her mother did not like Miss Kelly, although she could think of no reason for this. It was said that Miss Kelly sold the best ham in the town and the best creamery butter and the freshest of everything including cream, but Eilis did not think she had ever been in the shop, merely glanced into the interior as she passed and noticed Miss Kelly at the counter.

Miss Kelly slowly came down the stairs into the hallway and turned on a light.

"Now," she said, and repeated it as though it were a greeting. She did not smile.

Eilis was about to explain that she had been sent for, and to ask politely if this was the right time to come, but Miss Kelly's way of looking her up and down made her decide to say nothing. Because of Miss Kelly's manner, Eilis wondered if she had been offended by someone in the town and had mistaken her for that person.

"Here you are, then," Miss Kelly said.

Eilis noticed a number of black umbrellas resting against the hallstand.

"I hear you have no job at all but a great head for figures."

"Is that right?"

"Oh, the whole town, anyone who is anyone, comes into the shop and I hear everything."

Eilis wondered if this was a reference to her own mother's consistent dealing in another grocery shop, but she was not sure. Miss Kelly's thick glasses made the expression on her face difficult to read.

"And we are worked off our feet every Sunday here. Sure, there's nothing else open. And we get all sorts, good, bad and indifferent. And, as a rule, I open after seven mass, and between the end of nine o'clock mass until eleven mass is well over, there isn't room to move in this shop. I have Mary here to help, but she's slow enough at the best of times, so I was on the lookout for someone sharp, someone who would know people and give the right change. But only on Sundays, mind. The rest of the week we can manage ourselves. And you were recommended. I made inquiries about you and it would be seven and six a week, it might help your mother a bit."

Miss Kelly spoke, Eilis thought, as though she were describing a slight done to her, closing her mouth tightly between each phrase.

"So that's all I have to say now. You can start on Sunday, but come in tomorrow and learn off all the prices and we'll show you how to use the scales and the slicer. You'll have to tie your hair back and get a good shop coat in Dan Bolger's or Burke O'Leary's."

Eilis was already saving this conversation for her mother and Rose; she wished she could think of something smart to say to Miss Kelly without being openly rude. Instead, she remained silent.

"Well?" Miss Kelly asked.

Eilis realized that she could not turn down the offer. It would be better than nothing and, at the moment, she had nothing.

"Oh, yes, Miss Kelly," she said. "I'll start whenever you like."

"And on Sunday you can go to seven o'clock mass. That's what we do, and we open when it's over."

"That's lovely," Eilis said.

"So, come in tomorrow, then. And if I'm busy I'll send you home, or you can fill bags of sugar while you wait, but if I'm not busy, I'll show you all the ropes."

"Thank you, Miss Kelly," Eilis said.

"Your mother'll be pleased that you have something. And

your sister," Miss Kelly said. "I hear she's great at the golf. So go home now like a good girl. You can let yourself out."

Miss Kelly turned and began to walk slowly up the stairs. Eilis knew as she made her way home that her mother would indeed be happy that she had found some way of making money of her own, but that Rose would think working behind the counter of a grocery shop was not good enough for her. She wondered if Rose would say this to her directly.

On her way home she stopped at the house of her best friend Nancy Byrne to find that their friend Annette O'Brien was also there. The Byrnes had only one room downstairs, which served as a kitchen, dining room and sitting room, and it was clear that Nancy had news of some sort to impart, some of which Annette seemed already to know. Nancy used Eilis's arrival as an excuse to go out for a walk so they could talk in confidence.

"Did something happen?" Eilis asked once they were on the street.

"Say nothing until we are a mile away from that house," Nancy said. "Mammy knows there's something, but I'm not telling her."

They walked down Friary Hill and across the Mill Park Road to the river and then down along the prom towards the Ringwood.

"She got off with George Sheridan," Annette said.

"When?" Eilis asked.

"At the dance in the Athenaeum on Sunday night," Nancy said.

"I thought you weren't going to go."

"I wasn't and then I did."

"She danced all night with him," Annette said.

"I didn't, just the last four dances, and then he walked me home. But everybody saw. I'm surprised you haven't heard."

"And are you going to see him again?" Eilis asked.

"I don't know." Nancy sighed. "Maybe I'll just see him on the street. He drove by me yesterday and beeped the horn. If there had been anyone else there, I mean anyone of his sort, he would have danced with her, but there wasn't. He was with Jim Farrell, who just stood there looking at us."

"If his mother finds out, I don't know what she'll say," Annette said. "She's awful. I hate going into that shop when Jim isn't there. My mother sent me down once to get two rashers and that old one told me she didn't sell rashers in twos."

Eilis then told them that she had been offered a job serving in Miss Kelly's every Sunday.

"I hope you told her what to do with it," Nancy said.

"I told her I'd take it. It won't do any harm. It means I might be able to go to the Athenaeum with you using my own money and prevent you being taken advantage of."

"It wasn't like that," Nancy said. "He was nice."

"Are you going to see him again?" Eilis repeated.

"Will you come with me on Sunday night?" Nancy asked Eilis. "He mightn't even be there, but Annette can't come, and I'm going to need support in case he is there and doesn't even ask me to dance or doesn't even look at me."

"I might be too tired from working for Miss Kelly."

"But you'll come?"

"I haven't been there for ages," Eilis said. "I hate all those country fellows, and the town fellows are worse. Half drunk and just looking to get you up the Tan Yard Lane."

"George isn't like that," Nancy said.

"He's too stuck up to go near the Tan Yard Lane," Annette said.

"Maybe we'll ask him if he'd consider selling rashers in twos in future," Eilis said.

"Say nothing to him," Nancy said. "Are you really going to work for Miss Kelly? There's a one for rashers."

*   *   *

Over the next two days Miss Kelly took Eilis through every item in the shop. When Eilis asked for a piece of paper so she could note the different brands of tea and the various sizes of the packets, Miss Kelly told her that it would only waste time if she wrote things down; it was best instead to learn them off by heart. Cigarettes, butter, tea, bread, bottles of milk, packets of biscuits, cooked ham and corned beef were by far the most popular items sold on Sundays, she said, and after these came tins of sardines and salmon, tins of mandarin oranges and pears and fruit salad, jars of chicken and ham paste and sandwich spread and salad cream. She showed Eilis a sample of each object before telling her the price. When she thought that Eilis had learned these prices, she went on to other items, such as cartons of fresh cream, bottles of lemonade, tomatoes, heads of lettuce, fresh fruit and blocks of ice cream.

"Now there are people who come in here on a Sunday, if you don't mind, looking for things they should get during the week. What can you do?" Miss Kelly pursed her lips disapprovingly as she listed soap, shampoo, toilet paper and toothpaste and called out the different prices.

Some people, she added, also bought bags of sugar on a Sunday, or salt and even pepper, but not many. And there were even those who would look for golden syrup or baking soda or flour, but most of these items were sold on a Saturday.

There were always children, Miss Kelly said, looking for bars of chocolate or toffee or bags of sherbet or jelly babies, and men looking for loose cigarettes and matches, but Mary would deal with those since she was no good at large orders or remembering prices, and was often, Miss Kelly went on, more of a hindrance than a help when there was a big crowd in the shop.

"I can't stop her gawking at people for no reason. Even some of the regular customers."

The shop, Eilis saw, was well stocked, with many different brands of tea, some of them very expensive, and all of them at higher prices than Hayes's grocery in Friary Street or the L&N in Rafter Street or Sheridan's in the Market Square.

"You'll have to learn how to pack sugar and wrap a loaf of bread," Miss Kelly said. "Now, that's one of the things that Mary is good at, God help her."

As each customer came into the shop on the days when she was being trained, Eilis noticed that Miss Kelly had a different tone. Sometimes she said nothing at all, merely clenched her jaw and stood behind the counter in a pose that suggested deep disapproval of the customer's presence in her shop and an impatience for that customer to go. For others she smiled drily and studied them with grim forbearance, taking the money as though offering an immense favour. And then there were customers whom she greeted warmly and by name; many of these had accounts with her and thus no cash changed hands, but amounts were noted in a ledger, with inquiries about health and comments on the weather and remarks on the quality of the ham or the rashers or the variety of the bread on display from the batch loaves to the duck loaves to the currant bread.

"And I'm trying to teach this young lady," she said to a customer whom she seemed to value above all the rest, a woman with a fresh perm in her hair whom Eilis had never seen before. "I'm trying to teach her and I hope that she's more than willing, because Mary, God bless her, is willing, but sure that's no use, it's less than no use. I'm hoping that she's quick and sharp and dependable, but nowadays you can't get that for love or money."

Eilis looked at Mary, who was standing uneasily near the cash register listening carefully.

"But the Lord makes all types," Miss Kelly said.

"Oh, you're right there, Miss Kelly," the woman with the perm said as she filled her string bag with groceries. "And there's no use in complaining, is there? Sure, don't we need people to sweep the streets?"

On Saturday, with money borrowed from her mother, Eilis bought a dark green shop coat in Dan Bolger's. That night she asked her mother for the alarm clock. She would have to be up by six o'clock in the morning.

Since Jack, the nearest to her in age, had followed his two older brothers Pat and Martin to Birmingham to find work, Eilis had moved into the boys' room, leaving Rose her own bedroom, which their mother carefully tidied and cleaned each morning. As their mother's pension was small, they depended on Rose, who worked in the office of Davis's Mills; her wages paid for most of their needs. Anything extra came sporadically from the boys in England. Twice a year Rose went to Dublin for the sales, coming back each January with a new coat and costume and each August with a new dress and new cardigans and skirts and blouses, which were often chosen because Rose did not think they would go out of fashion, and then put away until the following year. Most of Rose's friends now were married women, often older women whose children had grown up, or wives of men who worked in the banks, who had time to play golf on summer evenings or in mixed foursomes at the weekends.

Rose, at thirty, Eilis thought, was more glamorous every year, and, while she had had several boyfriends, she remained single; she often remarked that she had a much better life than many of her former schoolmates who were to be seen pushing prams through the streets. Eilis was proud of her sister, of how much care she took with her appearance and how much care she put into whom she mixed with in the town and the golf club. She knew that Rose had tried to find her work in an office, and Rose was paying for her books now that she was studying bookkeeping and rudimentary accountancy, but she knew also that there was, at least for the moment, no work for anyone in Enniscorthy, no matter what their qualifications.

Eilis did not tell Rose about her offer of work from Miss Kelly; instead, as she went through her training, she saved up every detail to recount to her mother, who laughed and made her tell some parts of the story again.

"That Miss Kelly," her mother said, "is as bad as her mother and I heard from someone who worked there that that woman was evil incarnate. And she was just a maid in Roche's before she married. And Kelly's used to be a boarding house as well as a shop, and if you worked for her, or even if you stayed there, or dealt in the shop, she was evil incarnate. Unless, of course, you had plenty of money or were one of the clergy."

"I'm just there until something turns up," Eilis said.

"That's what I said to Rose when I was telling her," her mother replied. "And don't listen to her if she says anything to you."

Rose, however, never mentioned that Eilis was to begin work at Miss Kelly's. Instead, she gave her a pale yellow cardigan that she herself had barely worn, insisting that the colour was wrong for her and that it would look better on Eilis. She also gave her some lipstick. She was out late on Saturday night so she did not witness Eilis going to bed early, even though Nancy and Annette were going to the pictures, so that she would be fresh for work at Miss Kelly's on her first Sunday.

Only once, years before, had Eilis been to seven o'clock mass and that was on a Christmas morning when her father was alive and the boys were still at home. She remembered that she and her mother had tiptoed out of the house while the others were sleeping, leaving the presents under the tree in the upstairs living room, and coming back just after the boys and Rose and their father had woken and begun to open the packages. She remembered the darkness, the cold and the beautiful emptiness of the town. Now, leaving the house just after the twenty to seven bell rang, with her shop coat in a carrier bag and her hair tied in a ponytail, she walked through the streets to the cathedral, making sure she was in plenty of time.

She remembered that on that Christmas morning, years before, the seats in the central aisle of the cathedral had almost been full. Women with a long morning in the kitchen ahead of them wanted an early start. But now there was almost nobody. She looked around for Miss Kelly, but she did not see her until communion and then realized that she had been sitting across from her all along. She watched her walking down the main aisle with her hands joined and her eyes on the ground, followed by Mary, who was wearing a black mantilla. They both must have fasted, she thought, as she had been fasting, and she wondered when they would have their breakfast.

Once mass was over, she decided not to wait for Miss Kelly in the cathedral grounds but instead lingered at the news-stand as they unpacked bundles of newspapers and then stood outside the shop and waited for her there. Miss Kelly did not greet her or smile when she arrived but moved gruffly to the side door, ordering Eilis and Mary to wait outside. As she unlocked the main door of the shop and began to turn on the lights, Mary went to the back of the shop and started to carry loaves of bread towards the counter. Eilis realized that this was yesterday's bread; there was no bread delivered on a Sunday. She stood and watched as Miss Kelly opened a new strip of long sticky yellow paper to attract flies and told Mary to stand on the counter, fix it to the ceiling and take down the old one, which had dead flies stuck to every part of it.

"No one likes flies," Miss Kelly said, "especially on a Sunday."

Soon, two or three people came into the shop to buy cigarettes. Even though Eilis had already put her shop coat on, Miss Kelly ordered Mary to deal with them. When they had gone, Miss

Kelly told Mary to go upstairs and make a pot of tea, which she then delivered to the newspaper kiosk in exchange for what Eilis learned was a free copy of the *Sunday Press,* which Miss Kelly folded and put aside. Eilis noticed that neither Miss Kelly nor Mary had anything to eat or drink. Miss Kelly ushered her into a back room.

"That bread there," she said, pointing to a table, "is the freshest. It came yesterday evening all the way from Stafford's, but it is only for special customers. So you don't touch that bread whatever you do. The other bread'll do fine for most people. And we have no tomatoes. Those ones there are not for anybody unless I give precise instructions."

After nine o'clock mass the first crowd came. People who wanted cigarettes and sweets seemed to know to approach Mary. Miss Kelly stood back, her attention divided between the door and Eilis. She checked every price Eilis wrote down, informed her briskly of the price when she could not remember, and wrote down and added up the figures herself after Eilis had done so, not letting her give the customer the change until she had also been shown the original payment. As well as doing this, she greeted certain customers by name, motioning them forward and insisting that Eilis break off whatever she was doing to serve them.

"Oh, Mrs. Prendergast now," she said, "the new girl will look after you now and Mary will carry everything out to the car for you."

"I need to finish this first," Eilis said, as she was only a few items away from completing another order.

"Oh, Mary will do that," Miss Kelly said.

By this time people were five deep at the counter. "I'm next," a man shouted as Miss Kelly came back to the counter with more bread.

"Now, we are very busy and you will have to wait your turn."

"But I was next," the man said, "and that woman was served before me."

"So what is it you want?"

The man had a list of groceries in his hand.

"Eilis will deal with you now," Miss Kelly said, "but only after Mrs. Murphy here."

"I was before her too," the man said.

"I'm afraid you are mistaken," Miss Kelly said. "Eilis, hurry up now, this man is waiting. No one has all day, so he's next, after Mrs. Murphy. What price did you charge for that tea?"

It was like this until almost one o'clock. There was no break and nothing to eat or drink and Eilis was starving. No one was served in turn. Miss Kelly informed some of her customers, including two who, being friends of Rose, greeted Eilis familiarly, that she had lovely fresh tomatoes. She weighed them herself, seeming to be impressed that Eilis knew these customers, telling others firmly, however, that she had no tomatoes that day, none at all. For favoured customers she openly, almost proudly, produced the fresh bread. The problem was, Eilis realized, that there was no other shop in the town that was as well stocked as Miss Kelly's and open on a Sunday morning, but she also had a sense that people came here out of habit and they did not mind waiting, they enjoyed the crush and the crowd.

Although she had planned not to mention her new job in Miss Kelly's over dinner at home that day unless Rose raised the matter first, Eilis could not contain herself and began as soon as they sat down to describe her morning.

"I went into that shop once," Rose said, "on my way home from mass and she served Mary Delahunt before me. I turned and walked out. And there was a smell of something. I can't think what it was. She has a little slave, doesn't she? She took her out of a convent."

"Her father was a nice enough man," her mother said, "but she had no chance because her mother was, as I told you, Eilis, evil incarnate. I heard that when one of the maids got scalded she wouldn't even let her go to the doctor. The mother had Nelly working there from the time she could walk. She's never seen daylight, that's what's wrong with her."

"Nelly Kelly?" Rose asked. "Is that really her name?"

"In school they had a different name for her."

"What was it?"

"Everyone called her Nettles Kelly. The nuns couldn't stop us. I remember her well, she was a year or two behind me. She'd always have five or six girls following behind her coming from the Mercy Convent shouting 'Nettles.' No wonder she's so mad."

There was silence for a while as Rose and Eilis took this in.

"You wouldn't know whether to laugh or to cry," Rose said.

Eilis found as the meal went on that she could do an imitation of Miss Kelly's voice that made her sister and her mother laugh. She wondered if she was the only one who remembered that Jack, the youngest of her brothers, used to do imitations of the Sunday sermon, the radio sports commentators, the teachers at school and many characters in the town, and they all used to laugh. She did not know if the other two also realized that this was the first time they had laughed at this table since Jack had followed the others to Birmingham. She would have loved to say something about him, but she knew that it would make her mother too sad. Even when a letter came from him it was passed around in silence. So she continued mocking Miss Kelly, stopping only when someone called for Rose to take her to play golf, leaving Eilis and her mother to clear the table and wash the dishes.

*   *   *

That evening Eilis called at Nancy Byrne's at nine, aware that she had not made enough effort with her appearance. She had washed her hair and put on a summer dress, but she thought that she looked dowdy and was resigned to the idea that if Nancy danced more than one dance with George Sheridan then she was going home on her own. She was glad that Rose had not seen her before she left, as she would have made her do something more with her hair and put on some make-up and generally try to look smarter.

"Now, the rule is," Nancy said, "that we are not even looking at George Sheridan and he might be with a whole crowd from the rugby club, or he might not even be there at all. They often go to Courtown on a Sunday night, that crowd. So we are to be deep in conversation. And I'm not dancing with anyone else, just in case he came in and saw me. So if someone is coming over to ask us to dance, we just stand up and go to the ladies'."

It was clear that Nancy, using help from her sister and her mother, with both of whom she had finally shared the news that she had danced with George Sheridan the previous Sunday, had gone to a great deal of trouble. She had had her hair done the day before. She was wearing a blue dress that Eilis had seen only once before and she was now applying make-up in front of the bathroom mirror as her mother and sister made their way in and out of the room, offering advice and commentary and admiration.

They walked in silence from Friary Street into Church Street and then around to Castle Street and into the Athenaeum and up the stairs to the hall. Eilis was not surprised at how nervous Nancy was. It was a year since her boyfriend had let her down badly by turning up one night with another girl in this very same hall and staying with the other girl all night, barely acknowledging Nancy's existence as she sat watching. Later, he had gone to England, coming home briefly only to get married to the girl he had been with that night. It was not just that George Sheridan was handsome and had a car, but he ran a shop that did a thriving business in the Market Square; it was a business he would inherit in full on his mother's death. For Nancy, who worked in Buttle's Barley-Fed Bacon behind the counter, going out with George Sheridan was a dream that she did not wish to wake from, Eilis thought, as she and Nancy glanced around the hall, pretending they were not on the lookout for anyone in particular.

There were some couples dancing and a few men standing near the door.

"They look like they are at a cattle mart," Nancy said. "And God, it's the hair oil I hate."

"If one of them comes over, I'll stand up immediately," Eilis said, "and you tell them that you have to go with me to the cloakroom."

"We should have bottle glasses and buck teeth and have left our hair all greasy," Nancy said.

As the place filled up there was no sign of George Sheridan. And even as men crossed the hall to ask women to dance, no one approached either Nancy or Eilis.

"We'll get a name for being wallflowers," Nancy said.

"You could be called worse," Eilis said.

"Oh, you could. You could be called the Courtnacuddy Bus," Nancy replied.

Even when they had both stopped laughing and had gone back to looking around the hall, one of them would begin giggling again and it would start the other one off too.

"We must look mad," Eilis said.

Nancy beside her, however, had suddenly become serious. As Eilis looked over at the bar where soft drinks were on sale, she saw that George Sheridan, Jim Farrell and a number of their friends from the rugby club had arrived and there were a number of young women with them. Jim Farrell's father owned a pub in Rafter Street.

"That's it," Nancy whispered. "I'm going home."

"Wait, don't do that," Eilis said. "We'll go to the ladies' at the end of this set and then discuss what to do."

They waited and crossed the floor, empty of dancers; Eilis presumed that George Sheridan had spotted them. In the ladies' she told Nancy to do nothing, just to wait, and they would go back out when the next dance was in full swing. As they did so, and Eilis glanced over to where George and his friends had been, she caught George's eye. Nancy's face, as they searched for somewhere to sit, had turned a blotched red; she looked like someone whom the nuns had told to go and stand outside the door. They sat there without speaking as the dance went on. Everything Eilis thought of saying was ridiculous and so she said nothing, but she was aware that they both must seem a sad sight to anyone who paid any attention to them. She decided that if Nancy made even the weakest suggestion that they should go after this set, then she would agree immediately. Indeed, she longed to be outside already; she knew they would find some way of making a laugh of it later.

At the end of the set, however, George walked across the hall even before the music began and asked Nancy to dance. He smiled at Eilis as Nancy stood up and she smiled at him in return. As they began to dance, with George chatting easily, Nancy seemed to be making an effort to look cheerful. Eilis looked away in case her watching made Nancy uncomfortable, and then looked at the ground, hoping that no one would ask her to dance. It would be easier now, she thought, if George asked Nancy for the next dance when this set was over and she could slip quietly home.

Instead, George and Nancy came towards her and said they were going to get a lemonade at the bar and George would like to buy one for Eilis as well. She stood up and walked across the hall with them. Jim Farrell was standing at the bar holding a place for George. Some of their other friends, one or two of whom Eilis knew by name and the others by sight, were close by. As they approached, Jim Farrell turned and kept an elbow on the counter. He looked both Nancy and Eilis up and down without nodding or speaking, and then moved over and said something to George.

As the music began again, some of their friends took to the floor but Jim Farrell did not move. As George handed the glasses full of lemonade to Nancy and Eilis, he set about introducing them formally to Jim Farrell, who nodded curtly but did not shake hands. George seemed at a loss as he stood sipping his drink. He said something to Nancy and she replied. Then he sipped his drink again. Eilis wondered what he was going to do; it was clear that his friend did not like Nancy or Eilis and had no intention of speaking to them; Eilis wished she had not been brought to the bar like this. She sipped her drink and looked at the ground. When she glanced up, she saw Jim Farrell studying Nancy coldly and then, when he noticed he was being watched by Eilis, he shifted his ground and looked at her, his face expressionless. He was wearing, she saw, an expensive sports jacket and a shirt with a cravat.

George put the glass on the counter and turned to Nancy, inviting her to dance; he motioned to Jim, as if to suggest that he should do the same. Nancy smiled at George and then at Eilis and Jim, left her drink down and went to the dance floor with him. She seemed relieved and happy. As Eilis looked around, she was aware that she and Jim Farrell were alone at the bar counter and that there was no room at the ladies' side of the hall. Unless she went to the ladies' again, or went home, she was trapped. For a second, Jim Farrell looked as though he was stepping forward to ask her to dance. Eilis, since she felt she had no choice, was ready to accept; she did not want to be rude to George's friend. Just as she was about to accept him, Jim Farrell appeared to think better of it, stepped back and almost imperiously glanced around the hall, ignoring her. He did not look at her again and when the set was over she went and found Nancy and told her quietly that she was leaving and would see her soon. She shook hands with George and made the excuse that she was tired, and then walked from the hall with as much dignity as she could.

The following evening at tea she told her mother and Rose the story. They were interested at first in the news that Nancy had been dancing two Sunday nights in succession with George Sheridan, but they became far more animated when Eilis told them about the rudeness of Jim Farrell.

"Don't go near that Athenaeum again," Rose said.

"Your father knew his father well," her mother said. "Years ago. They went to the races together a few times. And your father drank in Farrell's sometimes. It's very well kept. And his mother is a very nice woman, she was a Duggan from Glenbrien. It must be the rugby club has him that way, and it must be sad for his parents having a pup for a son because he's an only child."

"He sounds like a pup all right and he looks like one," Rose said.

"Well, he was in a bad mood last night anyway," Eilis said. "That's all I have to say. I suppose he might think that George should be with someone grander than Nancy."

"There's no excuse for that," her mother said. "Nancy Byrne is one of the most beautiful girls in this town. George would be very lucky to get her."

"I wonder would his mother agree," Rose said.

"Some of the shopkeepers in this town," her mother said, "especially the ones who buy cheap and sell dear, all they have is a few yards of counter and they have to sit there all day waiting for customers. I don't know why they think so highly of themselves."

Although Miss Kelly paid Eilis only seven and sixpence a week for working on Sundays, she often sent Mary to fetch her at other

times—once when she wanted to get her hair done without closing the shop and once when she wanted all the tins on the shelves
taken down and dusted and then replaced. Each time she gave
Eilis two shillings but kept her for hours, complaining about Mary
whenever she could. Each time also, as she left, Miss Kelly handed
Eilis a loaf of bread, which Eilis knew was stale, to give to her
mother.

"She must think we're paupers," her mother said. "What
would we do with stale bread? Rose will go mad. Don't go there
the next time she sends for you. Tell her you're busy."

"But I'm not busy."

"A proper job will turn up. That's what I'm praying for every
day."

Her mother made breadcrumbs with the stale bread and
roasted stuffed pork. She did not tell Rose where the breadcrumbs came from.

One day at dinnertime Rose, who walked home from the office at
one and returned at a quarter to two, mentioned that she had
played golf the previous evening with a priest, a Father Flood,
who had known their father years before and their mother when
she was a young girl. He was home from America on holidays, his
first visit since before the war.

"Flood?" her mother asked. "There was a crowd of Floods out
near Monageer, but I don't remember any of them becoming a
priest. I don't know what became of them, you never see any of
them now."

"There's Murphy Floods," Eilis said.

"That's not the same," her mother replied.

"Anyway," Rose said, "I invited him in for his tea when he said
that he'd like to call on you and he's coming tomorrow."

"Oh, God," her mother said. "What would an American priest like for his tea? I'll have to get cooked ham."

"Miss Kelly has the best cooked ham," Eilis said, laughing.

"No one is buying anything from Miss Kelly," Rose replied. "Father Flood will eat whatever we give him."

"Would cooked ham be all right with tomatoes and lettuce, or maybe roast beef, or would he like a fry?"

"Anything will be fine," Rose said. "With plenty of brown bread and butter."

"We'll have it in the dining room, and we'll use the good china. If I could get a bit of salmon, maybe. Would he eat that?"

"He's very nice," Rose said. "He'll eat anything you put in front of him."

Father Flood was tall; his accent was a mixture of Irish and American. Nothing he said could convince Eilis's mother that she had known him or his family. His mother, he said, had been a Rochford.

"I don't think I knew her," her mother said. "The only Rochford we knew was old Hatchethead."

Father Flood looked at her solemnly. "Hatchethead was my uncle," he said.

"Was he?" her mother asked. Eilis saw how close she was to nervous laughter.

"But of course we didn't call him that," Father Flood said. "His real name was Seamus."

"Well, he was very nice," her mother said. "Weren't we awful to call him that?"

Rose poured more tea as Eilis quietly left the room, afraid that if she stayed she would be unable to disguise an urge to begin laughing.

When she returned she realized that Father Flood had heard about her job at Miss Kelly's, had found out about her pay and had expressed shock at how low it was. He inquired about her qualifications.

"In the United States," he said, "there would be plenty of work for someone like you and with good pay."

"She thought of going to England," her mother said, "but the boys said to wait, that it wasn't the best time there, and she might only get factory work."

"In Brooklyn, where my parish is, there would be office work for someone who was hard-working and educated and honest."

"It's very far away, though," her mother said. "That's the only thing."

"Parts of Brooklyn," Father Flood replied, "are just like Ireland. They're full of Irish."

He crossed his legs and sipped his tea from the china cup and said nothing for a while. The silence that descended made it clear to Eilis what the others were thinking. She looked across at her mother, who deliberately, it seemed to her, did not return her glance, but kept her gaze fixed on the floor. Rose, normally so good at moving the conversation along if they had a visitor, also said nothing. She twisted her ring and then her bracelet.

"It would be a great opportunity, especially if you were young," Father Flood said finally.

"It might be very dangerous," her mother said, her eyes still fixed on the floor.

"Not in my parish," Father Flood said. "It's full of lovely people. A lot of life centres round the parish, even more than in Ireland. And there's work for anyone who's willing to work."

Eilis felt like a child when the doctor would come to the house, her mother listening with cowed respect. It was Rose's silence that was new to her; she looked at her now, wanting her sister to ask a question or make a comment, but Rose appeared to be in a sort of dream. As Eilis watched her, it struck her that she had never seen Rose look so beautiful. And then it occurred to her that she was already feeling that she would need to remember this room, her sister, this scene, as though from a distance. In the silence that had lingered, she realized, it had somehow been tacitly arranged that Eilis would go to America. Father Flood, she believed, had been invited to the house because Rose knew that he could arrange it.

Her mother had been so opposed to her going to England that this new realization came to Eilis as a shock. She wondered if she had not taken the job in the shop and had not told them about her weekly humiliation at Miss Kelly's hands, might they have been so ready to let this conversation happen. She regretted having told them so much; she had done so mostly because it had made Rose and her mother laugh, brightened a number of meals that they had had with each other, made eating together nicer and easier than anytime since her father had died and the boys had left. It now occurred to her that her mother and Rose did not think her working for Miss Kelly was funny at all, and they offered no word of demurral as Father Flood moved from praising his parish in Brooklyn to saying that he believed he would be able to find Eilis a suitable position there.

In the days that followed no mention was made of Father Flood's visit or his raising the possibility of her going to Brooklyn, and it was the silence itself that led Eilis to believe that Rose and her mother had discussed it and were in favour of it. She had never considered going to America. Many she knew had gone to England and often came back at Christmas or in the summer. It was part of the life of the town. Although she knew friends who regularly received presents of dollars or clothes from America, it was always from their aunts and uncles, people who had emigrated long before the war. She could not remember any of these people ever appearing in the town on holidays. It was a long journey across the Atlantic, she knew, at least a week on a ship, and it must be expensive. She had a sense too, she did not know from where, that, while the boys and girls from the town who had gone to England did ordinary work for ordinary money, people who went to America could become rich. She tried to work out how she had come to believe also that, while people from the town who lived in England missed Enniscorthy, no one who went to America missed home. Instead, they were happy there and proud. She wondered if that could be true.

Father Flood did not visit again; instead, he wrote a letter to her mother when he returned to Brooklyn, saying that he had spoken, soon after he arrived, to one of his parishioners, a merchant of Italian origin, about Eilis and wanted to let Mrs. Lacey know that there would soon be a position vacant. It would not be in the office, as he had hoped, but on the shop floor of the large store that this gentleman owned and managed. But, he added, he had been assured that, were Eilis to prove satisfactory in her first job, there would be plenty of opportunity for promotion and very good prospects. He would also, he said, be able to provide suitable documentation to satisfy the Embassy, which was often not so easy nowadays, and would, he was sure, be able to find suitable accommodation for Eilis near the church and not far from her place of work.

Her mother handed her the letter when she had it read. Rose had already gone to work. There was silence in the kitchen.

"He seems very genuine," her mother said. "I'll say that for him."

Eilis read the sentence again about the shop floor. She presumed that he meant she would work behind a counter. Father Flood did not mention how much she would earn, or how she would raise the money to pay the fare. Instead, he suggested that she should get in touch with the American Embassy in Dublin and ascertain precisely what documents she would require before she travelled so they could all be arranged. As she read and reread, her mother moved about the kitchen with her back to her, saying nothing. Eilis sat at the table, not speaking either, wondering how long it would take her mother to turn towards her and say something, deciding that she would sit and wait, counting each second, knowing that her mother had no real work to do. She was, in fact, Eilis saw, making work for herself so that she would not have to turn.

Finally, her mother turned and sighed.

"Keep that letter safe now," she said, "and we'll show it to Rose when she comes in."

Within weeks, Rose had organized everything, even managing to befriend by telephone a figure in the American Embassy in Dublin who sent the necessary forms and a list of doctors authorized to write a report on Eilis's general health, and a list of other things the Embassy would require, including a precise offer of work, work that Eilis was singularly qualified to do, a guarantee that she would be looked after financially on her arrival and a number of character references.

Father Flood wrote a formal letter sponsoring Eilis and guaranteeing to take care of her accommodation as well as her general and financial welfare, and on headed notepaper came a letter from Bartocci & Company, Fulton Street, Brooklyn, offering her a permanent position in their main store at the same address and mentioning her bookkeeping skills and general experience. It was signed Laura Fortini; the handwriting, Eilis noted, was clear and beautiful, and even the notepaper itself, its light blue colour, the embossed drawing of a large building over the letterhead, seemed heavier, more expensive, more promising than anything of its kind she had seen before.

It was agreed that her brothers in Birmingham would, between them, pay her passage to New York. Rose would give her money to live on until she was settled in her job. She told the news to a few friends, asking them not to tell anyone else, but Eilis knew that some of Rose's colleagues at work had heard the phone calls to Dublin; she was aware also that her mother would not be able to keep the news to herself. Thus she felt that she should go and tell Miss Kelly before she heard it from someone else. It was best, she thought, to go during the week, when things were not so busy.

She found Miss Kelly standing behind the counter. Mary was at the top of a ladder stacking packets of marrowfat peas on the higher shelves.

"Oh, you've come at the worst time now," Miss Kelly said. "Just when we thought we would have a bit of peace. Now don't disturb that Mary one whatever you do." She inclined her head in the direction of the ladder. "She'd fall as soon as she'd look at you."

"Well, I just came to say that I'll be going to America in about a month's time," Eilis said. "I'm going to work there and I wanted to give you plenty of notice."

Miss Kelly stood back from the counter. "Is that right?" she asked.

"But I'll be here on Sundays of course until I go."

"Is it a reference you're looking for?"

"No. Not at all. I just came to let you know."

"Well, that's lovely now. So we'll see you when you come home on holidays, if you'll still be talking to everyone."

"I'll be here on Sunday," Eilis said.

"Ah, no, we won't be needing you at all. If you're going, you're best to go."

"But I could come."

"No, you couldn't. There'd be too much talk about you and

there'd be too much distraction and we're very busy on a Sunday, as you know, without that."

"I was hoping I could work until I left."

"Not here you can't. So be off with you now. We have plenty of work, more deliveries today and more stacking. And no time for talking."

"Well, thank you very much."

"And thank you too."

As Miss Kelly moved towards the store at the back of the shop, Eilis looked to see if Mary would turn so she could say goodbye to her. Since Mary did not, Eilis quietly left the shop and went home.

Miss Kelly was the only one who mentioned the possibility of her coming home on holidays. No one else mentioned it. Until now, Eilis had always presumed that she would live in the town all her life, as her mother had done, knowing everyone, having the same friends and neighbours, the same routines in the same streets. She had expected that she would find a job in the town, and then marry someone and give up the job and have children. Now, she felt that she was being singled out for something for which she was not in any way prepared, and this, despite the fear it carried with it, gave her a feeling, or more a set of feelings, she thought she might experience in the days before her wedding, days in which everyone looked at her in the rush of arrangements with light in their eyes, days in which she herself was fizzy with excitement but careful not to think too precisely about what the next few weeks would be like in case she lost her nerve.

There was no day that passed without an event. The forms that came from the Embassy were filled in and sent back. She went on the train to Wexford town for what seemed to her a cursory medical examination, the doctor appearing to be satisfied when she told him that no one in her family had suffered from tuberculosis. Father Flood wrote with more details, of where she would stay when she arrived and how close it would be to her place of work; her ticket arrived for the ship to New York, which would leave from Liverpool. Rose gave her some money for clothes and promised to buy her shoes and a complete set of underwear. The house was, she thought, unusually, almost unnaturally happy, and the meals they shared were full of too much talk and laughter. It reminded her of the weeks before Jack had left for Birmingham, when they would do anything to distract themselves from the thought that they were losing him.

One day, when a neighbour called and sat in the kitchen with them having tea, Eilis realized that her mother and Rose were doing everything to hide their feelings. The neighbour, almost casually, as a way of making conversation, said: "You'll miss her when she's gone, I'd say."

"Oh, it'll kill me when she goes," her mother said. Her face wore a dark strained look that Eilis had not seen since the months after their father died. Then, in the moments that followed, the neighbour appearing to have been taken aback by her mother's tone, her mother's expression became almost darker and she had to stand up and walk quietly out of the room. It was clear to Eilis that she was going to cry. Eilis was so surprised that, instead of following her mother into the hallway or the dining room, she made small talk with their neighbour, hoping her mother would soon return and they could resume what had seemed like an ordinary conversation.

Even when she woke in the night and thought about it, she did not allow herself to conclude that she did not want to go. Instead, she went over all the arrangements and worried about carrying two suitcases with all her clothes without any help, and making sure that she did not lose the handbag that Rose had given her, where she would keep her passport, and the addresses in Brooklyn where she would live and work, and Father Flood's address in case he did not turn up to meet her as he had promised to do. And money. And her make-up bag. And an overcoat maybe to be carried over her arm, although perhaps she would wear it, she thought, unless it was too hot. And it still might be hot in late September, she had been warned.

She had already packed one case and hoped, as she went over its contents in her mind, that she would not have to open it again. It struck her on one of those nights, as she lay awake, that the next time she would open that suitcase it would be in a different room in a different country, and then the thought came unbidden into her mind that she would be happier if it were opened by another person who could keep the clothes and shoes and wear them every day. She would prefer to stay at home, sleep in this room, live in this house, do without the clothes and shoes. The arrangements being made, all the bustle and talk, would be better if they were for someone else, she thought, someone like her, someone the same age and size, who maybe even looked the same as she did, as long as she, the person who was thinking now, could wake in this bed every morning and move as the day went on in these familiar streets and come home to the kitchen, to her mother and Rose.

Even though she let these thoughts run as fast as they would, she still stopped when her mind moved towards real fear or dread or, worse, towards the thought that she was going to lose this world for ever, that she would never have an ordinary day again in this ordinary place, that the rest of her life would be a struggle with the unfamiliar. Downstairs, once Rose and her mother were there, she talked about practical things and remained bright.

One evening, when Rose invited her into her room so that she could choose some pieces of jewellery to bring with her, something new occurred to Eilis that surprised her by its force and clarity. Rose was thirty now, and since it was obvious that their mother could never be left to live alone, not merely because her pension was small but because she would be too lonely without any of them, Eilis's going, which Rose had organized so precisely, would mean that Rose would not be able to marry. She would have to stay with her mother, living as she was now, working in Davis's office, playing golf at the weekends and on summer evenings. Rose, she realized, in making it easy for her to go, was giving up any real prospect of leaving this house herself and having her own house, with her own family. Eilis, as she fitted on some necklaces, seated in front of her dressing-table mirror, saw that in the future, as her mother got older and more frail, Rose would have to care for her even more, go up the steep steps of the stairs with trays of food and do the cleaning and cooking when her mother could not.

It occurred to her also, as she tried on some earrings, that Rose knew all this too, knew that either she or Eilis would have to leave, and had decided to let Eilis go. As she turned and looked at her sister, Eilis wanted to suggest that they change places, that Rose, so ready for life, always making new friends, would be happier going to America, just as Eilis would be quite content to stay at home. But Rose had a job in the town and she did not, and so it was easy for Rose to sacrifice herself, since it seemed that she was doing something else. In these moments, as Rose offered her some brooches to take with her, Eilis would have given anything to be able to say plainly that she did not want to go, that Rose could go instead, that she would happily stay here and take care of her mother and they would manage somehow and maybe she would find other work.

She wondered if her mother too believed that the wrong sister was leaving, and understood what Rose's motives were. She imagined that her mother knew everything. They knew so much, each one of them, she thought, that they could do everything except say out loud what it was they were thinking. She resolved as she went back to her room that she would do everything she could for them by pretending at all times that she was filled with excitement at the great adventure on which she was ready to embark. She would make them believe, if she could, that she was looking forward to America and leaving home for the first time. She promised herself that not for one moment would she give them the smallest hint of how she felt, and she would keep it from herself if she had to until she was away from them.

There was, she thought, enough sadness in the house, maybe even more than she realized. She would try as best she could not to add to it. Her mother and Rose could not be fooled, she was sure, but there seemed to her an even greater reason why there should be no tears before her departure. They would not be needed. What she would need to do in the days before she left and on the morning of her departure was smile, so that they would remember her smiling.

Rose took the day off from work and travelled with her to Dublin. They went to lunch together in the Gresham Hotel before it was time for the taxi to the boat to Liverpool, where Jack had agreed to meet her and spend the day with her before she set out on her long journey to New York. That day in Dublin Eilis was aware that going to work in America was different from just taking the boat to England; America might be further away and so utterly foreign in its systems and its manners, yet it had an almost compensating glamour attached to it. Even going to work in a shop in Brooklyn with lodgings a few streets away, all orga- nized by a priest, had an element of romance that she and Rose were fully alert to as they ordered their lunch in the Gresham, having left her luggage in the railway station. Going to work in a shop in Birmingham or Liverpool or Coventry or even London was sheer dullness compared to this.

Rose had dressed up beautifully for the day, and Eilis had tried to look as well as she could. Rose, merely by smiling at the hotel porter, seemed to be able to make him stand in O'Connell Street to get a taxi for them, insisting that they wait in the lobby. So too as many passengers made their way towards the boat Rose seemed in command. No one who did not have a ticket was allowed beyond a certain point; Rose, however, made an exception of herself with the assistance of the ticket collector, who fetched a colleague to help the ladies with their suitcases. He told Rose she could stay on the boat until half an hour before it was due to sail, when he would locate her, accompany her back and then find someone to keep an eye on her sister for the crossing to Liverpool. Even people with first-class tickets would not get this treatment, Eilis remarked to Rose, who smiled knowingly and agreed.

"Some people are nice," she said, "and if you talk to them properly, they can be even nicer."

They both laughed.

"That'll be my motto in America," Eilis said.

In the early morning when the boat arrived in Liverpool she was helped with her luggage by a porter who was Irish. When she told him she was not sailing to America until later that day, he advised her to take her cases immediately down to a shed where a friend of his worked, close to where the transatlantic liners docked; if she gave the man at the office his name, then she would be free of them for the day. She found herself thanking him in a tone that Rose might have used, a tone warm and private but also slightly distant though not shy either, a tone used by a woman in full possession of herself. It was something she could not have done in the town or in a place where any of her family or friends might have seen her.

She saw Jack as soon as she descended from the boat. She did not know whether she should embrace him or not. They had never embraced before. When he put his hand out to shake her hand, she stopped and looked at him again. He seemed embarrassed until he smiled. She moved towards him as though to hug him.

"That's enough of that now," he said as he gently pushed her away. "People will think . . ."

"What?"

"It's great to see you," he said. He was blushing. "Really great to see you."

He took her suitcases from the ship's attendant, calling him "mate" as he thanked him. For a second, as he turned, Eilis tried to hug him again, but he stopped her.

"No more of that now," he said. "Rose sent me a list of instructions, and they included one that said no kissing and hugging." He laughed.

They walked together down the busy docks as ships were being loaded and unloaded. Jack had already seen that the transatlantic liner on which Eilis was to sail had docked, and, once they had left the suitcases in the shed as arranged, they went to inspect it. It stood alone, massive and much grander and whiter and cleaner than the cargo ships around it.

"This is going to take you to America," Jack said. "It's like time and patience."

"What about time and patience?"

"Time and patience would bring a snail to America. Did you never hear that?"

"Oh, don't be so stupid," she said and nudged him and smiled.

"Daddy always said that," he said.

"When I was out of the room," she replied.

"Time and patience would bring a snail to America," he repeated.

The day was fine; they walked silently from the docks into the city centre as Eilis wished that she were back in her own bedroom or even on the boat as it moved across the Atlantic. Since she did not have to embark until five o'clock at the earliest, she wondered how they were going to spend the day. As soon as they found a café, Jack asked her if she was hungry.

"A bun," she said, "maybe and a cup of tea."

"Enjoy your last cup of tea, so," he said.

"Do they not have tea in America?" she asked.

"Are you joking? They eat their young in America. And they talk with their mouths full."

She noticed that, when a waiter approached them, Jack asked for a table almost apologetically. They sat by the window.

"Rose said you were to have a good dinner later in case the food on the boat was not to your liking," her brother told her.

Once they had ordered, Eilis looked around the café.

"What are they like?" she asked.

"Who?"

"The English."

"They're fair, they're decent," Jack said. "If you do your job, then they appreciate that. It's all they care about, most of them. You get shouted at a bit on the street, but that's just Saturday night. You pay no attention to it."

"What do they shout?"

"Nothing for the ears of a nice girl going to America."

"Tell me!"

"I certainly will not."

"Bad words?"

"Yes, but you learn to pay no attention and we have our own pubs so anything that would happen would be just on the way home. The rule is never to shout back, pretend nothing is happening."

"And at work?"

"No, work is different. It's a spare-parts warehouse. Old cars and broken machinery are brought in from all over the country. We take them to pieces and sell the parts on, down to the screws and the scrap metal."

"What exactly do you do? You can tell me everything." She looked at him and smiled.

"I'm in charge of the inventory. As soon as a car is stripped, I get a list of every single part of it, and with old machines some parts can be very rare. I know where they're kept and if they're sold. I worked out a system so everything can be located easily. I have only one problem."

"What's that?"

"Most people who work in the company think they're free to liberate any spare part that their mates might need them to take home."

"What do you do about that?"

"I convinced the boss that we should let anyone working for us have anything they want within reason at half the price and that means we have things under control a bit more, but they still take stuff. Why I'm in change of the inventory is that I came recommended by a friend of the boss. I don't steal spare parts. It's not that I'm honest or anything. I just know I'd get caught so I wouldn't risk it."

As he spoke, he looked innocent and serious, she thought, but nervous as well as though he was on display and worried how she would view him and the life he had now. She could think of nothing which might make him more natural, more like himself. All she could think of were questions.

"Do you see Pat and Martin much?"

"You sound like a quiz master."

"Your letters are great but they never tell us anything we want to know. And Pat and Martin's letters are worse."

"There's not much to say. Martin moves around too much but he might settle in the job he has now. But we all meet on a Saturday night. The pub and then the dancehall. We get nice and clean on a Saturday night. It's a pity you're not coming to Birmingham, there'd be a stampede for you on a Saturday night."

"You make it sound horrible."

"It's great gas. You'd enjoy it. There are more men than women."

*　　*　　*

They moved around the city centre, slowly becoming more relaxed, beginning to even laugh sometimes as they talked. At times, it struck her, they spoke like responsible adults—he told her stories about work and about weekends—and then they were suddenly back as children or teenagers, jeering one another or telling jokes. It seemed odd to her that Rose or their mother could not come at any moment and tell them to be quiet, and then she realized in the same second that they were in a big city and answerable to no one and with nothing to do until five o'clock, when she would have to collect her suitcases and hand in her ticket at the gate.

"Would you ever think of going home to live?" she asked him as they continued to walk aimlessly around the city centre before having a meal at a restaurant.

"Ah, there's nothing there for me," he said. "In the first few months I couldn't find my way around at all and I was desperate to go home. I would have done anything to go home. But now I'm used to it, and I like my wage packet and my independence. I like the way the boss at work, or even the boss in the place I was before, never asked me any questions; they both just made up their minds about me because of the way I worked. They never bother me, and if you suggest something to them, a better way of doing things, they'll listen."

"And what are English girls like?" Eilis asked.

"There's one of them very nice," Jack replied. "I couldn't vouch for the rest of them." He began to blush.

"What's her name?"

"I'm telling you nothing more."

"I won't tell Mammy."

"I heard that before. I've told you enough now."

"I hope you don't make her come to some flea-pit on a Saturday night."

"She's a good dancer. She doesn't mind. And it's not a flea-pit."

"And do Pat and Martin have girlfriends as well?"

"Martin is always getting stood up."

"And is Pat's girlfriend English as well?"

"You're just fishing for information. No wonder they told me to meet you."

"Is she English too?"

"She's from Mullingar."

"If you don't tell me your girlfriend's name, I'm going to tell everybody."

"Tell them what?"

"That you make her come to a flea-pit on a Saturday night."

"I'm telling you nothing more. You're worse than Rose."

"She's probably got one of those posh English names. God, wait until Mammy finds out. Her favourite son."

"Don't say a word to her."

It was difficult to carry her suitcases down the narrow stairs of the liner and Eilis had to move sideways on the corridor as she followed the signs that led to her berth. She knew that the liner was fully booked for the journey and she would have to share the berth.

The room was tiny, with a bunk bed, no window, not even an air hole, and a door into a minuscule bathroom that also, as she had been told, served the room on the other side. A notice said that passengers should unlock the other door when the bathroom was not in use, thus facilitating access for passengers in the adjoining room.

Eilis put one of her suitcases on the rack provided, placing the other against the wall. She wondered if she should change her clothes or what she should do between now and the evening meal that would be served to third-class passengers once the boat had set sail. Rose had packed two books for her, but she saw that the light was too weak for her to read. She lay down on the bed and put her hands behind her head, glad that the first part of the journey was over and there was still a week left without anything to do before she arrived. If only the rest of it could be as easy as this!

One thing that Jack had said remained with her because it was unlike him to be so vehement about anything. His saying that at the beginning he would have done anything to go home was strange. He had said nothing about this in his letters. It struck her that he might have told no one, not even his brothers, how he felt, and she thought how lonely that might have been for him. Maybe, she thought, all three of her brothers went through the same things and helped each other, sensing the feeling of homesickness when it arose in one of the others. If it happened to her, she realized, she would be alone, so she hoped that she would be ready for whatever was going to happen to her, however she was going to feel, when she arrived in Brooklyn.

Suddenly, the door opened and a woman came in, pulling a large trunk behind her. She ignored Eilis, who stood up immediately and asked her if she needed help. The woman dragged the trunk into the tiny berth and tried to close the door behind her but there was not enough space.

"This is hell," she said in an English accent as she now attempted to stand the trunk on its side. Having succeeded, she stood in the space between the bunk beds and the wall beside Eilis. There was barely room for the two of them. Eilis saw that the upturned trunk was almost blocking the door.

"You're on the top bunk. Number one means bottom bunk and that's on my ticket," the woman said. "So move. My name is Georgina."

Eilis did not check her own ticket but instead introduced herself.

"This is the smallest room," Georgina said, "you couldn't keep a cat in here, let alone swing one."

Eilis had to stop herself from laughing, and she wished Rose were close by so she could tell her that she was on the verge of asking Georgina if she were going all the way to New York or if she planned to get off somewhere on the journey.

"I need a fag but they won't let us smoke down here," Georgina said.

Eilis began to climb up the little ladder to the top bunk.

"Never again," Georgina said. "Never again."

Eilis could not resist. "Never again such a big trunk or never again going to America?"

"Never again in third class. Never again the trunk. Never again going home to Liverpool. Just never again. Does that answer your question?"

"But you like the bottom bunk?" Eilis asked.

"Yes, I do. Now, you're Irish so come and have a cigarette with me."

"I'm sorry. I don't smoke."

"Just my luck. No bad habits."

Georgina slowly made her way out of the room by edging around the trunk.

Later, when the engine of the ship, which seemed remarkably close to their berth, began to fire up and a large hooting whistle started to blow at regular intervals, Georgina returned to the room to fetch her coat and, having brushed her hair in the bathroom, invited Eilis to come on deck with her and see the lights of Liverpool as they departed.

"We could meet someone we like," she said, "who could invite us to the first-class lounge."

Eilis found her coat and scarf and followed her, inching with difficulty past the trunk. She could not understand how Georgina had managed to get it down the stairs. It was only when they were standing on deck in the dwindling evening light that she was able to get a good look at the woman with whom she was sharing the berth. Georgina, she thought, was anything between thirty and forty, although she could have been more. Her hair was a bright blond, and her hairstyle was like a film star's. She moved with confidence, and when she lit a cigarette and pulled on it, the way she pursed her lips and narrowed her eyes and released the smoke from her nose made her seem immensely poised and glamorous.

"Look at them," she said, pointing to a group of people standing on the other side of a barrier, who were also watching the city as it grew smaller. "They're the first-class passengers. They get the best view. But I know a way around. Come on with me."

"I'm all right here," Eilis said. "There'll be no view in a minute anyway."

Georgina turned and looked at her and shrugged. "Suit yourself. But, by the look of it and from what I've heard, it's going to be one of those nights, one of the worst. The steward who carried my trunk down said it was going to be one of those nights."

It grew dark quickly and windy on deck. Eilis found the third-class dining room and sat alone as a single waiter set the tables around her, eventually noticing her and bringing her first, without even showing her a menu, a bowl of oxtail soup, followed by what she thought was boiled mutton in gravy with potatoes and peas. As she ate she looked around but saw no sign of Georgina and was surprised at the number of empty tables. She wondered if most of the cabins were first class and second class, and if third class was just the small number of people she saw now in the dining room, or had seen on deck. She thought this was unlikely, and asked herself where the rest of them were, or how they were going to eat.

By the time the waiter brought her jelly and custard, there was no one else in the dining room. She thought that Georgina, since there was no other restaurant in third class, must have slipped into first or second but she did not think it could be easily done. There was nothing for her to do, in any case, since there was no third-class lounge or bar, but to go back to her cabin and settle down for the night. She was tired and she hoped now that she might sleep.

In the cabin, when she went to brush her teeth and wash her face before going to bed, she discovered that the people on the other side had locked the door; she believed that they must be using the bathroom and stood waiting for them to finish and then unlock the door. She listened but heard no sound, except the engine, which she thought loud enough to muffle any bathroom noise. After a while she went into the corridor and spent time outside the door of the adjoining room but could hear nothing. She wondered if the people in there had gone to sleep and waited in the corridor hoping that Georgina would come. Georgina, she thought, would know what to do, as would Rose or her mother, or indeed Miss Kelly, whose face came into her mind for one brief moment. But she had no idea what to do.

When some time had gone by, she knocked gently on the door and, on receiving no reply, banged harder with her knuckles in case they could not hear her. Still there was no reply. Since the liner was full, and since there was no one in the dining room, which was by now surely closed, she presumed that all the passengers were in their cabins; some of them could even have been asleep. In her agitation and worry, she suddenly realized that not only did she need to brush her teeth and wash her face, but she needed to empty her bladder and her bowels as well, and do so quickly, almost urgently. She went into her own cabin again and tried the door of the bathroom, but it was still locked.

She went back into the corridor and made her way towards the dining room, her need more and more urgent, but she could find no bathroom. She went up the two flights of stairs towards the deck but found that the door had been locked. She walked down a number of corridors, checking at the end of each one for a bathroom or a toilet, but there was nothing except the sound of the engines and the beginning of a movement as the liner lunged forward, which made it necessary for her to hold the rails carefully as she went back down the stairs so she could keep her balance.

She was desperate now and did not think she could manage much longer without finding a toilet. She had noticed earlier that towards each end of her own corridor there was a small alcove where a bucket and some mops and brushes were kept. She realized that since she had met no one, then, if she were lucky, no one would see her now as she went to the alcove on the right. She was glad when she saw that there was already some water in the bottom of the bucket. She moved fast, trying to relieve herself as quickly as she could, keeping inside the alcove so that even if someone came along the corridor they might not spot her unless they had to pass. She used the soft mop to wipe herself when she had finished and then tiptoed back to the cabin, hoping that Georgina would come and know how to wake their neighbours to make them unlock the bathroom door. She would not, it struck her, be able to complain about this to the ship's authorities in case they associated her with what they would, she was sure, discover in the bucket the following morning.

She went into her berth and changed into her nightdress and turned off the light before climbing up to the top bunk. Soon she fell asleep. She did not know for how long she slept, but when she woke, she found herself covered in sweat. It soon became clear to her what was wrong. She was going to vomit. In the darkness she almost tumbled from the bunk and could not stop herself throwing up parts of her evening meal as she tried to keep her balance while searching for the cabin light.

As she found it, she moved past Georgina's trunk towards the door, and as soon as she reached the corridor she began to vomit copiously. She got down on her knees; it was the only way she could manage since the ship was swaying so much. She realized that she should try to vomit everything up as quickly as possible before she was discovered by one of her fellow passengers, or by the ship's authorities, but each time she stood up thinking she had finished, the nausea returned. As she began to return to the cabin, longing to cover herself with blankets on the top bunk, hoping that no one would realize that she was the one who had made the mess in the corridor, the urge to be sick became even more intense than before, forcing her to get down on her hands and knees and vomit a thick liquid with a vile taste that made her shudder with revulsion when she lifted her head.

The ship's movements took on a harsh rhythm, and replaced the sense of lunging forward and then being pushed back she had felt when she woke first. They seemed to be making progress only with great difficulty, almost banging against something hard and forceful that attempted to withstand their progress. A noise, as though the massive liner were creaking, appeared louder sometimes than the engine itself. But, once back in the cabin, when she leaned against the door of the bathroom, she heard another sound, faint until she put her ear right up against the door, and then unmistakable, of someone retching. She listened: it was a heaving sound. She banged on the door, angry when she understood why it had remained locked. The people on the other side must have known how rough the night was going to be and known they would need to use the bathroom all the time. The retching came at intervals from the other side, and there was no sign that the door into her berth was going to be opened.

She felt strong enough to look at where she had vomited in the cabin. Having put on her shoes and a coat over her nightdress, she went into the corridor and walked to the alcove on the left, where she found a mop and a brush and a bucket. She was careful where she stepped and careful also not to lose her balance. She wondered now if many of the third-class passengers had known what this night was going to be like and had therefore kept away from the dining room and the deck and the corridors, had decided to lock themselves in their cabins, where they were going to stay until the worst was over. She did not know if this often happened when a liner sailed out of Liverpool destined for New York, but, remembering that Georgina had said that it was going to be one of those nights, she presumed that it was worse than usual. They were now, she imagined, close to the coast somewhere south of Ireland, but she could not be sure of that.

She carried a mop and brush back to the cabin, hoping that the smell could be got rid of by pouring some of the perfume that Rose had given her on the parts of the floor and the blankets where she had vomited. But the mopping appeared only to make things worse and the brush was no use. She decided to bring them back to where she had found them. Suddenly, as she left them in the alcove, she felt nauseous again and could not stop herself vomiting in the corridor once more. There was hardly anything to vomit, just a sour bile that left a taste in her mouth that made her cry as she banged on the door of the cabin beside hers and kicked it hard. But no one opened the door as the liner shuddered and seemed to lunge forward, and then shuddered again.

She had no idea how far under the sea she was except that her cabin was deep in the belly of the ship. As her stomach began dry heaves, she realized that she would never be able to tell anyone how sick she felt. She pictured her mother standing at the door waving as the car took her and Rose to the railway station, the expression on her mother's face strained and worried, managing a final smile when the car turned down Friary Hill. What was happening now, she hoped, was something that her mother had never even imagined. If it had been somehow easier, just rocking back and forth, then she might have been able to convince herself that it was a dream, or it would not last, but every moment of it was absolutely real, totally solid and part of her waking life, as was the foul taste in her mouth and the grinding of the engines and the heat that seemed to be increasing as the night wore on. And with all this came the feeling that she had done something wrong, that it was somehow her fault that Georgina had gone else-where and that her neighbours had locked the bathroom door, and her fault that she had vomited all over the cabin and had not suc-ceeded in cleaning up the mess.

She was breathing now through her nose, concentrating, mak-ing every effort to stop her stomach heaving again, using all of the force of will she had left to climb the ladder to the top bunk and lie there in the dark, imagining that the boat was moving forward, even though the shuddering sound became fiercer as the liner seemed to hit a wave stronger than it was. She imagined for a while that she herself was the sea outside, pushing hard to resist the weight and force of the liner. She fell into a light, dreamless sleep.

She was woken by a soft hand on her forehead. She knew exactly where she was when she opened her eyes.

"Oh, the poor little pet," Georgina said.

"They wouldn't open the bathroom door," Eilis said. She made her voice sound as weak as she could.

"The bastards!" Georgina said. "They do that every time, some of them, whoever gets in first locks the door. Watch me dealing with them."

Eilis sat up and slowly made her way down the ladder. The smell of vomit was dreadful. Georgina had taken a nail file from her handbag and was already busy working at the lock on the bathroom door. She opened it without too much difficulty. Eilis followed her into the bathroom, where the passengers in the other berth had left their toilet things.

"Now, we have to block their door because tonight is going to be even worse," Georgina said.

Eilis saw that the lock was a simple metal bar that could eas-ily be lifted by a nail file.

"There's only one solution," Georgina said. "If I put my trunk in here, we won't be able to close the door, we'll have to sit sideways on the toilet, but they won't have a chance of getting in. You poor pet."

She looked at Eilis again with sympathy. She was wearing make-up and seemed untouched by the ravages of the night.

"What did you have for dinner?" Georgina asked as she set about moving the trunk into the bathroom.

"I think it was mutton."

"And peas, plenty of peas. And how do you feel?"

"I have never felt worse. Did I leave a big mess in the corridor?"

"Yes, but the whole ship's a mess. Even first class is a mess. They'll start the cleaning there and it'll be hours before they make it down here. Why did you eat such a big dinner?"

"I didn't know."

"Did you not hear them saying it when we were coming on board? It's the worst storm in years. It's always bad, especially down here, but this one is terrible. Just drink water, nothing else, no solids. It'll do wonders for your figure."

"I'm sorry about the smell."

"They'll come and clean it all up. We'll move the trunk again when we hear them coming and we'll put it back when they go. I got spotted in first class and I've been warned to stay down here until we dock or I'll be arrested at the other side. So I'm afraid you've got company. And, darling, when I vomit, you'll know all about it. And that's all's going to happen for the next day or so, vomiting, plenty of it. And then I'm told we'll be in calm waters."

"I feel terrible," Eilis said.

"It's called seasickness, duck, and it turns you green."

"Do I look terrible?"

"Oh, yes, and so does every person on this boat."

As she spoke, a loud knocking came from the other cabin. Georgina went into the bathroom.

"Fuck off!" she shouted. "Can you hear me? Good! Now, fuck off!"

Eilis stood behind her in her nightdress and her bare feet. She was laughing.

"I need to go to the toilet now," she said. "I hope you don't mind."

Later in the day they came with buckets of water filled with disinfectant and they washed the floors of the corridors and the rooms. They took away the sheets and blankets that had been soiled and brought new ones and fresh towels. Georgina, who had been watching out for them, pushed the trunk back to its place inside the door. When the neighbours, two elderly American ladies, whom Eilis now saw for the first time, complained to the cleaners that the bathroom had been locked, the cleaners shrugged and carried on working. The second they had gone, Georgina and Eilis edged the trunk back into the bathroom before their neighbours got a chance to block the door from the other side. When they banged on both the bathroom door and the door of the cabin, Eilis and Georgina laughed.

"They missed their chance. That will teach them now!" Georgina said.

She went to the dining room and came back with two jugs of water.

"They have only one waiter," she said, "so you can take what you like. This is your ration for tonight. Eat nothing and drink plenty, that's the key. It won't stop you being sick, but it won't be as bad."

"It feels as if the boat is being pushed back all the time," Eilis said.

"From down here it always feels like that," Georgina replied. "But stay still and save your breath and vomit to your heart's content when you feel like it and you'll be a new woman tomorrow."

"You sound like you have been on this boat thousands of times."

"I have," Georgina said. "I go home once a year to see my mam. It's a lot of suffering for a week. By the time I've recovered I have to go back. But I love seeing them all. We're not getting any younger, any of us, so it's nice to spend a week together."

After another night of constant retching, Eilis was exhausted; the liner seemed to hammer against the water. But then the sea became calm. Georgina, who moved regularly up and down the corridor, met the couple in the adjoining cabin and made an agreement with them that neither side would prevent the other from using the bathroom, but they would instead attempt to share it in a spirit of harmony now that the storms were over. She moved her trunk out of the bathroom and warned Eilis, who admitted to being hungry, not to eat anything at all, no matter how hungry she was, but to drink plenty of water and try not to fall asleep during the day, despite the overwhelming temptation to do so. If she could sleep a full night, Georgina said, she would feel much better.

Eilis could not believe she had four more nights to spend in this cramped space, with stale air and weak light. It was only when she went into the bathroom to wash herself that she found moments of relief from the vague nausea mixed with terrible hunger that stayed with her and the claustrophobia that seemed to become more intense whenever Georgina left her in the cabin.

Since they had only a bath in her mother's house, she had never had a shower before, and it took her a while to work out how to get the water at the right temperature without turning it off altogether. As she soaped herself and put shampoo on her wet hair, she wondered if this could be heated sea water and, if not, then how the ship managed to carry so much fresh water. In tanks, maybe, she thought, or perhaps it was rainwater. Whatever it was, standing under it brought her ease for the first time since the ship had left Liverpool.

*   *   *

On the night before they were due to dock, she went to the dining room with Georgina, who told her that she looked wretched and that if she did not take care she would be stopped at Ellis Island and put in quarantine, or at least given a thorough medical examination. Back in the cabin, Eilis showed Georgina her passport and papers to prove to her that she would not have a problem entering the United States. She told her that she would be met by Father Flood. Georgina was surprised, she said, that Eilis had a full, rather than a temporary, work permit. She did not think it was easy to get such a document any more, even with the help of a priest. She made Eilis open her suitcase and show her what clothes she had brought so that she could select suitable attire for her when she was disembarking and make sure that nothing she wore was too wrinkled.

"Nothing fancy," she said. "We don't want you looking like a tart."

She chose a white dress with a red floral pattern that Rose had given Eilis and a plain cardigan and a plain-coloured scarf. She looked at the three pairs of shoes that Eilis had packed and selected the plainest, insisting that the shoes would have to be polished.

"And wear your coat over your arm and look as though you know where you're going and don't wash your hair again, the water on this boat has made it stand out like a ball of steel wool. You'll need to spend a few hours brushing it to get it into any shape at all."

In the morning, between arranging to have her trunk carried on deck, Georgina began to put make-up on, getting Eilis to comb her hair out even straighter now that the brushing was done so that it could be tied back into a bun.

"Don't look too innocent," she said. "When I put some eye-liner on you and some rouge and mascara, they'll be afraid to stop you. Your suitcase is all wrong, but there's nothing we can do about that."

"What's wrong with it?"

"It's too Irish and they stop the Irish."

"Really?"

"Try not to look so frightened."

"I'm hungry."

"We're all hungry. But, darling, you don't need to look hungry. Pretend you are full."

"And I almost never wear make-up at home."

"Well, you're about to enter the land of the free and the brave. And I don't know how you got that stamp on your passport. The priest must know someone. The only thing they can stop you for is if they think you have TB, so don't cough whatever you do, or if they think you have some funny eye disease, I can't remember the name of it. So keep your eyes open. Sometimes, they don't stop you at all, except to look at your papers."

Georgina made Eilis sit on the bottom bunk and turn her face towards the light and close her eyes. For twenty minutes she worked slowly, applying a thin cake of make-up and then some rouge, with eye-liner and mascara. She backcombed her hair. When she finished, she sent Eilis into the bathroom with some lipstick and told her to put it on very gently and make sure that she did not spread it all over her face. When Eilis looked at herself in the mirror she was surprised. She seemed older and, she thought, almost good-looking. She thought that she would love to know how to put make-up on properly herself in the way that Rose knew and Georgina knew. It would be much easier, she imagined, to go out among people she did not know, maybe people she would never see again, if she could look like this. It would make her less nervous in one way, she thought, but maybe more so in another, because she knew that people would look at her and might have a view on her that was wrong if she were dressed up like this every day in Brooklyn.

Part Two

Eilis woke in the night and pushed the blanket onto the floor and tried to go back to sleep with just a sheet covering her, but it was still too hot. She was bathed in sweat. This was, they told her, probably the last week of the heat; soon, the temperature would drop and she would need blankets, but for the moment it would remain muggy and humid and everyone would move slowly and wearily in the streets.

Her room was at the back of the house and the bathroom was across the corridor. The floorboards creaked and the door, she thought, was made of light material and the plumbing was loud so she could hear the other boarders if they went to the bathroom in the night or came back home late at the weekends. She did not mind being woken as long as it was still dark outside and she could curl up in her own bed knowing there was time to doze. She could manage then to keep all thoughts of the day ahead out of her mind. But if she woke when it was bright, then she knew she had only an hour or two at most before the alarm clock would sound and the day would begin.

Mrs. Kehoe, who owned the house, was from Wexford town and loved to talk to her about home, about Sunday trips to Curracloe and Rosslare Strand, or hurling matches, or the shops along the Main Street in Wexford town, or characters she remembered. Eilis had presumed at the beginning that Mrs. Kehoe was a widow and had asked about Mr. Kehoe and where he had come from, to be met with a sad smile as Mrs. Kehoe informed her that he came from Kilmore Quay and said nothing more. Later, when Eilis had mentioned this to Father Flood, he had told her that it was best not to say too much about Mr. Kehoe, who had gone out west with all of their money, leaving his wife with debts, the house on Clinton Street and no income at all. This was why, Father Flood said, Mrs. Kehoe was letting out the rooms in the house and had five other girls as lodgers besides Eilis.

Mrs. Kehoe had her own sitting room and bedroom and bathroom on the ground floor. She had her own telephone, but would not, she made clear to Eilis, take phone messages under any circumstances for any of the lodgers. There were two girls in the basement and four on the upper floors; between them they had the use of the large kitchen on the ground floor, where Mrs. Kehoe served them their evening meal. They could make tea or coffee there at any time, Eilis was told, as long as they used their own cups and saucers, which they were to wash and dry themselves and put away.

On Sundays, Mrs. Kehoe had a rule that she did not appear and it was up to the girls to cook, making sure to leave no mess behind them. Mrs. Kehoe went to early mass on Sundays, she told Eilis, and then had friends around in the evening for an old-fashioned and serious poker game. She made the poker game, Eilis noted in a letter home, sound as though it was another form of Sunday duty that she performed only because it was in the rules.

Before dinner each evening they stood up solemnly and joined their hands and Mrs. Kehoe led them in saying grace. As they sat at the table, she did not like the girls talking among themselves, or discussing matters she knew nothing about, and she did not encourage any mention of boyfriends. She was mainly interested in clothes and shoes, and where they could be bought and at what price and at what time of the year. Changing fashions and new trends were her daily topic, although she herself, as she often pointed out, was too old for some of the new colours and styles. Yet, Eilis saw, she dressed impeccably and noticed every item each of her lodgers was wearing. She also loved discussing skin care and different types of skin and problems. Mrs. Kehoe had her hair done once a week, on a Saturday, using the same hairdresser each time, spending several hours with her so that her hair would be perfect for the rest of the week.

On Eilis's own floor, in the front bedroom, was Miss McAdam from Belfast, who worked as a secretary and had least to say at the table about fashions, unless the subject of rising prices came up. She was very prim, Eilis wrote in a letter home, and had asked Eilis as a special favour not to leave all her toilet things around the bathroom as the other girls did. The other girls, on the floor above them, were younger than Miss McAdam, Eilis wrote in her letter, and had to be regularly corrected by both Mrs. Kehoe and Miss McAdam. One of them, Patty McGuire, had been born in upstate New York, she told Eilis, and was now working as Eilis was in one of the large department stores in Brooklyn. She was man-mad, Eilis noted. Patty's best friend was in the basement; she was called Diana Montini, but her mother was Irish and she had red hair. Like Patty, she spoke with an American accent.

Diana complained constantly about the food that Mrs. Kehoe cooked, insisting that it was too Irish. She and Patty dressed up, taking hours to do so, every Friday and Saturday night and went out to amusements or movies or dances, any place where there were men, as Miss McAdam sourly said. There was always trouble between Patty and Sheila Heffernan, who shared the top floor, over noise at night. Sheila, who was also older than Patty and Diana, came from Skerries and worked as a secretary. When the reason for the trouble between Sheila and Patty was explained to Eilis by Mrs. Kehoe, Miss McAdam, who was in the room, interrupted to say that she saw no difference between them and the mess they made and the way they used her soap and her shampoo and even her toothpaste when she was foolish enough to leave them in the bathroom.

She complained all the time, to Patty and Sheila themselves, and to Mrs. Kehoe, about the noise their shoes made on the stairs and the floor above.

In the basement with Diana was Miss Keegan from Galway, who never said much, unless the talk turned to Fianna Fáil and De Valera, or the American political system, which it seldom did, as Mrs. Kehoe had, she said, a complete revulsion of political discussion of any sort.

The first two weekends Patty and Diana asked Eilis if she would like to come out with them, but Eilis, who had not yet been paid, preferred to stay in the kitchen until bedtime even on the Saturday nights. And on her second Sunday she had gone for a walk on her own in the afternoon, having made the mistake the previous week of going with Miss McAdam, who had nothing good to say about anyone and had sniffed her nose disapprovingly if anyone passed by them who she thought was Italian or Jewish.

"I didn't come all the way to America, thank you, to hear people talking Italian on the street or see them wearing funny hats," she said.

In another letter home Eilis described the system they had at Mrs. Kehoe's for washing clothes. Mrs. Kehoe did not have many rules, Eilis told her mother and Rose, but they included no visitors, no dirty cutlery or cups and saucers left lying around and no washing of clothes of any sort on the premises. Once a week, on a Monday, an Italian woman and her daughter from a nearby street came to collect the washing. Every boarder had a bag, and a list had to be attached of what was in the bag, which would then be returned with the washing on Wednesdays with a price at the bottom that Mrs. Kehoe would pay, to be reimbursed by each boarder when she came home from work. They would then find their clean clothes hanging in their closets or folded and placed in the chest of drawers. There would also be clean sheets on the beds and fresh towels. The Italian women, Eilis wrote, ironed everything beautifully and put starch into her dresses and blouses, which she loved.

She had dozed for a while and now she woke. She looked at the clock: it was twenty to eight. If she got up immediately, she thought, she would reach the bathroom before Patty or Sheila; Miss McAdam would, she knew, have already gone to work by now. She moved quickly to the door and across the landing with her toilet bag. She wore a shower cap because she did not want to destroy her hair, which became fuzzy when it was washed in the water of the house as it had on the ship and took hours then to comb out. When she got paid, she thought, she would go to the hairdresser's and have it cut shorter, made more manageable.

Downstairs, she was glad to be alone in the kitchen. Since she did not want to talk, she did not sit down so that she could leave instantly if any of the others arrived. She made tea and toast. She still had not found bread anywhere that she liked and even the tea and the milk tasted strange. The butter had a flavour she did not like either, it tasted almost of grease. One day on the street as she walked home from work she had noticed a woman at a stall selling jam. The woman spoke no English; Eilis did not think she was Italian and could not guess where she came from, but the woman had smiled at her as she examined the different pots of jam. She selected one and paid, thinking she was buying gooseberry jam, but when she tried it at Mrs. Kehoe's the flavour was new to her. She was not sure what it was, but she liked it because it masked the taste of the bread and the butter, just as three spoons of sugar managed to mask the taste of the tea and milk.

She had spent some of Rose's money on shoes. The first pair

she had bought had looked comfortable but after a few days had begun to pinch her feet slightly. The second pair were flat and plain but fitted perfectly; she carried them in her bag and changed into them once she arrived at work.

She hated it when Patty or Diana paid too much attention to her. She was the new girl, and the youngest, and they could not stop giving her advice, or making criticisms or comments. She wondered how long it would go on for, and was trying to let them know how little appreciated their interest was by smiling faintly at them when they spoke or, a few times, especially in the morning, by looking at them vacantly as though she did not understand a word they said.

Having had her breakfast and washed her cup and saucer and plate, paying no heed to Patty, who had just arrived, Eilis slipped quietly out of the house, leaving herself plenty of time to get to work. This was her third week, and, although she had written a number of times to her mother and Rose and once to her brothers in Birmingham, she still had received no letters from them. It struck her as she crossed the street that by the time she arrived home at six thirty a whole world of things would have happened that she could tell them about; each moment appeared to bring some new sight or sensation or piece of information. The days at work so far had not been boring for her, the hours passing easily enough.

It was later, when she got home and lay in the bed after her evening meal, that the day she had just spent would seem like one of the longest of her life as she would find herself going through it scene by scene. Even tiny details stayed in her mind. When she deliberately tried to think about something else, or leave her mind blank, events from the day would come quickly back. For each day, she thought, she needed a whole other day to contemplate what had happened and store it away, get it out of her system so that it did not keep her awake at night or fill her dreams with flashes of what had actually happened and other flashes that had nothing to do with anything familiar, but were full of rushes of colour or crowds of people, everything frenzied and fast.

She liked the morning air and the quietness of these few leafy streets, streets that had shops only on the corners, streets where people lived, where there were three or four apartments in each house and where she passed women accompanying their children to school as she went to work. As she walked along, however, she knew she was getting close to the real world, which had wider streets and more traffic. Once she arrived at Atlantic Avenue, Brooklyn began to feel like a strange place to her, with so many gaps between buildings and so many derelict buildings. And then suddenly, when she arrived at Fulton Street, there would be so many people crowding to cross the street, and in such dense clusters, that on the first morning she thought a fight had broken out or someone was injured and they had gathered to get a good view. Most mornings she stood back for a minute or two, waiting for the crowds to disperse.

In Bartocci's, she had to clock in, which was easy, and then go to her locker in the women's room downstairs and change into the blue uniform that girls on the shop floor had to wear. She was there most mornings before most of the other girls arrived. Some of them often did not appear until the last second. Miss Fortini, who was the supervisor, disapproved of this, Eilis knew. On her first day, Father Flood had taken her to the main office and she had had an interview with Elisabetta Bartocci, the daughter of the owner, who she thought was the most perfectly dressed woman she had ever seen. She wrote to her mother and Rose about Miss Bartocci's flaring red costume and white plain blouse, her red high-heeled shoes, her hair, which was shiny black and perfect. Her lipstick was bright red and her eyes were the blackest Eilis had ever seen.

"Brooklyn changes every day," Miss Bartocci said as Father

Flood nodded. "New people arrive and they could be Jewish or Irish or Polish or even coloured. Our old customers are moving out to Long Island and we can't follow them, so we need new customers every week. We treat everyone the same. We welcome every single person who comes into this store. They all have money to spend. We keep our prices low and our manners high. If people like it here, they'll come back. You treat the customer like a new friend. Is that a deal?"

Eilis nodded.

"You give them a big Irish smile."

As Miss Bartocci went to fetch the supervisor, Father Flood told Eilis to take a look at the people working in the office. "A lot of them started like you, on the shop floor. And they did night classes and studied and now they're in the office. Some of them are actual accountants, fully qualified."

"I'd like to study bookkeeping," Eilis said. "I've already done a basic course."

"It'll be different here, different systems," Father Flood said. "But I'll find out if there are any courses nearby with places open. Even if they don't have places open, we'll see if we can get one open. But it'd be best not to mention this to Miss Bartocci and concentrate for the moment, as far as she is concerned, on the job you have."

Eilis nodded. Soon Miss Bartocci came back with Miss Fortini, who said "yes" after everything Miss Bartocci said, barely opening her mouth as she spoke. Every so often her eyes darted around the office and then, as though she had been doing something wrong, fixed quickly again on Miss Bartocci's face.

"Miss Fortini is going to teach you how to use the cash system, which is easy once you know it. And if you have any problems, go to her first, even the smallest thing. The only way for the customers to be happy is for the staff to be happy. You work nine to six, Monday through Saturday, with forty-five minutes for lunch and one half-day a week. And we encourage all our staff to do night classes—"

"We were speaking about that just now," Father Flood interrupted.

"So if you wanted to do night classes, we would pay part of the tuition. Not all of it, mind. And if you want to purchase anything in the store, you tell Miss Fortini and with most things there will be a reduction in the price."

Miss Fortini asked Eilis if she was ready to start. Father Flood took his leave as Miss Bartocci went to her desk and briskly began to open the post. When Miss Fortini led her to the shop floor and showed her the cash system, Eilis did not want to say that they had exactly the same system in Bolger's in Rafter Street at home, where the cash and a docket were put into a metal holder that was sent through the shop by a system of tubes until it arrived at the cash office, where the docket was marked paid, put back in the container with the change and returned. Eilis allowed Miss Fortini to explain it to her carefully, as though she had never seen anything like it before.

Miss Fortini then alerted the cash office that she would be sending a number of dummy dockets, each with five dollars enclosed. She showed Eilis how to fill out the dockets, writing her own name and the date at the top, then below the item purchased with the quantity on the left-hand side and the price on the right-hand side. She should also, Miss Fortini said, note the amount of money she was sending on the back of the docket, just so there would be no misunderstanding. Most customers would have to wait for their change, Miss Fortini said. Hardly anyone ever came up with the right amount, and most items, in any case, cost some number of dollars and then ninety-nine cents, or an uneven number of cents. If a customer were purchasing more than one item, Miss Fortini advised, Eilis should do the maths herself, but it would always be checked as well in the cash office.

"If you don't make mistakes, they'll notice you and they'll get to like you," she added.

Eilis watched as Miss Fortini wrote out several dockets for her and sent them and then waited for them to return. She then filled some out herself, the first for a single item purchased, the second for a number of the same item, and the third for a complicated mixture of items. Miss Fortini stood over her as she did the addition.

"It's better to go slowly and then you won't make mistakes," she said.

Eilis did not tell Miss Fortini that she never made mistakes when she did addition. Instead, she worked slowly, as she had been advised, making sure that the figures were correct.

She was surprised by some of the items of clothing for sale. The cups of some of the brassieres seemed much more pointed than anything she had seen before, and an item called a two-way stretch, which looked as though it had plastic bones in the middle, was new to her. The first thing she sold was called a brasalette, and she decided that, when she knew the other boarders at Mrs. Kehoe's well enough, she would ask one of them to take her through these items of American women's underwear.

The work was easy. Miss Fortini was interested only in time-keeping and tidiness and making sure that the slightest complaint or query was immediately conveyed to her. She was not hard to locate, Eilis discovered, as she was always watching, and if you seemed to be having the slightest difficulty with a customer and if you were not seen to be smiling, Miss Fortini would notice and begin to move towards you signalling to you, stopping only if she saw that you looked both busy and pleasant.

Eilis learned quickly where she could have a fast lunch at a counter and then have twenty minutes to explore the other shops around Fulton Street. Diana and Patty and Mrs. Kehoe all told her that the best clothes shop near Bartocci's was Loehmann's on Bedford Avenue. Downstairs at Loehmann's at lunchtime was always busier than Bartocci's, and the clothes seemed cheaper, but the minute Eilis made her way upstairs she thought of Rose because it was the most beautiful shop floor she had ever seen, not really like a shop at all, closer to a palace, with fewer people shopping and elegantly dressed assistants. When she looked at the prices she had to convert them into pounds to make any sense of them. They appeared very low. She tried to remember some of the dresses and costumes and their prices so she could give Rose a precise description of them, but each time she went there she had only a few minutes to spare, as she did not want to return late to the shop floor at Bartocci's. She had had no difficulties so far with Miss Fortini and she did not want to have any problems so early in her time working for her.

One morning, when she had been there for three weeks and was on her fourth, Eilis knew that something strange had happened as soon as she reached the other side of Fulton Street and could see the windows of Bartocci's. They were covered in huge banners saying FAMOUS NYLON SALE. She did not know that they had planned to have a sale, presuming that they would not do so until January. In the locker room she met Miss Fortini, to whom she expressed surprise.

"Mr. Bartocci always keeps it a secret. He supervises all the work himself overnight. The whole floor is nylon, everything nylon, and most at half price. You can buy four items yourself. And this is a special bag to keep the money in because you can only accept exact change. We've put even prices on everything. So no dockets today. And there will be tight security. It will be the biggest scramble you've ever seen in your life because even the nylon stockings are half price. And there's no lunch break, instead there will be free sandwiches and soda down here, but don't come more than twice. I'll be watching. We need everyone working."

Within half an hour of opening there were queues outside. Most women wanted stockings; they took three or four pairs before moving to the back of the store, where there were nylon sweater sets in every possible colour and in most sizes, everything at least half off the regular price. The job of the sales assistant was to follow the crowd with Bartocci carrier bags in one hand and the cash bag in the other. All the customers seemed to know that there would be no change given.

Miss Bartocci and two of the office staff manned the doors, which had to be kept shut from ten o'clock as the crowds surged. The people who normally worked in the cash department had special uniforms and worked on the shop floor as well. A few stood outside and made sure that the queue was orderly. The shop, Eilis thought, was the hottest and busiest place she had ever seen. Mr. Bartocci walked through the crowd taking the cash bags and emptying them into a huge canvas sack that he carried.

The morning was full of frenzy; she did not for one moment have peace to look around her. Everyone's voice was loud, and there were times when she thought in a flash of an early evening in October walking with her mother down by the prom in Enniscorthy, the Slaney River glassy and full, and the smell of leaves burning from somewhere close by, and the daylight going slowly and gently. This scene kept coming to her as she filled the bag with notes and coins and women of all types approached her asking where certain items of clothing could be found or if they could return what they had bought in exchange for other merchandise, or simply wishing to purchase what they had in their hands.

Although Miss Fortini was not especially tall, she appeared to be able to oversee everything, answering questions, picking things up from the floor that had fallen there, tidying and stacking goods neatly. The morning had gone by quickly, but as the afternoon wore on Eilis found herself watching the clock, discovering after a while that she was checking every five minutes in between dealing with what seemed like hundreds of customers as the supply of nylon goods began to dwindle slowly, enough for Miss Fortini to tell her to take what she needed herself, four items only, downstairs now. She could, she was told, pay for them later.

She selected a pair of nylon stockings for herself, one she thought might suit Mrs. Kehoe, and then one each for her mother and for Rose. Having taken them downstairs and put them in her locker, she sat with one of the other assistants and drank a soda and then opened another that she sipped until she thought that Miss Fortini would notice her absence. When she went back upstairs, she discovered that it was only three o'clock and some of the nylon items that were running short were being replaced, were being almost dumped on to the display cases by men who were overseen by Mr. Bartocci. Later, when she was having her evening meal at Mrs. Kehoe's, she discovered that both Patty and Sheila had found out about the sale and had rushed around during their lunch break, running in to get some items and running out again so that they did not have time in the middle of all the crush to see where she was and say hello.

Mrs. Kehoe seemed pleased by the pair of stockings and offered to pay for them, but Eilis said they were a gift. That evening, during supper, they all talked about Bartocci's Famous Nylon Sale, which always happened without warning, yet they were amazed when Eilis told them that even she who worked there had no idea the sale was going to happen.

"Well, if you ever hear, even a rumour," Diana said, "you'll have to let us all know. And the nylon stockings are the best, they don't run as easily as some of the others. They'd sell you garbage, some of those other stores."

"That's enough now," Mrs. Kehoe said. "I'm sure all the stores are doing their best."

With all the excitement and discussion surrounding the nylon sale, Eilis did not notice until the end of the meal that there were three letters for her. The minute she came back from work every day she had checked the side table in the kitchen where Mrs. Kehoe left letters. She could not believe that she had forgotten to check this evening. She drank a cup of tea with the others, holding the letters in her hand nervously, feeling her heart beating faster when she thought about them, waiting to go to her room and open them and read the news from home.

The letters, she knew by the handwriting, were from her mother and Rose and Jack. She decided to read her mother's first and leave Rose's until the end. Her mother's letter was short and there was no news in it, just a list of the people who were asking for her with some details of where her mother had met them and when. Jack's letter was much the same, but with references to the crossing that she had told him about in her letter and had said very little about in her letter to her mother and Rose. Rose's handwriting was, she saw, very beautiful and clear, as usual. She wrote about golf and work and how quiet and dull the town was and how lucky Eilis was to be in the bright lights. In a postscript, she suggested that Eilis might like sometimes to write to her separately about private matters or things that might worry their mother too much. She suggested that Eilis might use her work address for these letters.

The letters told Eilis little; there was hardly anything personal in them and nothing that sounded like anyone's own voice. Nonetheless, as she read them over and over, she forgot for a moment where she was and she could picture her mother in the kitchen taking her Basildon Bond notepad and her envelopes and setting out to write a proper letter with nothing crossed out. Rose, she thought, might have gone into the dining room to write on paper she had taken home from work, using a longer, more elegant white envelope than her mother had. Eilis imagined that Rose when she was finished might have left hers on the hall table, and her mother would have gone with both letters in the morning to the post office, having to get special stamps for America. She could not imagine where Jack had written his letter, which was briefer than the other two, almost shy in its tone, as though he did not want to put too much in writing.

She lay on the bed with the letters beside her. For the past few weeks, she realized, she had not really thought of home. The town had come to her in flashing pictures, such as the one that had come during the afternoon of the sale, and she had thought of course of her mother and Rose, but her own life in Enniscorthy, the life she had lost and would never have again, she had kept out of her mind. Every day she had come back to this small room in this house full of sounds and gone over everything new that had happened. Now, all that seemed like nothing compared to the picture she had of home, of her own room, the house in Friary Street, the food she had eaten there, the clothes she wore, how quiet everything was.

All this came to her like a terrible weight and she felt for a second that she was going to cry. It was as though an ache in her chest was trying to force tears down her cheeks despite her enormous effort to keep them back. She did not give in to whatever it was. She kept thinking, attempting to work out what was causing this new feeling that was like despondency, that was like how she felt when her father died and she watched them closing the coffin, the feeling that he would never see the world again and she would never be able to talk to him again.

She was nobody here. It was not just that she had no friends and family; it was rather that she was a ghost in this room, in the streets on the way to work, on the shop floor. Nothing meant anything. The rooms in the house on Friary Street belonged to her, she thought; when she moved in them she was really there. In the

town, if she walked to the shop or to the Vocational School, the
air, the light, the ground, it was all solid and part of her, even if
she met no one familiar. Nothing here was part of her. It was false,
empty, she thought. She closed her eyes and tried to think, as she
had done so many times in her life, of something she was looking
forward to, but there was nothing. Not the slightest thing. Not
even Sunday. Nothing maybe except sleep, and she was not even
certain she was looking forward to sleep. In any case, she could
not sleep yet, since it was not yet nine o'clock. There was nothing
she could do. It was as though she had been locked away.

In the morning, she was not sure that she had slept as much as
lived a set of vivid dreams, letting them linger so that she would
not have to open her eyes and see the room. One of the dreams
was about the courthouse at the top of Friary Hill in Enniscorthy.
She remembered now how much the neighbours had dreaded the
day when the court sat, not because of the cases that were reported
in the papers of petty theft, or drunkenness, or disorderly behav-
iour, but because sometimes the court ordered children to be
taken into care, put into orphanages or industrial schools or fos-
ter homes because they mitched from school or caused trouble or
because of problems with their parents. Sometimes, inconsolable
mothers could be found screaming, howling outside the courthouse as their children were taken away. But her dream had no
screaming women, just a group of silent children, Eilis among
them, standing in a line, knowing that they would soon be led
away on the orders of the judge.

What was strange for her now as she lay awake was that she
had seemed to be looking forward to being led away, she had felt
no fear of it. Her fear, instead, was of seeing her mother in front
of the courthouse. In her dream she found a way of avoiding her
mother. She was taken out of the line, and through a side door and
then on a car journey that appeared to last as long as she could
stay asleep.

She got up and used the bathroom very quietly; she thought that she would have breakfast in one of the diners on Fulton Street, as she had seen people do on her way to work. Once she was dressed and ready, she tiptoed out of the house. She did not want to meet any of the others. It was only half past seven. She would, she thought, sit somewhere for an hour, having a coffee and a sandwich, and then go to work early.

As she walked, she began to dread the day. Later, as she sat at the counter of a diner looking at a menu, snatches of another dream that she had only half remembered when she woke came to her. She was flying, as though in a balloon, over the calm sea on a calm day. Below, she could see the cliffs at Cush Gap and the soft sand at Ballyconnigar. The wind was propelling her towards Blackwater, then the Ballagh, then Monageer, then Vinegar Hill and Enniscorthy. She was lost so much in the memory of this dream that the waiter behind the counter asked her if she was all right.

"I'm fine," she said.

"You look sad," he replied.

She shook her hair and tried to smile and ordered a coffee and a sandwich.

"Cheer up," he said in a louder voice. "Come on, cheer up. It'll never happen. Give us a smile."

A few of the other customers at the counter looked at her. She knew that she would not be able to hold back the tears. She did not wait for her order to arrive but ran out of the diner before anyone could say anything else to her.

During the day she felt that Miss Fortini was looking at her more than usual and this made her acutely conscious of how she appeared when she was not dealing directly with a customer. She tried to look towards the door and the front windows and the street, she tried to seem busy, but she found that she could, if she did not stop herself, move easily into a sort of trance, thinking over and over of the same things, about everything she had lost, and wondering how she would face going back to the evening meal with the others and the long night alone in a room that had nothing to do with her. Then she would find Miss Fortini staring at her across the shop floor and she would try once again to seem cheerful and helpful to customers as though it were a normal day at work.

The evening meal was not as difficult as she had imagined, as both Patty and Diana had bought new shoes and Mrs. Kehoe, before she could give them her full approval, needed to see what costume or dress and other accessories they would be worn with. The kitchen before and after supper became like a fashion parade, with both Miss McAdam and Miss Keegan withholding approval each time Patty or Diana came into the room wearing the shoes and some new set of clothes with a different handbag.

Mrs. Kehoe was not sure, once she had seen Diana's shoes with the costume they were intended to match, that they were dressy enough.

"They are neither fish nor fowl," she said. "You couldn't wear them to work and they mightn't look great on a night out somewhere. I can't see why you bought them unless there was a sale."

Diana looked crestfallen as she admitted that there had been no sale.

"Oh, then," Mrs. Kehoe said. "All I can say is that I hope you kept the receipt."

"Well, I quite like them," Miss McAdam said.

"So do I," Sheila Heffernan added.

"But when would you wear them?" Mrs. Kehoe asked.

"I just like them," Miss McAdam said and shrugged.

Eilis slipped away, glad no one had noticed that she had not spoken once at the meal. She wondered if she could go out now, do anything rather than face her tomb of a bedroom and all the thoughts that would come when she lay awake and all the dreams that would come when she slept. She stood in the hall, and then turned upstairs, realizing that she was afraid too of the outside, and even if she were not she would have no idea where to go at this time of the evening. She hated this house, she thought, its smells, its noises, its colours. She was already crying as she went up the stairs. She knew that as long as the others were discussing their wardrobes in the kitchen below, she would be able to cry as loudly as she pleased without their hearing her.

That night was the worst she had ever spent. It was only as the dawn came that she remembered something Jack had said to her on the day in Liverpool before she had caught the boat, a time that now seemed like years ago. He had said that he found being away hard at first, but he did not elaborate and she did not think of asking him what it really had been like. His manner was so mild and good-humoured, just as her father's had been, that he would not in any case want to complain. She considered writing to him now asking him if he too had felt like this, as though he had been shut away somewhere and was trapped in a place where there was nothing. It was like hell, she thought, because she could see no end to it, and to the feeling that came with it, but the torment was strange, it was all in her mind, it was like the arrival of night if you knew that you would never see anything in daylight again. She did not know what she was going to do. But she knew that Jack was too far away to be able to help her.

None of them could help her. She had lost all of them. They would not find out about this; she would not put it into a letter. And because of this she understood that they would never know her now. Maybe, she thought, they had never known her, any of them, because if they had, then they would have had to realize what this would be like for her.

She lay there as the light of day began; she did not think she would be able to manage another night like this. For a while she was quietly resigned to the prospect that nothing would change, but she did not know what the consequences would be, or what form they would take. Once more, she got up early and left the house without making a sound and walked the streets for an hour before going to have a cup of coffee. She noticed the cold in the air for the first time; it seemed to her that the weather had changed. But it hardly mattered now what the weather was like. She found a place in a diner where she could have her back to everybody, and no one could comment on the expression on her face.

By the time she drank the coffee and had a bun and managed to get the waitress's attention to pay the bill, she realized that she had left herself too short a time to get to work. If she did not hurry, she was going to be late for the first time. There were crowds in the streets and she could not easily get past people. She wondered at one point if people were not deliberately blocking her way. It took a long time for the traffic lights to change. Once she was on Fulton Street, it was even harder; it was as though crowds were coming out of a football game. Even moving at a normal pace was hard. She arrived at Bartocci's with just a minute to spare. She did not know how she was going to spend the day standing on the shop floor trying to look pleasant and attentive. The minute she appeared upstairs in her work clothes she caught Miss Fortini's gaze, which seemed disapproving as she began to move towards her, only for her then to be distracted by a customer. Once the customer had been dealt with, Eilis was careful not to look Miss Fortini's way again. She kept her back to her for as long as she could.

"You don't look well," Miss Fortini said when she approached.

Eilis could feel her eyes filling with tears.

"Why don't you go downstairs and have a glass of water and I'll be down in a second?" Miss Fortini said. Her voice sounded kind but she did not smile.

Eilis nodded. It struck her that she had not yet been paid; she was still living on the money Rose had given her. If they sacked her, she did not know if they would pay her. If they did not, within a short time she would have no money at all. It would be hard, she thought, to find another job, but even if she did she would have to be paid at the end of the first week, otherwise she would not be able to pay the rent to Mrs. Kehoe.

Downstairs, she went into the bathroom and washed her face. She stared at herself in the mirror for a moment and then stood tidying her hair. Then in the staff room she waited for Miss Fortini.

"Now you'll have to tell me what's wrong," she said as she came into the room and closed the door behind her. "Because I can see that there's something wrong and soon some of the customers will begin to notice and then we'll all be in trouble."

Eilis shook her head. "I don't know what's wrong."

"Is it your time of the month?" Miss Fortini asked.

Eilis shook her head again.

"Eilis"—she pronounced the name strangely, with too much emphasis on the second syllable—"why are you upset?" She stood in front of her and waited. "Would you like me to call Miss Bartocci?" she asked.

"No."

"Then what?"

"I don't know what it is."

"Are you sad?"

"Yes."

"All the time?"

"Yes."

"Do you wish you were with your family at home?"

"Yes."

"Do you have family here?"

"No."

"No one?"

"No one."

"When did the sadness begin? You were happy last week."

"I got some letters."

"Bad news?"

"No, no, nothing."

"Just the letters? Have you been out of Ireland before?"

"No."

"Away from your father and mother?"

"My father is dead."

"Your mother?"

"I've never been away from her before."

Miss Fortini looked at her but did not smile.

"I'll need to talk to Miss Bartocci and the priest you came with."

"Please don't."

"They won't cause a problem. But you cannot work here if you're sad. And of course you're sad if you're not with your mother for the first time in your life. But the sadness won't last so we'll do what we can for you."

Miss Fortini told her to sit down and filled her another glass of water and left the room. It was clear to Eilis as she waited there that she was not going to be sacked. As a result, she was almost proud of how she had managed Miss Fortini, letting her ask all the questions and answering as little as she could, but enough not to seem surly or ungrateful. She felt almost strong as she contemplated what had just happened and she resolved that no matter who came into the room now, even if it were Mr. Bartocci himself, she would be able to elicit their sympathy. It was not as though there was nothing wrong; whatever darkness she felt had not lifted. But she could not tell them that she dreaded their shop and their customers, and that she hated Mrs. Kehoe's house, and there was nothing any of them could do for her. Yet she would have to keep her job. And she believed she had achieved that much and it gave her a feeling of satisfaction that appeared to melt into her sadness, or float on its surface, distracting her, as least for now, from the worst parts of it.

After a while Miss Fortini arrived with a sandwich that she had brought from a diner near the store. She said that she had spoken to Miss Bartocci and assured her that it was a simple problem, that it had never happened before and might never happen again. But Miss Bartocci had then spoken to her father, who was a special friend of Father Flood, and he had telephoned the priest and left a message with his housekeeper.

"Mr. Bartocci says you are to stay down here until he hears from Father Flood and he told me to get you this sandwich. You are one lucky girl. He is sometimes nice the first time like this. But I wouldn't cross him twice. No one crosses Mr. Bartocci twice."

"I didn't cross him," Eilis said quietly.

"Oh, you did, dear. Turning up in that state to work and having that look on your face. Oh, you crossed Mr. Bartocci and it's something that he'll never forget."

As the day went on, some of the other sales girls from the floor came down to see Eilis, studying her with curiosity, some asking if she was all right, others pretending to search for something in their lockers. As she sat there, she realized that, unless she wanted to lose her job, she would have to make a decision to lift herself out of whatever it was that was affecting her.

Miss Fortini did not reappear, but at around four Father Flood opened the door.

"I hear there's trouble," he said.

She tried to smile.

"It's all my fault," he said. "They said you were doing great here and Mrs. Kehoe says you're the nicest girl she's ever had staying and so I thought you don't want me coming around checking up on you."

"I was all right until I got the letters from home," Eilis said.

"Do you know what's wrong with you?" Father Flood asked.

"What do you mean?"

"There's a name for it."

"For what?" She thought that he was going to mention some private female complaint.

"You're homesick, that's all. Everybody gets it. But it passes. In some it passes more quickly than in others. There's nothing harder than it. And the rule is to have someone to talk to and to keep busy."

"I am busy."

"Eilis, I hope you don't mind if I try and enrol you in a night class. Do you remember we mentioned bookkeeping and accountancy? It would be two or three nights a week, but it would keep you busy and you could get a very good qualification."

"Is it not too late to enrol for this year? Some of the girls said that you have to apply in the spring."

"It's a funny place, Brooklyn," Father Flood said. "As long as the guy in charge is not Norwegian—and in a college that's unlikely—then I can pull strings most places. The Jews are the best, they always love doing something for you. Say a prayer it's a Jewish fellow who believes in the power of the collar. We'll try the best college first, and that's Brooklyn College. I love breaking all the rules. So I'll go down there now and Franco says you are to go home, but be here on time in the morning with a big smile. And I'll drop by Ma Kehoe's later."

Eilis almost laughed out loud when he said "Ma Kehoe." His accent was, for the first time, pure Enniscorthy. She understood that Franco was Mr. Bartocci, and she was interested in the familiar way in which Father Flood had described him. As soon as he left, she found her coat and slipped quietly out of the shop. She was sure that Miss Fortini had seen her pass, but she did not turn as she made her way quickly along Fulton Street and then home towards Mrs. Kehoe's.

As she let herself into the hall with her own key, she found Mrs. Kehoe waiting for her.

"You go into the sitting room there now," Mrs. Kehoe said. "I'm going to make tea for the two of us."

The sitting room, which gave on to the front of the house, was surprisingly beautiful, with old rugs and heavy, comfortable-looking furniture and some dark pictures in gold frames. Double doors opened into a bedroom, and, since one of the doors was open, Eilis could see that the bedroom was decorated in the same heavy, rich style. She looked at the old round dining table and supposed that that was where the game of poker was played on Sunday nights. Her mother, she thought, would love this room. She saw an old gramophone and a wireless in another corner and noticed that the tassels on the tablecloth and the curtains seemed to match. She began to take note of all the details, thinking, for the first time in days, how she could include an account of them in a letter to her mother and Rose. She would write it as soon as she got to her room after supper, she thought, and she would put nothing in about how she had spent the last two days. She would try to put those two days behind her. No matter what she dreamed about, no matter how bad she felt, she had no choice, she knew, but to put it all swiftly out of her mind. She would have to get on with her work if it was during the day and go back to sleep if it was during the night. It would be like covering a table with a tablecloth, or closing curtains on a window; and maybe the need would lessen as time went on, as Jack had hinted it would, as Father Flood had suggested. In any case, that was what she would have to do. As soon as Mrs. Kehoe appeared with tea things on a tray, Eilis clenched her fist when she felt that she was ready to begin.

After the evening meal Father Flood came and Eilis was summoned once more into Mrs. Kehoe's private quarters. Father Flood was smiling and went towards the fireplace as soon as Eilis appeared as if to warm his hands, even though there was no fire lit. He rubbed his hands together and turned towards her.

"Now I'll leave the two of you in peace," Mrs. Kehoe said. "If you need me, I'm in the kitchen."

"The power of the Holy Roman and Apostolic Church is not to be underestimated," Father Flood said. "The first thing I found was a nice devout Italian secretary who told me what courses are full and what courses are really full, and most important told me what not to ask for. I told her the whole story. I had her in tears."

"I'm glad you think it's funny," Eilis said.

"Oh, cheer up. I got you into the night class in bookkeeping and preliminary accountancy. I told them how brilliant you were. You're the first Irish girl. It's full of Jews and Russians and those Norwegians I told you about and they'd like to have even more Italians, but they're too busy making money. The Jewish fellow who runs the place looked like he never saw a priest in his life before. He stood to attention when he saw me like it was the army. Brooklyn College, only the best. I paid your tuition for the first semester. It's Monday, Tuesday and Wednesday, seven to ten, and Thursday, seven to nine. If you do it for two years and pass all their tests, there's no office in New York won't want you."

"Will I have time?" she asked.

"Of course you will. And start next Monday. I'll get you the books. I have a list here. And you can spend your spare time studying them."

His good humour seemed strange to her; it seemed he was putting on a show. She tried to smile.

"Are you sure this is okay?"

"It's done."

"Did Rose ask you to do this? Is that why you are doing it?"

"I'm doing it for the Lord," he said.

"Tell me really why you are doing it."

He looked at her carefully and left silence for a moment. She returned his gaze calmly, making clear that she wanted a reply.

"I was amazed that someone like you would not have a good job in Ireland. When your sister mentioned that you had no work in Ireland, then I said I would help you to come here. That's all. And we need Irish girls in Brooklyn."

"Would any Irish girl do?" Eilis asked.

"Don't be sour. You asked me why I was doing it."

"I'm very grateful to you," Eilis said. She had used a tone that she had heard her mother use, which was very dry and formal. She knew that Father Flood could not tell whether she meant what she said or not.

"You'll make a great accountant," he said. "But a bookkeeper first. And no more tears? Is that a deal?"

"No more tears," she said quietly.

When she came back from work the following evening he had left a pile of books for her as well as ledgers and copy books and a set of pens. He had also arranged with Mrs. Kehoe that she could take a packed meal with her the first three days of each week at no extra charge.

"Now, it will be just ham or a slice of tongue and some salad and brown bread. You'll have to get tea somewhere along the way," Mrs. Kehoe said. "And I told Father Flood that since I would already be getting my reward in heaven, I have that nicely arranged, thank you, he owes me a favour that I would like repaid on this earth. And before too long. You know it's about time someone spoke up to him."

"He's very nice," Eilis said.

"He's nice to those he's nice to," Mrs. Kehoe said. "But I hate a priest rubbing his hands together and smiling. You see that a lot

with the Italian priests and I don't like it. I wish he was more dignified. That's all I have to say about him."

Some of the books were simple; one or two appeared so basic that
she wondered if they could be used in a college at all, but the first
chapter that she read in the book on commercial law was all new
to her and she could not see how it might apply to bookkeeping.
She found it difficult, with many references to judgments of the
courts. She hoped that this would not be an important part of the
course.

Slowly, she became used to the timetable at Brooklyn College,
the three-hour sessions with ten-minute breaks, the strange way
in which everything was explained from first principles, including the simple matter of writing down in an ordinary ledger all
money going into the bank and all money going out and the date
and the name of the person making the deposit or making the
withdrawal or writing the cheque. This was easy, as were the types
of accounts you could have in a bank and the different sorts of
interest rates. But when it came to drawing up annual accounts,
the system was different from the system she had learned, with
many more factors added in, and many more complex features,
including city, state and federal taxes.

She wished she could tell the difference between Jews and Italians. Some of the Jews wore skullcaps and many more of them
appeared to wear glasses than did the Italians. But most of the students were dark-skinned with brown eyes and most were diligent
and serious-looking young men. There were very few women in
her class and no one Irish at all, no one even English. They all
seemed to know each other and they moved in groups but they
were polite to her, careful to make space for her and make her feel
at ease without anyone offering to see her home. No one asked her
any questions about herself, or sat beside her more than once. The

classes were much larger than the classes she had attended at home and she wondered if this was why the instructors went so slowly.

The law instructor, who took the class after the break on Wednesdays, was clearly Jewish; she thought that the name Rosenblum was Jewish, but he also made jokes about being Jewish and spoke in a foreign accent that she guessed was not Italian. He talked big, asking them all the time to imagine that they were the president of a large corporation, larger than that owned by Henry Ford, being sued by another corporation or by the federal government. He then drew their attention to real cases in which the issues he had outlined were actually argued. He knew the names of the lawyers who had done the arguing and the track records and the temperaments of the judges who decided the cases and the further judges of the appeal courts.

Eilis had no trouble understanding Mr. Rosenblum's accent, and even when he made mistakes in grammar or syntax or used the wrong word she could follow him. Like the other students, she took notes when he spoke, but she could find nothing in her book on basic commercial law about most of the cases he mentioned. When she wrote home about Brooklyn College, she tried to describe to her mother and Rose some of the jokes Mr. Rosenblum made in which there was always a Pole and an Italian; it was easier to describe the atmosphere he created, how much the students looked forward to Wednesdays after the break, and how easy and exciting he made corporate litigation sound. But she worried about the exam questions that Mr. Rosenblum would set. One day after class, she asked one of her fellow students, a young man with glasses and curly hair and a friendly yet studious appearance.

"Maybe we'd better ask him what book he's reading from," the young man said and looked worried for a moment.

"I don't think he's reading from a book," Eilis said.

"Are you British?"

"No, Irish."

"Oh, Irish," he said and nodded and smiled. "Well, see you next week. Maybe we can ask him then."

The weather grew cold and sometimes in the morning it was icy when the wind blew. She had read her law book twice and taken notes on it and bought a second book that Mr. Rosenblum had recommended and it lay on her bedside table close to the alarm clock, which rang each morning at seven fifty-five just as Sheila Heffernan was starting her shower in the bathroom across the landing. What she loved most about America, Eilis thought on these mornings, was how the heating was kept on all night. She wrote to her mother and Rose and to Jack and the boys about it. The air was like toast, she said, even on winter mornings, and you had no fear when getting out of bed that your feet were going to freeze on the floor. And if you woke in the night with the wind outside howling, you could turn over happily in your warm bed. Her mother wrote back wondering how Mrs. Kehoe could afford to keep the heating on all night, and Eilis replied to say that it was not just Mrs. Kehoe, who was not in any way extravagant, it was everyone in America, they all kept their heating on all night.

As she began to buy Christmas presents to send to her mother and Rose, and Jack, Pat and Martin, checking how early she would have to post them so that they would arrive on time, she pondered on what Christmas Day would be like at Mrs. Kehoe's kitchen table; she wondered if each of the lodgers would exchange presents. In late November she received a formal letter from Father Flood asking her if she would, as a special favour to him, work in the parish hall on Christmas Day serving dinners to people who did not have anywhere else to go. He knew, he said, that it would be a great sacrifice for her to make.

She wrote back immediately to let him know that, as long as she was not working, she would be available during the Christmas period, including Christmas Day, any time he needed her. She let Mrs. Kehoe know that she would not be spending Christmas in the house, but working for Father Flood.

"Well, I wish you would take a few of the others with you," Mrs. Kehoe said. "I won't name them or anything, but it's the one day of the year I like a bit of peace. Indeed, I might end up presenting myself to you and Father Flood as a person in need. Just to get a bit of peace."

"I'm sure you would be very welcome, Mrs. Kehoe," Eilis said, and then, having realized how offensive that remark might sound, added quickly as Mrs. Kehoe glared at her: "But of course you'll be needed here. And it's nice to be in your own house for Christmas."

"I dread it, to be honest," Mrs. Kehoe said. "And if it wasn't for my religious convictions, I'd ignore it like the Jews do. In parts of Brooklyn, it could be any day of the week. I always think that's why you get a biting cold on a Christmas Day, to remind you. And we'll miss you now for the dinner. I was looking forward to having a Wexford face."

One day as she was walking to work, crossing State Street, Eilis saw a man selling watches. She was early for work and so had time to linger at his stand. She knew nothing about types of watches but thought the prices were very low. She had enough money in her handbag to buy one for each of her brothers. Even if they already had watches—and she knew that Martin wore her father's watch—these could serve them if the old ones broke or had to be repaired, and they were from America, which might mean something in Birmingham, and they would be easy to package and cheap to send. In Loehmann's one lunchtime she found beautiful angora wool cardigans that cost more than she had in mind, but she came back the next day and bought one for her mother and one for Rose and wrapped them together with the nylon stockings she had bought on the sale and sent them to Ireland.

Slowly, Christmas decorations began to appear in the stores and streets of Brooklyn. After supper one Friday evening, when Mrs. Kehoe had left the kitchen, Miss McAdam wondered when Mrs. Kehoe would put up the decorations.

"Last year she waited until the last minute, and that took all the good out of it," Miss McAdam said.

Patty and Diana were going to stay near Central Park, they said, with Patty's sister and her children and have a real Christmas, with presents and visits to Santa Claus. Miss Keegan said that it was not really Christmas if you were not in your own house in Ireland, and she was going to be sad all day and there was no point in pretending that she wouldn't be.

"Do you know something?" Sheila Heffernan interjected. "There's no taste off American turkeys, even the one we had at Thanksgiving tasted of nothing except sawdust. It isn't Mrs. Kehoe's fault, it's the same all over America."

"All over America?" Diana asked. "In every part?" She and Patty began to laugh.

"It'll be quiet anyway," Sheila said pointedly, glancing in their direction. "We won't have so much useless chatter."

"Oh, I wouldn't bet on that," Patty said. "We might come down the chimney to fill your stocking when you're least expecting us, Sheila."

Patty and Diana both laughed again.

Eilis did not tell any of them what she was doing for Christmas; at breakfast one day the following week, however, it was clear that Mrs. Kehoe had told them.

"Oh, God," Sheila said, "they take in every oul' fella off the street. You'd never know what they'd have."

"I heard about it all right," Miss Keegan said. "They put funny hats on the down and outs and give them bottles of stout."

"You're a saint, Eilis," Patty said. "A living saint."

At work Miss Fortini asked Eilis if she would stay on late in the evenings in the week before Christmas and she agreed, as the college had closed for a two weeks' holiday. She also agreed to work Christmas Eve up to the very last minute, since some of the other girls on the floor wanted to leave early to catch trains and buses and be with their families.

When she finished at Bartocci's on Christmas Eve she went directly as arranged to the parish hall so that she could take instructions for the next day. Long tables were being carried in from a truck parked outside, followed by benches. She had heard Father Flood before mass asking some women to lend him table-cloths that they could then retrieve when Christmas was over. After his sermon he had asked for donations of cutlery and glasses and cups and saucers and plates to add to his store. He also made clear that the parish hall would be open from eleven in the morning until nine in the evening on Christmas Day and anyone passing, irrespective of creed or country of origin, would be welcome in God's name; even those not in need of food or refreshment could drop by at any time to add to the day's cheer, but not, he added, between twelve thirty and three, please, when Christmas dinner would be served. He also announced that, beginning in the middle of January, he was going to run a dance in the parish hall every Friday night with a live band but no alcohol to raise funds for the parish and he would like everyone to spread the word.

As soon as Eilis had pushed past the men setting the tables and benches down evenly in rows and women hanging Christmas decorations from the ceiling, she saw Father Flood.

"I wonder would you count the silverware to make sure we have enough?" he said. "Otherwise, we'll have to go out into the highways and byways."

"How many are you expecting?"

"Two hundred last year. They cross the bridges, some of them come down from Queens and in from Long Island."

"And are they all Irish?"

"Yes, they are all leftover Irishmen, they built the tunnels and the bridges and the highways. Some of them I only see once a year. God knows what they live on."

"Why don't they go back home?"

"Some of them are here fifty years and they've lost touch with everyone," Father Flood said. "One year I got home addresses for some of them, the ones I thought needed help most, and I wrote to Ireland for them. Mostly, I got silence, but for one poor old divil I got a stinker of a letter from his sister-in-law saying that the farm, or the homestead, or whatever it was, wasn't his, and he wasn't to think of ever setting foot in it. She'd scatter him at the gate. I remember that. That's what she said."

Eilis went to midnight mass with Mrs. Kehoe and Miss Keegan, discovering on the way home that Mrs. Kehoe was among the parishioners who were roasting a turkey and potatoes and boiling a ham for Father Flood, who had arranged for it all to be collected at twelve.

"It's like the war," Mrs. Kehoe said. "Feeding the army. Has to be done like clockwork. I'll carve what our own small needs will be from the turkey, the biggest one I could get, it'll be six hours in the oven, before I send it off. And we'll eat, just the four of us, myself, Miss McAdam, Miss Heffernan and Miss Keegan here, as soon as the turkey is off our hands. And if there's anything left over, we'll save it for you, Eilis."

By nine o'clock Eilis was in the parish hall peeling vegetables in the big kitchen at the back. There were women working beside her whom she had never met before, all of them older than she, some with faint American accents but all of Irish origin. Most of them were just here for this part of the morning, she was told, before going home to feed their families. Soon it became clear that two women were in charge. When Father Flood arrived he introduced Eilis to them.

"They are the Miss Murphys from Arklow," he said. "Though we won't hold that against them."

The two Miss Murphys laughed. They were tall, cheerful-looking women in their fifties.

"It'll be just the three of us," one of them said, "here all day. The other helpers will come and go."

"We're the ones with no homes to go to," the other Miss Murphy said and smiled.

"Now, we'll feed them in sets of twenty," her sister said.

"Each of us prepares sixty-five dinners, it might even be more, in three sittings. I'm in Father Flood's own kitchen and the two of you are here in the hall. As soon as a turkey arrives, or when the ones we have cooking upstairs are ready, Father Flood will attack them and the hams and carve them. The oven here is just for keeping things hot. For an hour people will bring us turkeys and hams and roast potatoes and the thing is to have vegetables cooked and hot and ready to be served."

"Rough and ready might be a better way of putting it," the other Miss Murphy interrupted.

"But we have plenty of soup and stout for them while they're waiting. They're very nice, all of them."

"They don't mind waiting, and if they do, they don't say."

"Are they all men?" Eilis asked.

"A few couples come because she is too old to cook, or they're too lonely, or whatever, but the rest are men," Miss Murphy said. "And they love the company and it's Irish food, you know, proper stuffing and roast potatoes and Brussels sprouts boiled to death." She smiled at Eilis and shook her head and sighed.

As soon as ten o'clock mass was over people began to call by. Father Flood had filled one of the tables with glasses and bottles of lemonade and sweets for the children. He made everyone who came in, including women with fresh hairdos, put on a paper hat. Thus as the men began to arrive to spend all of Christmas Day in the hall they were barely noticed among the crowd. It was only later, after midday, when the visitors began to disperse, that they could be seen clearly, some of them sitting alone with a bottle of stout in front of them, others huddled in groups, many of them stubbornly still wearing cloth caps instead of paper hats.

The Miss Murphys were anxious for the men who came first to gather at one or two of the long tables, enough to make a group who could be served soon with bowls of soup so that the bowls could be washed and used again by the next group. As Eilis, on instructions, went out to encourage the men to sit down at the top table nearest to the kitchen, she observed coming into the hall a tall man with a slight stoop; he was wearing a cap low over his forehead and an old brown overcoat with a scarf at the neck. She paused for a moment and stared at him.

He stood still as soon as he had closed the main door behind him, and it was the way he took in the hall, surveying the scene with shyness and a sort of mild delight, that made Eilis sure, for one moment, that her father had come into her presence. She felt as though she should move towards him as she saw him hesitantly opening his overcoat and loosening his scarf. It was how he stood, taking full slow possession of the room, searching almost shyly for the place where he might be most comfortable and at ease, or looking around carefully to see if he knew anybody. As she realized that it could not be him, that she was dreaming, he took off his cap and she saw that the man did not look like her father at all. She glanced around her, embarrassed, hoping that no one had noticed her. It was something, she thought, that she could tell no one, that she had imagined for an instant that she had seen her father, who was, she remembered quickly, dead for four years.

Although the first table had not been filled, she turned and went back to the kitchen and set about checking the number of plates for the first serving, even though she knew she had the right number, and then lifting the lid of the huge saucepan to check if the Brussels sprouts were boiling, even though she knew that the water was not hot enough yet. When one of the Miss Murphys asked her if the nearest table had been filled up and if every man had a glass of stout, Eilis turned and said that she had done her best to move the men to the tables but maybe Miss Murphy could do better. She tried to smile, hoping that Miss Murphy did not notice anything strange.

For the next two hours she was busy, piling food on to plates, carrying them out two at a time. Father Flood carved turkeys and hams as they arrived, piling stuffing and roast potatoes into bowls. For a while, one Miss Murphy devoted herself entirely to washing up and drying and cleaning and clearing space as her sister and Eilis served the men, making sure to leave nothing out—turkey, ham, stuffing, roast potatoes and Brussels sprouts—and making sure in their haste not to give anyone too much or too little.

"There's plenty of food now, so don't worry," Father Flood shouted, "but no more than three potatoes a head and go easy on the stuffing."

When they had enough meat carved, he went outside and busied himself opening more bottles of stout.

At first the men seemed shabby to Eilis and she noticed body odours from a good number of them. As they sat down and drank their stout waiting for the soup or the food, she could not believe there were so many of them, some of them so poor-looking and so old, but even the younger ones had bad teeth and appeared worn down. Many were still smoking, even as the soup came. She did her best to be polite to them.

She observed a change in them soon, however, as they began to talk to each other or shout greetings down the table or enter into low, intense conversations. At first they had reminded her of men who sat on the bridge in Enniscorthy or gathered at the seat at Arnold's Cross or the Louse Bank by the Slaney, or men from the County Home, or men from the town who drank too much. But by the time she served them and they turned to thank her, they seemed more like her father and his brothers in the way they spoke or smiled, the toughness in their faces softened by shyness, what had appeared stubborn or hard now strangely tender. As she served the man she had thought was her father, she looked at him carefully, amazed at how little he actually resembled him, as though it had been a trick of the light or something she had completely imagined. She was surprised also to find that he was talking to the man beside him in Irish.

"This was the miracle of the turkey and the ham," Miss Murphy said to Father Flood when large plates of second helpings had been left on all the tables.

"Brooklyn-style," her sister said.

"I'm glad it's trifle now," she added, "and not plum pudding and we don't have to worry about keeping it hot."

"Wouldn't you think they'd take off their caps when they are eating?" her sister asked. "Don't they know they're in America?"

"We have no rules here," Father Flood said. "And they can smoke and drink all they like. If we can get them all home safely, that's the main thing. We always have a few a bit too under the weather to go home."

"Too drunk," one Miss Murphy said.

"Ah, on Christmas Day we call it under the weather, and I have a rake of beds made up for them in my own house," Father Flood said.

"What we'll do now is have our own dinner," Miss Murphy said. "And I'll set the table and I've kept a nice dinner for each of us hot and everything."

"Well, I was wondering if we were going to eat at all," Eilis said.

"Poor Eilis. She's starving. Will you look at her?"

"Should we not serve the trifle first?" Eilis asked.

"No, we'll wait," Father Flood said. "It'll stretch the day out."

By the time they were removing the trifle dishes, the hall was a mass of smoke and animated talk. Men sat in groups with one or two standing behind them; others moved from group to group, some with bottles of whiskey in brown paper bags that they passed around. When all the cleaning of the kitchen and the filling of garbage cans had been completed, Father Flood suggested that they go into the hall and join the men for a drink. Some visitors had arrived, including a few women, and Eilis thought, as she sat down with a glass of sherry in her hand, that it could have been a parish hall anywhere in Ireland on the night of a concert or a wedding when the young people were all elsewhere dancing or standing at the bar.

After a while Eilis noticed that two men had taken out fiddles and another a small accordion; they had found a corner and were playing as a few others stood around and listened. Father Flood was moving about the hall with a notebook now, writing down names and addresses and nodding as old men spoke to him. After a while he clapped his hands and called for silence but it took a few minutes before he could get everyone's attention.

"I don't want to interrupt the proceedings," he said, "but we'd like to thank a nice girl from Enniscorthy and two nice women from Arklow for their hard day's work."

There was a round of applause.

"And, as a way of thanking them, there's one great singer in this hall and we're delighted to see him this year again."

He pointed to the man whom Eilis had mistaken for her father. He was sitting away from Eilis and Father Flood, but he stood up when his name was called and walked quietly towards them. He stood with his back to the wall so that everyone could see him.

"That man," Miss Murphy whispered to Eilis, "has made LPs."

When Eilis looked up the man was signalling to her. He wanted her, it seemed, to come and stand with him. It struck her for a second that he might want her to sing so she shook her head, but he kept beckoning and people began to turn and look at her; she felt that she had no choice but to leave her seat and approach him. She could not think why he wanted her. As she came close she saw how bad his teeth were.

He did not greet her or acknowledge her arrival but closed his eyes and reached his hand towards hers and held it. The skin on the palm of his hand was soft. He gripped her hand tightly and began to move it in a faint circular motion as he started to sing. His voice was loud and strong and nasal; the Irish he sang in, she thought, must be Connemara Irish because she remembered one teacher from Galway in the Mercy Convent who had that accent. He pronounced each word carefully and slowly, building up a wildness, a ferocity, in the way he treated the melody. It was only when he came to the chorus, however, that she understood the words—"*Má bhíonn tú liom, a stóirín mo chroí*"—and he glanced at her proudly, almost possessively, as he sang these lines. All the people in the hall watched him silently. There were five or six verses; he sang the words out with pure innocence and charm so that at times, when he closed his eyes, leaning his large frame against the wall, he did not seem like an old man at all; the strength of his voice and the confidence of his performance had taken over. And then each time he came to the chorus he looked at her, letting the melody become sweeter by slowing down the pace, putting his head down then, managing to suggest even more that he had not merely learned the song but that he meant it. Eilis knew how sorry this man was going to be, and how sorry she would be, when the song had ended, when the last chorus had to be sung and the singer would have to bow to the crowd and go back to his place and give way to another singer as Eilis too went back and sat in her chair.

As the night wore on, some of the men fell asleep or had to be helped to the toilet. The two Miss Murphys made pots of tea and there was Christmas cake. Once the singing ended some of the men found their coats and came up to thank Father Flood and the Miss Murphys and Eilis, wishing them a happy Christmas before setting out into the night.

When most of the men had left and several who remained seemed to be very drunk, Father Flood told Eilis that she could go if she wanted and he would ask the Miss Murphys to accompany her to Mrs. Kehoe's house. Eilis said no, she was used to walking home alone, and it would in any case, she said, be a quiet night. She shook hands with the two Miss Murphys and with Father Flood and wished each of them a happy Christmas before she set out to walk through the dark, empty streets of Brooklyn. She would, she thought, go straight to her room and avoid the kitchen. She wanted to lie on the bed and go over everything that had happened before falling asleep.

Part Three

In January, Eilis felt the fierce sharp cold in the mornings as she went to work. No matter how fast she walked, and even when she bought thick socks, her feet felt frozen by the time she arrived at Bartocci's. Everyone in the streets was covered up as though afraid to show themselves, wearing thick coats, scarves, hats, gloves and boots. She noticed that they even covered their mouths and noses with thick scarves or mufflers as they moved along. All she could see was their eyes, and the expression seemed alarmed by the cold, made desperate by the wind and the freezing temperatures. At the end of the lectures in the evening, the students huddled in the hallway of the college, putting on layer after layer of clothes as a defence against the cold night. It was, she thought, like a preparation for a strange play, with all of them trying on costumes, their gestures slow and deliberate, looks of blank determination on their faces. It appeared impossible to imagine a time when it was not cold and she could walk these streets thinking about something other than the warm hallway of Mrs. Kehoe's house, the warm kitchen and her own warm bedroom.

One evening, as she was about to go upstairs to bed, Eilis saw Mrs. Kehoe standing in the doorway of her own sitting room, hovering there in the shadows as though afraid to be seen. She beckoned to Eilis without speaking, motioned her into the room and then quietly closed the door. Even as she crossed the room and sat in the armchair by the fire, indicating to Eilis that she should sit in the armchair opposite, she said nothing. The look on her face was grave as she put her right hand out and lowered it, suggesting to Eilis that if she were to speak her voice should not be loud.

"Now," she said and looked into the fire, which was burning brightly in the grate, before placing a log and then another on the flames. "Not a word that you ever even came in here? Promise?"

Eilis nodded.

"The truth is that Miss Keegan is departing and the sooner the better as far as I'm concerned. I have her sworn not to say a word to anyone. She's very West of Ireland and they're better at saying nothing than we are. So it suits her because she doesn't have to say any farewells. She'll be gone on Monday and I want you to move into her room in the basement. It's not damp now so don't look at me like that."

"I'm not looking at you," Eilis said.

"Well, don't."

Mrs. Kehoe studied the fire for a moment and then the floor.

"It's the best room in the house, the biggest, the warmest, the quietest and the best-appointed. And I don't want any discussion about it. You are getting it and that's that. So if you pack your things on Sunday, on Monday when you're at work I'll have them moved down, and that'll be the end of it. You'll need a key for down below because you have your own entrance, which you share with Miss Montini, but of course even if you lose the key, there's still the stairs between the basement and this floor so don't look so worried."

"Will the others not mind that I'm getting the room?" Eilis asked.

"They will," Mrs. Kehoe said and smiled at her. She then looked into the fire, nodding her head in satisfaction. She raised her head and gazed bravely at Eilis. It took Eilis a moment to realize that this was a signal from Mrs. Kehoe that she should leave. She stood up quietly as Mrs. Kehoe once more stretched out her right hand to make clear that Eilis should not make a sound.

It struck Eilis, as she made her way up the stairs to her bedroom, that the basement room could, in fact, be damp and small. She had never heard anyone say before that it was the best room in the house. She wondered if all this secrecy was not merely a way of landing her there without giving her a chance to see where she was going or make any protest. She would have to wait, she realized, until she came back from her classes on Monday night.

Over the next few days she began to dread the move and resent the idea of Mrs. Kehoe moving her cases when she was out of the house and putting them into a place from which Miss Keegan emerged daily in a state that did not seem to Eilis to suggest that she had the best room in the house. She realized also that she could not appeal to Father Flood were the room dingy or dark or damp. She had used up enough of his sympathy and she knew that Mrs. Kehoe was fully aware of this.

On the Sunday, as she packed her cases and left them by the bed, finding that she had acquired more belongings than she could fit into them and having to go downstairs and quietly ask Mrs. Kehoe for some carrier bags, she felt that Mrs. Kehoe had taken advantage of her, and she found herself suffering the beginnings of the terrible homesickness she had gone through before. That night, she did not sleep.

In the morning there was a biting wind that was new to her. It seemed to blow fiercely in every direction; it carried ice with it and people moved in the streets with their heads bowed, some of them dancing up and down with the cold as they waited to cross the street. It made her almost smile at the idea that no one in Ireland knew that America was the coldest place on earth and its people on a cold morning like this the most deeply miserable. They would not believe it if she put it in a letter. All day in Bartocci's people roared at anyone who left the door open for a second longer than necessary and there was a brisk trade in heavy woollen underwear, even more than usual.

That evening as she took notes during the lectures Eilis was struggling so hard to stay awake that she put no thought into what she would find when she returned to Mrs. Kehoe's and, when walking home from the trolley-car, decided she did not care what her new room was like as long as it was warm and had a bed where she could sleep. The night was still, the wind having died down, and there was a dryness and a punishing intensity in how the icy air bit into her toes and fingers and hurt the skin on her face and made her pray that this journey by foot would end even when she knew that she was only halfway there.

As soon as she had opened the front door Mrs. Kehoe appeared in the hallway and put her fingers to her lips. She motioned for Eilis to wait, returned a moment later and, having checked that no one was coming into the hallway from the kitchen, handed Eilis a key; she then directed her back out into the night, closing the front door softly behind her. Eilis walked down the steps to the basement. By the time she had opened the door Mrs. Kehoe was already waiting for her.

"Don't make a sound," she whispered.

She opened the door that led into the front room of the basement, the room recently vacated by Miss Keegan. A standard lamp in the corner and a lamp by a bedside table were already lit, and these, with the low ceiling and the dark velvet curtains and the richly patterned bedspread and the rugs on the floor, made the room seem luxurious, like something from a painting or an old photograph. Eilis noticed a rocking chair in the corner and saw that there were logs in the fireplace and paper under them waiting to be lit. The room was twice the size of her old bedroom; it also had a desk where she could study and an easy chair on the other side of the hearth to the rocking chair. It had none of the functional, almost Spartan aura of the room she had slept in until now. She knew that all of her fellow lodgers would have wanted this room.

"If any of them ask you, just say that your own room is being decorated," Mrs. Kehoe said as she opened a large built-in closet whose wood was stained a dark reddish colour, to show Eilis where the suitcases and bags were. Because of the way Mrs. Kehoe stood watching her, her gaze proud but almost soft and sad as well, it struck Eilis that this room might have been created in the time before Mr. Kehoe left home. As she looked at the double bed she wondered if this had been their bedroom. She wondered if they had rented out the rooms on the upper floors.

"The bathroom is at the end of the corridor," Mrs. Kehoe said. She stood in the shadowy room uneasily, as though she were trying to regain her composure.

"And say nothing to anyone," she added. "You can never go wrong if you follow that policy to the letter."

"The room is lovely," Eilis said.

"And you can light a fire," Mrs. Kehoe said. "But Miss Keegan only ever did on Sundays because it eats wood. I don't know why."

"Will the others not be raging?" Eilis asked.

"It's my house so they can rage all they like, the more the merrier."

"But—"

"You are the only one of them with any manners."

Mrs. Kehoe's tone, as she tried to smile, caused, Eilis felt, a sadness to come into the room. She believed that Mrs. Kehoe was giving her too much without knowing her well enough and just now had also said too much. She did not want Mrs. Kehoe to become close to her or come to depend on her in any way. Eilis left silence for a few moments, even though she knew that this might make her seem ungrateful. She nodded almost formally at Mrs. Kehoe.

"When will the others know that I am here for good?" she asked eventually.

"In their own good time. It's none of their business anyway."

As she took in the implications of what Mrs. Kehoe had done and the trouble it was now likely to cause her with her fellow lodgers, Eilis wished she had been left alone in her old bedroom.

"I hope they won't blame me."

"Pay no attention to any of them. I don't think either of us needs to lose a night's sleep over them."

Eilis stood up straight, attempting to make herself taller, and stared coldly at Mrs. Kehoe. It was clear to her that her landlady's last remark carried with it the firm idea that she and Eilis stood apart from the other lodgers and were prepared to intimate to them that they had conspired in this. Eilis believed that this was a piece of gross presumption on Mrs. Kehoe's part but also that the decision to give her, the most recently arrived, the best room in the house not only would cause bitterness and difficulty between herself and Patty, Diana, Miss McAdam and Sheila Heffernan but would come to mean, in time, that Mrs. Kehoe herself would feel free to call in the favour she had done her.

She could, Eilis saw, do this if she needed something urgently, or allow it to cause a familiarity in their relationship, a sort of friendship or close connection. As they stood in the room, Eilis felt almost angry with Mrs. Kehoe, and this feeling, mixed with tiredness, seemed to give her courage.

"It's always better to be honest," she said, imitating Rose when Rose found her dignity or sense of propriety challenged in any way. "I mean with everybody," she added.

"When you've gone through the world like I have," Mrs. Kehoe replied, "you'll find that that only works some of the time."

Eilis looked at her landlady, not flinching at the wounded aggression in the way her look was returned. She was determined not to speak again, no matter what Mrs. Kehoe said. She felt the older woman's irritation directed against her as though she had betrayed her in some incalculable way, until she realized that giving her this room, the act of generosity, had released something in Mrs. Kehoe, some deep resentment against the world, that Mrs. Kehoe was now putting carefully back in its place.

"The bathroom as I said is down the corridor," she finally said. "And I'm leaving the key here."

She put the key on a side table and left the room, banging the door so that the whole house would hear her.

Eilis wondered if the others would ever believe her if she told them that she had not asked for the room. She avoided the kitchen at breakfast-time and, on meeting Diana at the bathroom door on the second morning, rushed by her without saying a word. She knew, however, that when the weekend came it would be impossible to avoid a discussion with the others. Thus on the Friday evening, when Mrs. Kehoe had left the kitchen, and Miss McAdam said that she would like to speak to her alone, Eilis was not surprised. Under Miss McAdam's watchful gaze, as though she were a prisoner on parole who might try to abscond, she lingered in the kitchen after all the others had gone.

"I suppose you heard what happened," Miss McAdam said to her.

Eilis tried to look blank.

"You had better sit down."

Miss McAdam moved over to the kettle as it began to boil and she filled the teapot before she spoke again.

"Do you know why Miss Keegan left?" she asked.

"Why should I know?"

"So you don't know? I thought so. Well, that Kehoe woman knows and all the others know."

"Where has Miss Keegan gone? Was she in trouble?"

"To Long Island. And for good reasons."

"What happened?"

"She was followed home." Miss McAdam's eyes seemed to glitter with excitement as she spoke. She poured the tea slowly.

"Followed?"

"Not one night but two, or maybe more for all I know."

"You mean followed to this house?"

"That's exactly what I mean."

Miss McAdam sipped her tea while looking at Eilis sharply all the time.

"Who followed her?"

"A man."

As Eilis put milk and sugar into her tea, she remembered something that her mother always said.

"But sure if a man ran off with Miss Keegan, he'd drop her the minute he got to the first lamp-post and he could see her clearly."

"But it wasn't an ordinary man."

"What do you mean?"

"The last time he followed her he exposed himself to her. He was that sort of man."

"Who told you this?"

"Miss Keegan spoke to Miss Heffernan and myself privately before she left. She was followed to the very door of this house. And as she walked down the steps, the man exposed himself."

"Did she call the police?"

"She certainly did, and then she packed her bags. She thinks she knows where the man lives. And he followed her before."

"Did she tell the police all of this?"

"Yes, but there is nothing they can do unless she is ready to identify him and she isn't ready to do that. So she packed her bags. And she's moved in with her brother and his wife in Long Island. And then, to make matters worse, the Kehoe woman wanted to move me down to Miss Keegan's room. She went on about it being the best room in the house. I put her in her place.

And Miss Heffernan is in a terrible state. And Diana has refused to stay in the basement on her own. So she put you down there because none of the others would go."

Eilis noticed how pleased with herself Miss McAdam seemed. As she watched the older woman sipping her tea, it occurred to Eilis that this could easily be her revenge on Eilis and Mrs. Kehoe over the room. On the other hand, she reckoned, it could be true. Mrs. Kehoe could have used her, the only lodger who did not seem to know why Miss Keegan had left. But then she thought that Mrs. Kehoe could not have been sure in the days before she moved her to the basement that Eilis would not find out. The more she watched Miss McAdam, the more she was convinced that if she was not inventing the story of the man who exposed himself, then she was exaggerating it. She wondered if Miss McAdam had been encouraged to do this by the other lodgers or if she were doing it alone.

"It's a lovely room," Eilis said.

"Lovely it may be," Miss McAdam replied. "And you know we all wanted that room when Miss Keegan got it, all the better to stop that Kehoe woman snooping around you every time you came in the door. But I wouldn't want to be down there now with the light on for all to see. Maybe I shouldn't say any more."

"Say what you like."

"Well, for someone who walks home alone at night, you seem very calm."

"If anyone exposes himself to me, you'll be the first to know."

"If I am still here," Miss McAdam said. "It might be Long Island for us all."

In the days that followed, Eilis could not make her mind up about what Miss McAdam had told her. At meals in the kitchen with the rest of the lodgers she veered from believing that all of them had conspired to frighten her in revenge for her being installed in Miss Keegan's room to believing that Mrs. Kehoe had placed her there not because she favoured her but because she thought she was the least likely to protest. She studied their faces as they addressed her, but nothing became clear. She wanted to allow for the possibility that everyone's motives were good, but it was unlikely, she thought, unlikely that Mrs. Kehoe had genuinely given her the room out of pure generosity and unlikely also that Miss McAdam and the others really did not mind this and had merely wanted to warn her about the man who had followed Miss Keegan so that she would be careful. She wished she had a real friend among the lodgers whom she could consult. And she wondered then if she herself were the problem, reading malice into motives when there was none intended. If she woke in the night, or found time going slowly at work, she went over it all again, blaming Mrs. Kehoe one moment, Miss McAdam and her fellow lodgers the next, and then blaming herself, eventually coming to no conclusion except that it would be best if she stopped thinking about it altogether.

The following Sunday, Father Flood announced that the parish hall was now ready to run dances to raise funds for charities in the parish, that he had procured Pat Sullivan's Harp and Shamrock Orchestra and that he would ask the parishioners to spread the word that the first dance would be held on the last Friday of January and then every Friday night after that until further notice.

When Mrs. Kehoe came briefly into the kitchen that evening, having left her poker session, and sat at the table, the lodgers were discussing the dance.

"I hope Father Flood knows what he's doing," Mrs. Kehoe said. "They ran a dance in that selfsame parish hall after the war and they had to close it because of immorality. Some of the Italians started to come looking for Irish girls."

"Well, I don't see what's wrong with that," Diana said. "My father is Italian and I think he met my mother at a dance."

"I'm sure he is very nice," Mrs. Kehoe said, "but after the war some of the Italians were very forward."

"They're lovely-looking," Patty said.

"Be that as it may," Mrs. Kehoe said, "and I'm sure some of them are lovely and all, but from what I heard great care should be taken with many of them. But that's enough about Italians. It might be better for us all if we changed the subject."

"I hope there's not going to be Irish dancing," Patty said.

"Pat Sullivan's band are lovely," Sheila Heffernan said. "They can do everything from Irish tunes to waltzes and foxtrots and American tunes."

"That's good for them," Patty said, "as long as I can sit it out for the céilí stuff. God, it should be abolished. In this day and age!"

"If you're not lucky," Miss McAdam said, "you'll be sitting down all night, unless of course it's ladies' choice."

"That's enough about the dance," Mrs. Kehoe said. "I shouldn't have come into the kitchen at all. Just be careful. That's all I have to say. You have your whole life ahead of you."

Over the next while, as the night of the dance approached, the house broke into two factions: the first, which consisted of Patty and Diana, wanted Eilis to come with them to a restaurant where they would meet other people going to the dance, but the others—Miss McAdam and Sheila Heffernan—insisted that the restaurant in question was really a saloon bar and that the people who would gather there often were not sober or indeed decent. They wanted Eilis to go with them directly from Mrs. Kehoe's house to the parish hall only as a way of supporting a good cause and to leave as early as was polite.

"One of the things I don't miss about Ireland is the cattle mart on a Friday and Saturday night, and I'd be happy to stay single rather than have half-drunk fellows with terrible hair oil pushing me around."

"Where I'm from," Miss McAdam said, "we didn't go out at all and none of us were any the worse for it."

"And how did you meet fellows?" Diana asked.

"Will you look at her?" Patty interjected. "She's never met a fellow in her life."

"Well, when I do," Miss McAdam said, "it will not be in a saloon bar."

In the end Eilis waited at home with Miss McAdam and Sheila Heffernan and they did not set out for the parish hall until after ten o'clock. She noticed that both of them were carrying high-heeled shoes in their bags that they would change into once they arrived. Both, she saw, had backcombed their hair and were wearing make-up and lipstick. When she saw them first she was afraid that she herself would look dowdy beside them; she felt uncomfortable at spending the rest of the evening, no matter how short their stay in the parish hall, in their company. They seemed to have made so much effort, whereas she had merely tidied herself and put on the only good dress that she owned and a brand-new pair of nylon stockings. She decided, as they walked to the hall through the freezing night, that she would look carefully at what other women were wearing at the dance and make sure the next time that she did not look too plain.

As they approached she felt nothing but dread and wished she could have found an excuse to stay at home. Patty and Diana had laughed so much before they left, running up and down the stairs, forcing the others to admire them as they travelled from floor to floor of the house, even knocking on Mrs. Kehoe's door before they finally departed so that she could see them. Eilis was glad she had not gone with them, but now, in the strange tense silence that developed between Miss McAdam and Sheila Heffernan as they entered the hall, she felt their nervousness and was sorry for them and sorry too that she would have to stay with them for the evening and leave when they wanted to.

The hall was almost empty; once they had paid they went to the ladies' cloakroom, where Miss McAdam and Sheila Heffernan checked themselves in the mirrors and applied more make-up and lipstick, offering Eilis lipstick and mascara as well. As all three looked in the mirror, Eilis realized that her hair looked terrible. Even if she were never to go to a dance again, she thought, she would have to do something about it. Her dress, which Rose had helped her to buy, also looked terrible. Since she had some money saved, she thought that she should buy some new clothes, but she knew that she would never easily be able to do so alone and that her two companions would be as little use to her as Patty and Diana. The first pair were too formal and stiff in their attire and the second too modern and loud. She determined that once her exams were over in May she would spend time looking at stores and prices and trying to work out what sort of American clothes would suit her best.

When they walked out into the hall and across the bare boards to sit on benches on the opposite side, passing a number of middle-aged couples waltzing to the music, they saw Father Flood, who came and shook hands with them.

"We're expecting a crowd," he said. "But they never come when you want them."

"Oh, we know where they are," Miss McAdam said. "Getting Dutch courage."

"Ah, well, it's Friday night, I suppose."

"I hope they won't be drunk," Miss McAdam said.

"Oh, we have good men on the door. And we hope it will be a good night."

"If you opened a bar you'd make a fortune," Sheila Heffernan said.

"Don't think I haven't thought of it," Father Flood replied and rubbed his hands together, laughing as he moved away from them, crossing the dance floor towards the main entrance.

Eilis looked at the musicians. There was a man with an accordion who seemed very sad and wistful as he played the slow waltz and a younger man playing the drums and an older man at the back with a double bass. She noticed some brass instruments on stage and a microphone set up for a singer, so she presumed that when the hall filled there would be more musicians.

Sheila Heffernan fetched a lemon soda for each of them and they quietly sipped their drinks and sat on the bench as the hall filled up. There was still no sign, however, of Patty and Diana and their group.

"They probably found a better dance somewhere else," Sheila said.

"It would be too much to expect for them to support their own parish," Miss McAdam added.

"And I heard that some dances on the Manhattan side of the bridge can be very dangerous," Sheila Heffernan said.

"You know, the sooner this is over and I am at home in my own warm bed the happier I'll be," Miss McAdam said.

At first Eilis did not see Patty and Diana but spotted instead a crowd of young people who had come noisily into the hall. A few of the men were dressed in brightly coloured suits with their hair slicked back with oil. One or two were remarkably good-looking, like film stars. Eilis could imagine what they would think of her and her two companions as the new arrivals took in the hall, their gaze shiny, excited, brilliant, full of expectation. And then she saw Diana and Patty among them, both looking radiant, everything about them perfect including their warm smiles.

Eilis would have given anything now to have been with them, dressed like them, to be glamorous herself, too easily distracted by the jokes and smiles of those around her to watch anyone with the same breath-filled intensity as she was watching them. She was afraid to turn to check on Miss McAdam and Sheila Heffernan; she knew that they might share her feelings, but she was aware also how hard they would try to suggest that they deeply disapproved of the new arrivals. She could not bear to look at her two fellow lodgers, afraid that she would see something of her own gawking unease in their faces, her own sense of being unable to look as though she were enjoying herself.

Once the music changed, no more Irish tunes were performed. The accordion player began to play slow tunes on the saxophone, tunes that most of the dancers seemed to recognize. By now, the hall was full. The dancers moved slowly, and they appeared to Eilis, in how they responded to the music, more elegant than the dancers at home. As the rhythms grew slower, she was surprised at how close some of them danced; some of the women seemed almost wrapped around their partners. She saw Diana and Patty move with confidence and skill and noticed that Diana shut her eyes as she came close to her fellow lodgers, as though she meant to concentrate better on the music and the tall man with whom she was dancing and the pleasure she was taking in the night. Once she had passed, Miss McAdam said she thought it was time for them to go.

As they made their way across the hall to get their coats, Eilis wished they had waited until the set was over so that they might not be seen making such an early departure. As they walked home silently, she did not know how she felt. The tunes the band had played were so soft and beautiful. The way the couples who danced were dressed was to her eyes so fashionable and so right. She knew that it was something she would never be able to do.

"That Diana should be ashamed of herself," Miss McAdam said. "God only knows what time she'll come in at."

"Is that her boyfriend?" Eilis asked.

"Who knows?" Sheila Heffernan said. "She has a different one for every day of the week and two on Sundays."

"He looks lovely," Eilis said. "He was a great dancer."

Neither of her companions replied. Miss McAdam quickened her pace and forced the other two to follow. Eilis was pleased at what she had said even though it was clear that she had annoyed them. She wondered if she could think of something stronger to say so that they might not ask her to accompany them to the dance the following week. Instead, she determined that she would buy something, even just new shoes, which would make her feel more like the girls she had seen dancing. She thought for a moment that she would ask Patty and Diana for advice about clothes and make-up but reasoned that that might be going too far. As Miss McAdam and Sheila Heffernan barely said goodnight to her when they reached home, she decided that, no matter what, she would never go to a dance with them again.

At work on Monday, Miss Fortini was waiting for her. Eilis thought at first that she had done something wrong, as Miss Fortini asked her and Miss Delano, one of the other sales assistants, to follow her to Miss Bartocci's office. When they entered the room, Miss Bartocci seemed grave as she signalled to them to sit down opposite her.

"There is going to be a big change in the store," she said, "because there is a change going on outside the store. Coloured people are moving into Brooklyn, more and more of them."

As she looked at all of them, Eilis could not tell whether they viewed this as a good thing for business or a piece of ominous news.

"We're going to welcome coloured women into our store as shoppers. And we're starting with nylon stockings. This is going to be the first store on this street to sell Red Fox stockings at cheap prices and soon we're going to add Sepia and Coffee."

"These are colours," Miss Fortini said.

"Coloured women want Red Fox stockings and we are selling them and you two are going to be polite to anyone who comes into this store, coloured or white."

"Both of them are always very polite," Miss Fortini said, "but I'll be watching once the first notice goes in the window."

"We may lose customers," Miss Bartocci interjected, "but we're going to sell to anyone who will buy and at the best prices."

"But the Red Fox stockings will be apart, away from the other normal stockings," Miss Fortini said. "At least at first. And you two will be at that counter, Miss Lacey and Miss Delano, and your job is to pretend that it's no big deal."

"The sign is going in the window this morning," Miss Bartocci added. "And you stand there and smile. Is that agreed?"

Eilis and her companion looked at one another and nodded.

"You probably won't be busy today," Miss Bartocci said, "but we're going to hand leaflets out in the right places and by the end of the week you won't have a moment if we're lucky."

Miss Fortini then led them back to the shop floor, where to the left at a long table men were piling up new packages with nylon stockings that were almost red in colour.

"Why did they choose us?" Miss Delano asked her.

"They must think we are nice," Eilis said.

"You're Irish, that makes you different."

"And what about you?"

"I'm from Brooklyn."

"Well, maybe you are nice."

"Maybe I'm just easy to kick around. Wait until my dad hears about this."

Eilis saw that Miss Delano had perfectly plucked eyebrows. She had an image of her in front of the mirror for hours with a tweezers.

All day they stood at the counter chatting quietly, but no one approached them to look at the red-coloured nylon stockings. It was only the next day that Eilis spotted two middle-aged coloured women coming into the store and being approached by Miss Fortini and directed towards her and Miss Delano. She found herself staring at the two women and then, when she checked herself, looked around the store to find that everyone else was staring at them. The two women were, she saw when she looked at them again, beautifully dressed, both in cream-coloured woollen coats and each chatting casually to the other as though there were nothing unusual about their arrival in the store.

Miss Delano, she observed, stood back as they came close, but Eilis stayed where she was as the two women began to examine the nylon stockings, looking at different sizes. She studied their painted fingernails and then their faces; she was ready to smile at them if they looked at her. But they did not once glance up from the stockings and, even as they selected a number of pairs and handed them to her, they did not catch her eye. She saw Miss Fortini watching her across the store as she added up what they owed and showed it to them. As she was handed the money, she noticed how white the inside of the woman's hand was against the dark skin on the back of her hand. She took the money as busily as she could and put it in the container and sent it to the cash department.

As she waited for the receipt and the change to be returned, her two customers continued talking to each other as though no one else existed. Despite the fact that they were middle-aged, Eilis thought that they were glamorous and had taken great care with their appearance, their hair perfect, their clothes beautiful. She could not tell if either of them was wearing make-up; she could smell perfume but did not know what the scent was. When she handed them the change and the nylon stockings wrapped carefully in brown paper, she thanked them but they did not reply, merely took the change and the receipt and the package and moved elegantly towards the door.

As the week went on more of them came and as each one entered Eilis noticed a change in the atmosphere in the store, a stillness, a watchfulness; no one else appeared to move when these women moved in case they would get in their way; the other assistants would look down and seem busy and then glance up in the direction of the counter where the stockings in Red Fox were heaped before looking down again. Miss Fortini, however, never lifted her eyes from the scene at the counter. Each time the new customers approached, Miss Delano stood back and let Eilis serve them, but if a second set of customers came she moved forward as though it were part of some arrangement. Not once did a coloured woman come into the store alone, and most who came did not look at Eilis or address her directly.

The few who did speak to her used tones of such elaborate politeness that they made her feel awkward and shy. When the new colours of Coffee and Sepia came it was her job to point out to the customers that these were lighter colours but most of them ignored her. By the end of each of these days she felt exhausted and found her lectures in the evening almost relaxing, relieved that there was something to take her mind off the fierce tension in the store, which lay heaviest around her counter. She wished she had not been singled out to stand at this counter and wondered if, in time, she would be moved to another part of the store.

Eilis loved her room, loved putting her books at the table opposite the window when she came in at night and then getting into her pyjamas and the dressing gown she had bought in one of the sales and her warm slippers and spending an hour or more before she went to bed looking over the lecture notes and then rereading the manuals on bookkeeping and accounting she had bought. Her only problem remained the law lectures. She enjoyed watching the gestures that Mr. Rosenblum made and the way he spoke, sometimes acting out an entire case for them, the litigants vividly described even if they were a company, but neither she nor any of the other students she spoke to knew what was expected of them, how this might appear as a question in an examination paper. Since Mr. Rosenblum knew so much she wondered if he might expect all of them to have the same detailed knowledge of cases and what they meant, and precedents, and the judgments, prejudices and peculiarities of individual judges.

It worried her enough to decide to explain to him exactly what her problem was. Just as he spoke quickly in his lectures, moving from one case to another, from what a certain law could mean in theory to how it had been applied up to then, so he disappeared as soon as the lecture was over, as though he had another pressing appointment. Eilis determined to sit in the front row and approach him the very second he had finished speaking, but as it came to the time she was nervous. She hoped that he would not think that she was criticizing him; she also worried that he might begin talking in a way that she would not understand. She had never come across anyone like him before. He reminded her of waiters in some cafés near Fulton Street who had no patience, who needed her to make up her mind about everything there and then and always had a further question for her no matter what she asked for, if she wanted small or large, or if she wanted it heated or with mustard. In Bartocci's she had learned to be brave and decisive with the customers, but once she herself was a customer she knew she was too hesitant and slow.

She would have to approach Mr. Rosenblum. He seemed so clever and he knew so much that she still wondered as she walked towards the podium how he would respond to a simple request. Once she had his attention, however, she found that she had become, without too much effort or hesitation, almost poised.

"Is there a book I could buy that would help me with this part of the course?" she asked.

Mr. Rosenblum appeared puzzled and did not reply.

"Your lectures are interesting," she said, "but I'm worried about the exam."

"You like them?" He seemed younger now than he did when he was addressing all of the students on the law.

"Yes," she said, and smiled. She was surprised at herself, that she had not stammered. She did not think she was even blushing.

"Are you British?" he asked.

"No, Irish."

"All the way from Ireland." He spoke as though to himself.

"I wondered if you could recommend another textbook or a manual that I can study for the exams."

"You look worried."

"I don't know if the notes I'm taking or the books I have are enough."

"You want to read more?"

"I would like to have a book that I could study."

He looked around the lecture hall, which was emptying quickly. He seemed deep in thought, as though the question perplexed him.

"There are some good books on basic corporate law."

She presumed that he was about to give her the names of these books, but he stopped for a moment.

"Do you think I am going too fast?"

"No. I'm just not sure my notes will be enough for the exam."

He opened his briefcase and took out a notepad.

"Are you the only Irish student here?"

"I think so."

She watched him as he wrote a number of titles on a blank sheet of paper.

"There's a special law book store on West Twenty-third Street," he said. "In Manhattan. You'll have to go there to get these."

"And will they be the right books for the exam?"

"Sure. If you know the rudiments of corporate law and tort, then you will get through."

"Is that book store open every day?"

"I think so. You'll have to go and check it out, but I think so."

As she nodded and tried to smile, he appeared even more preoccupied.

"But you can follow the lectures?"

"Of course," she said. "Yes, of course."

He put the notepad into his briefcase and turned away brusquely.

"Thank you," she said, but he did not reply. Instead, he quickly left the hall. The porter was waiting to lock up when she pushed open the lecture-hall doors. She was the last to leave.

She asked Diana and Patty about West Twenty-third Street, showing them the full address. They explained to her that west meant west of Fifth Avenue and that the number she had been given signified that the store was between Sixth and Seventh avenues. They showed her a map, spreading it out on the kitchen table, amazed that Eilis had never been in Manhattan.

"It's wonderful over there," Diana said.

"Fifth Avenue is the most heavenly place," Patty said. "I'd give anything to live there. I'd love to marry a rich man with a mansion on Fifth Avenue."

"Or even a poor man," Diana said, "as long as he had a mansion."

They told her how to take the subway to West Twenty-third Street, and she decided she would go when she had her next half-day free from Bartocci's.

When the prospect of Friday night arose Eilis could not face asking Miss McAdam or Sheila Heffernan if they were going to the dance at the hall and she knew that it would be too disloyal to go with Patty and Diana, and maybe too expensive as well, since they went to a restaurant first and since she would need to buy new clothes to match the style that they were wearing.

On Friday night after work she came to supper with a handkerchief in her hand, warning the others not to come too close in case they caught the chill from her. She blew her nose loudly and sniffled as best she could several times throughout the meal. She did not care whether they believed her or not, but having a cold, she thought, would be the best excuse for her not to go to the dance. She knew as well that it would encourage Mrs. Kehoe to discuss winter ailments, which was one of the landlady's favourite subjects.

"Chilblains, now," she said, "you'd want to be very careful with the chilblains. When I was your age they were the death of me."

"I'd say in that store," Miss McAdam said to Eilis, "you could get all sorts of germs."

"You can get germs in offices as well," Mrs. Kehoe said, taking in Eilis with a glance as she spoke, making clear that she understood Miss McAdam's intention to belittle her because she worked in a store.

"But you'd never know who'd—"

"That's enough now, Miss McAdam," Mrs. Kehoe said. "And maybe it's best early bed for all of us in this cold weather."

"I was just going to say that I heard there are coloured women going into Bartocci's," Miss McAdam said.

For a moment no one spoke.

"I heard that too," Sheila Heffernan said after a while in a low voice.

Eilis looked down at her plate.

"Well, we mightn't like them but the Negro men fought in the overseas war, didn't they?" Mrs. Kehoe asked. "And they were killed just the same as our men. I always say that. No one minded them when they needed them."

121

"But I wouldn't like—" Miss McAdam began.

"We know what you wouldn't like," Mrs. Kehoe interrupted.

"I wouldn't like to have to serve them in a store," Miss McAdam insisted.

"God, I wouldn't either," Patty said.

"And is it their money you wouldn't like?" Mrs. Kehoe asked.

"They're very nice," Eilis said. "And some of them have beautiful clothes."

"So it's true, then?" Sheila Heffernan asked. "I thought it was a joke. Well, that's it, then. I'll pass Bartocci's, all right, but it'll be on the other side of the street."

Eilis suddenly felt brave. "I'll tell Mr. Bartocci that. He'll be very upset, Sheila. You and your friend here are famous for your style, especially for the ladders in your stockings and the fussy old cardigans you wear."

"That's enough from the whole lot of you," Mrs. Kehoe said. "I intend to eat the rest of my dinner in peace."

By the time silence had descended and Patty had stopped shrieking with laughter, Sheila Heffernan had left the room, but Miss McAdam, white-faced, was staring directly at Eilis.

Eilis could see no difference between Brooklyn and Manhattan when she went there the following Thursday afternoon except that the cold as she walked from the subway seemed more severe and dry and the wind more fierce. She was not sure what exactly she had expected, but glamour certainly, more glamorous shops and better-dressed people and a sense of things less broken-down and dismal than they seemed to her sometimes in Brooklyn.

She had been looking forward to writing to her mother and Rose about her first trip to Manhattan, but she realized now that it would have to join the arrival of coloured customers in Bartocci's or the fight with the other lodgers on the matter; it would be something that she could not mention in a letter home as she did not want to worry them or send them news that might cause them to feel that she could not look after herself. Nor did she want to write them letters that might depress them. Thus as she walked along a street that seemed interminable with dingy shops and poor-looking people, she knew that this would be no use to her when she needed news for her next letter unless, she thought, she made a joke of it, letting them believe that, since Manhattan was no better than Brooklyn, despite everything she had heard, she was missing nothing by not living there and by not planning to go there too soon again.

She found the bookshop easily and was amazed, once she was inside, at the number of law books on sale and the size and weight of some of them. She wondered if in Ireland there were as many law books and if the solicitors in Enniscorthy had immersed themselves in books like this when they were studying. It would, she knew, be a good subject to write to Rose about since Rose played golf with one of the solicitors' wives.

Eilis walked around the store first, studying titles on the shelves, aware now that some of the books were old and maybe second-hand. It was easy for her to imagine Mr. Rosenblum here, browsing, with one or two big books open in front of him, or using the ladder to get something from the higher shelves. When she had mentioned him several times in letters home, Rose replied to ask if he was married. It was hard to explain in return that he seemed to Eilis so full of knowledge and so steeped in the detail of his subject and its intricacies and so serious that it was impossible to imagine him with a wife or children. Rose in her letter had also suggested once more that if Eilis had something private to discuss, something that she did not want their mother to know about, then she could write to Rose at the office and Rose would, she said, make sure that no one else ever saw the letter.

Eilis smiled to herself at the thought that all she had to report was the first dance; and that she had felt free to write to her mother about it, mentioning it only in passing and as a joke. She had nothing private to report to Rose.

She knew, as she browsed, that she would have no hope of finding the three books on her list in the middle of all the other books, so when she was approached by an old man who had come from behind the desk she simply handed him the list and said that these were the books she had come looking for. The man, who was wearing thick glasses, had to raise them onto his forehead so that he could read. He squinted.

"Is this your handwriting?"

"No, it's my lecturer's. He recommended these books."

"Are you a law student?"

"Not really. But it's part of the course."

"What's your lecturer's name?"

"Mr. Rosenblum."

"Joshua Rosenblum?"

"I don't know his first name."

"What are you studying?"

"I'm doing a night course at Brooklyn College."

"That's Joshua Rosenblum. I'd know his writing."

He peered again at the piece of paper and the titles.

"He's clever," the man said.

"Yes, he's very good," she replied.

"Can you imagine . . . ," the man began but turned towards the cash desk before he finished. He was agitated. She followed him slowly.

"You want these books, then?" He spoke almost aggressively.

"Yes, I do."

"Joshua Rosenblum?" the man asked. "Can you imagine a country that would want to kill him?"

Eilis stepped back but did not reply.

"Well, can you?"

"What do you mean?" she asked.

"The Germans killed everyone belonging to him, murdered every one of them, but we got him out, at least we did that, we got Joshua Rosenblum out."

"You mean in the war?"

The man did not reply. He moved across the store and found a small footstool onto which he climbed to fetch a book. As he descended he turned towards her angrily. "Can you imagine a country that would do that? It should be wiped off the face of the earth."

He looked at her bitterly.

"In the war?" she asked again.

"In the holocaust, in the *churben.*"

"But was it in the war?"

"It was, it was in the war," the man replied, the expression on his face suddenly gentle.

As he busied himself finding the other two books, he had a resigned, almost stubborn look; by the time he returned to the counter and prepared the bill for her he had come to seem distant and forbidding. She did not ask him any questions as she handed him the money. He wrapped the books for her and gave her the change. She sensed that he wanted her to leave the shop and there was nothing she could do to make him tell her anything more.

She loved unwrapping the law books and placing them on the table beside the notebooks and her books on accountancy and bookkeeping. When she opened the first of them and looked at it she immediately found it difficult, worrying that she should have bought a dictionary as well so she could check the difficult words. She sat until suppertime going through the introduction, no wiser at the end as to what the "jurisprudence" mentioned at the beginning might be.

That evening at supper, when she had noticed that neither Miss McAdam nor Sheila Heffernan was still speaking to her, Eilis thought of asking Patty and Diana if she could go to the dance with them the following night, or meet them before it somewhere. She did not, she realized, want to go at all but she knew that Father Flood would miss her and, since it would be the second week for her not to be there, he would ask about her. There was another girl at supper that evening, Dolores Grace, who had taken Eilis's old room. She had red hair and freckles and came from Cavan, it emerged, but she was mainly silent and seemed embarrassed to be at the table with them. Eilis learned that this was her third evening among them, but she had missed her at the previous meals because she had been at her lectures.

After supper, as she was settling back down to see if she could follow one of the other two law books any better, a knock came to the door. It was Diana in the company of Miss McAdam, and Eilis thought it was strange to see the two of them together. She stood at her door and did not invite them into her room.

"We need to talk to you," Diana whispered.

"What's up now?" Eilis asked almost impatiently.

"It's that Dolores one," Miss McAdam butted in. "She's a scrubber."

Diana began to laugh and had to put her hand to her mouth.

"She cleans houses," Miss McAdam said. "And she's cleaning for the Kehoe woman here to pay part of her rent. And we don't want her at the table."

Diana let out what was close to a shriek of laughter. "She's awful. She's the limit."

"What do you want me to do?" Eilis asked.

"Refuse to eat with her when the rest of us do. And the Kehoe woman listens to you," Miss McAdam said.

"And where will she eat?"

"Out in the street for all I care," Miss McAdam said.

"We don't want her, none of us," Diana said. "If word got around—"

"That this was a house where people like her were staying—" Miss McAdam continued.

Eilis felt an urge to close the door in their faces and go back to her books.

"We're just letting you know," Diana said.

"She's a scrubber from Cavan," Miss McAdam said as Diana began to laugh again.

"I don't know what you're laughing at," Miss McAdam said, turning to her.

"Oh, God, I'm sorry. It's just awful. No decent fellow will have anything to do with us."

Eilis looked at both of them as though they were nuisance customers in Bartocci's and she was Miss Fortini. Since they both worked in offices, she wondered if they had spoken about her in the same way when she first came because she would be working in a shop. She firmly closed the door in their faces.

In the morning Mrs. Kehoe knocked on the window as Eilis reached the street from the basement. Mrs. Kehoe beckoned her to wait and then appeared at the front door.

"I was wondering if you would do me a special favour," she said.

"Of course I would, Mrs. Kehoe," Eilis said. It was something her mother had taught her to say if anyone asked her to do them a favour.

"Would you take Dolores to the dance in the hall tonight? She's dying to go."

Eilis hesitated. She wished she had guessed in advance that she was going to be asked to do this so she could have a reply prepared.

"All right." She found herself nodding.

"Well, that's great news. I'll tell her to be ready," Mrs. Kehoe said.

Eilis wished she could think of some quick excuse, some reason why she could not go, but she had used a cold the previous week and she knew that she would have to make an appearance at some stage, even if just for a short time.

"I'm not sure how long I'll be staying," she said.

"That's no problem," Mrs. Kehoe said. "No problem at all. She won't want to stay that long either."

Later, after work, when Eilis went upstairs, she found Dolores Grace alone working in the kitchen and made an arrangement to collect her at ten o'clock.

At supper, none of them spoke about the dance in the hall; Eilis presumed from the atmosphere and from the way in which Miss McAdam pursed her lips and seemed openly irritated every time Mrs. Kehoe spoke and from the fact that Dolores remained silent throughout the meal that something had been said. Eilis understood also by the way both Miss McAdam and Diana avoided her eyes that they knew she was taking Dolores to the dance. She hoped they did not believe that she had offered to do so and wondered if she could let them know that she had been press-ganged by Mrs. Kehoe.

Eilis was shocked by Dolores's appearance when she went upstairs at ten o'clock and found her. She was wearing a cheap leather jacket, like a man's, and a frilly white blouse and a white skirt and almost black stockings. The red lipstick seemed garish against her freckled face and bright hair. She struck Eilis as looking like a horse-dealer's wife in Enniscorthy on a fair day. Eilis almost fled downstairs as soon as she saw her. Instead, she had to smile as Dolores said that she would need to go upstairs and fetch her winter coat and a hat. Eilis did not know how she was going to sit beside her in the hall with Miss McAdam and Sheila Heffernan avoiding her on one side and Patty and Diana arriving with all their friends.

"Are there great fellas at this?" Dolores asked when they reached the street.

"I have no idea," Eilis replied coldly. "I go only because it is organized by Father Flood."

"Oh, God, does he hang around all night? It'll be just like home."

Eilis did not reply and tried to walk in a way that was dignified, as though she were going to eleven o'clock mass in the cathedral in Enniscorthy with Rose. Each time Dolores asked her a question she answered quietly and did not tell her much. It would be better, she thought, if they could walk in silence to the hall, but she could not ignore Dolores completely, although she found that, as they stood waiting for traffic lights to change, she was clenching her fists in pure irritation each time her companion spoke.

She had imagined that, when they were in the hall, Miss McAdam and Sheila Heffernan would sit away from them once they had left their coats in the cloakroom and found a position from which to survey the dancers. But instead their two fellow lodgers moved closer to them, all the more to emphasize that they had no intention of speaking to them or consorting with them in any way. Eilis observed how Dolores let her eyes dart around the hall, her brow knitted in watchfulness.

"God, there's no one here at all," she said.

Eilis stared straight in front of her pretending that she had not heard.

"I'd love a fella, would you?" Dolores asked and nudged her. "I wonder what the American fellas are like."

Eilis looked at her blankly.

"I'd say they're different," Dolores added.

Eilis responded by moving away from her slightly.

"They're awful bitches, those other ones," Dolores went on.

"That's what the boss-woman said. Bitches. The only one of them is not a bitch is you."

Eilis looked at the band and then stole a glance at Miss McAdam and Sheila Heffernan. Miss McAdam held her gaze and then smiled archly, dismissively.

When Patty and Diana arrived, they came with an even larger group than before. Everyone in the hall seemed to notice them. Patty had her hair tied back in a bun and was wearing heavy black eye-liner. It made her appear very severe and dramatic. Eilis noticed that Diana pretended not to see her. It was as though the very arrival of this group was a signal to the musicians, who had been playing old waltzes with just the piano and some of the bass players, to play some tunes that Eilis knew from the girls at work were called swing tunes and were very fashionable.

As the music changed, some of Patty and Diana's group began to applaud and cheer, and when Eilis caught Patty's eye, Patty signalled to her to come towards them. It was a tiny gesture but it was unmistakable and, having made it, Patty kept staring over at her almost impatiently. Suddenly, Eilis decided she would stand up and walk over towards their group, smiling confidently at them all, as though they were old friends. She kept her back straight as she moved and tried to appear as if she were in full possession of herself.

"It's so good to see you," she said quietly to Patty.

"I think I know what you mean," Patty replied.

When Patty suggested that they go to the bathroom, Eilis nodded and followed her.

"I don't know what you looked like sitting there," she said, "but you sure didn't look happy."

She offered to show Eilis how to put on the black eye-liner and some mascara and they spent time at the mirror together, ignoring everyone who came in and out. With extra clips that she carried in her bag, Patty put Eilis's hair up for her.

"Now, you look like a ballet dancer," she said.

"No, I don't," Eilis said.

"Well, at least you don't look like you've just come in from milking the cows any more."

"Did I look like that?"

"Just a bit. Nice clean cows," Patty said.

Finally, when they went back into the body of the hall, the place was crowded and the music was fast and loud and many couples were dancing. Eilis was careful where she looked or moved. She did not know if Dolores had remained seated where she had left her. She had no intention of going back there and no intention either of catching Dolores's eye in the hall. She stood with Patty and a group of her friends, including a young man with heavily oiled hair and an American accent who tried to explain the dance steps to her above the noise of the music. He did not ask her to dance, seeming to prefer to stay with the group; he glanced at his friends regularly as he took her through the steps, showing her how to move in time to the swing tunes that were becoming faster now as the dancers on the floor responded to them.

Eilis slowly became aware of a young man looking at her. He was smiling warmly, amused at her efforts to learn the dance steps. He was not much taller than she was, but looked strong, with blond hair and clear blue eyes. He seemed to think what was happening was funny as he swayed to the music. He stood alone, and when she caught his eye, having turned away for a moment, she was surprised at the expression on his face, which was unembarrassed at the fact that he was still looking at her. She was sure that he was not part of Patty and Diana's group; his clothes were too ordinary and he was not in any way dressed up. As the band lifted the tempo once more, everyone began to cheer and the man who had been trying to teach her the steps attempted to say something to her but she could not make out the words. When she turned towards him she discovered that he was saying that maybe they could dance together later when the beat was not so fast. She nodded at him and smiled and moved towards Patty, who was still surrounded by some of her friends.

When the music stopped some couples separated, others went to the bar for sodas or remained on the dance floor. Eilis saw that the man who had been teaching her the steps was now going to dance with Patty, and it struck her that Patty must have asked him to pay attention to her and he had done so merely to be kind. As Diana brushed by her, making clear that she was not speaking to her, the young man who had been looking at her approached.

"Are you with that guy who was teaching you the steps?" he asked. She noticed his American accent and his white teeth.

"No," she said.

"So, can I dance with you?"

"I'm not sure I know the steps."

"No one does. The trick is to look as though you do."

The music started up and they moved among the dancers. Her companion's eyes, she thought, were too big for his face but then when he smiled at her he appeared too happy for that to matter. He was a good dancer but not showy in any way and did not try to impress her or do better than she did and she liked that. She studied him as closely as she could because she was sure that if she let her eyes wander she would find Dolores still sitting where she had left her, waiting for her to return.

When she had danced the first set with him and the music stopped he introduced himself as Tony and asked her if he could buy her a soda. She knew this meant that she would have to stay with him for the next dance, and since by then Dolores might have gone home or found someone of her own to dance with, she agreed. As they passed Diana and Patty, she saw both of them taking Tony in, looking him up and down. Patty made a sign as if to say that he was not quite up to her standard. Diana simply looked away.

The next dance was slow and Eilis was worried about moving too close to Tony, although it was difficult not to, as there were many dancers on the floor. For the first time she was aware of him, sensing that he too was trying not to move too near, and she wondered if he was being considerate or if this meant that he did not like her very much. At the end of this set, she thought, she would thank him and go to the cloakroom, get her coat and go home. If Dolores complained about her to Mrs. Kehoe, she could say that she did not feel well and had to leave early.

Tony was able to move easily to the music without making an exhibition of himself or of her. As they made their way around the floor to the sound of a moody show tune on the saxophone, Eilis knew that no one was paying any attention to them. She felt the heat from him, and when he tried to say something she smelled a sweetness from his breath. For a second she looked at him again. He was carefully shaved and his hair tightly cut. His skin looked soft. When he caught her looking at him he twisted his mouth in amusement and this made his eyes seem even larger than before. For the last tune in the set, which was by far, she thought, the most romantic, he moved his body closer to her. He did this tactfully and gradually; she could feel the pressure and strength of him against her as she, in turn, moved closer too, until they were wrapped around each other for the last minutes of the dance.

As they turned to applaud the band, he did not catch her eye but stood beside her as though it were inevitable, already decided, that they would stay together for the next dance. There was too much noise around them for her to hear what he said when he attempted to speak but it seemed to be just a friendly comment about something so she nodded and smiled in reply. He looked happy and she liked that. The music that began now was even slower than before and it had a beautiful melody. She closed her eyes and let him touch her cheek with his. They were hardly dancing at all, just swaying to the sound, as were most other couples on the floor.

She wondered who he was, this young man she was dancing with, and where he came from. He did not seem Irish to her; he was too clean-cut and friendly and open in his gaze. But she could not be sure. There was nothing at all of the tailored poise of Patty and Diana's friends. It was also hard to imagine what he did for a living. She did not know as they smooched together on the dance floor if she would ever get a chance to ask him.

At the end of the set the man playing the saxophone took up the microphone and, in an Irish accent, explained that the best part of the evening was ahead, in fact was about to start now, since they were going to play some céilí tunes as they had the previous weeks. They were going to ask those who knew the dance steps to take the floor first, and, he added to cheers and whistles, he hoped they would not all be from County Clare. When he gave the signal, he said, everyone else could join in; then it would be the same free-for-all that they had enjoyed the previous weeks.

"Are you from County Clare?" her companion asked her.

"No."

"I saw you the first week but you didn't stay until the end so you missed the free-for-all and you weren't here last week."

"How do you know?"

"I looked for you and didn't see you."

Suddenly a tune began; when she glanced at the stage she saw that the band had transformed itself. The two saxophone players had become a banjo player and an accordion player and there were two fiddle players as well as a woman playing an upright piano. There was also the same drummer. A number of dancers moved into the centre of the hall and now became the focus of attention as they managed a set of intricate movements with immense confidence and speed. Soon, they were joined by others, equally skilful, to the sound of whoops and cheers from the crowd. The music grew faster; all the instruments together were led by the accordion player; the dancers made a loud noise with their shoes against the wooden floor.

When the accordion player announced that they were going to do "The Siege of Ennis" more dancers took to the floor, and they began to change from ordered dancing towards the free-for-all the man had mentioned earlier. As Tony suggested they take the floor also, Eilis quickly agreed, even though she did not know how to do the steps. They found a group who were standing in two lines facing each other, with a man giving instructions through a microphone on what should happen next. A dancer from each end—a man and a woman—moved into the centre and swung around before returning to their original place. Then it was the turn of the next dancer until each had had a moment in the centre. The two lines of dancers then came forward to confront one another and, once that was done, one line put their arms in the air and let the other through, thus finding themselves opposite a new line of dancers. As the playing went on, the shouting and laughing and roaring instructions grew louder and more intense. Great energy was put into the whirling and turning in the centre and banging the floor with their shoes. By the time the last tunes were played and everyone seemed to understand the basic steps and movements, Eilis could see that Tony loved this and put as much effort as he could into getting it right while making sure also that he did not do more than she did. She felt that he was holding himself back for her.

As soon as the music stopped he asked her where she lived; when she told him he said that it was on his way home. There was something about him now, something so innocent and eager and shiny, that she almost laughed out loud as she said yes, that he could walk her home. She told him that she would meet him outside when she had fetched her coat. When she went to the cloakroom, she watched out for any sign of Dolores in the queue.

It was freezing outside; they moved slowly through the streets huddled against each other, hardly speaking at all. When they came close to Clinton Street, however, he stopped and turned and faced her.

"There's something you've got to know," he said. "I'm not Irish."

"You don't sound Irish," she said.

"I mean I'm not Irish at all."

"None of you?" She laughed.

"Not a single bit."

"So where are you from?"

"I'm from Brooklyn," he said, "but my mom and dad are from Italy."

"And what were you doing—"

"I know," he interrupted. "I heard about the Irish dance and I thought I'd go and look at it and I liked it."

"Do the Italians not have dances?"

"I knew you were going to ask me that."

"I'm sure they're wonderful."

"I could take you some night but you would have to be warned. They behave like Italians all night."

"Is that good or bad?"

"I don't know, but bad because if I had gone to an Italian dance I wouldn't be walking you home now."

They continued in silence until they reached the front of Mrs. Kehoe's house.

"Can I collect you next week? Maybe get something to eat first?"

Eilis realized that this invitation would mean that she could go to the dance without having to take the feelings of any of her fellow lodgers into account. Even for Mrs. Kehoe, she thought, it would serve as an excuse not to have to accompany Dolores.

*   *   *

Later, during the week, as she was making her way from Bartocci's to Brooklyn College, she forgot what she was looking forward to; sometimes she actually believed that she was looking forward to thinking about home, letting images of home roam freely in her mind, but it came to her now with a jolt that, no, the feeling she had was only about Friday night and being collected from the house by a man she had met and going to the dance with him in the hall, knowing that he would be walking her back to Mrs. Kehoe's afterwards. She had been keeping the thought of home out of her mind, letting it come to her only when she wrote or received letters or when she woke from a dream in which her mother or father or Rose or the rooms of the house on Friary Street or the streets of the town had appeared. She thought it was strange that the mere sensation of savouring the prospect of something could make her think for a while that it must be the prospect of home.

Around Mrs. Kehoe's table, Eilis's ditching of Dolores, which Patty, having fully witnessed, informed the others about before breakfast on Saturday morning, meant that they were all speaking to her again, including Dolores herself, who viewed being ditched, since it had resulted in Eilis meeting a man, as eminently reasonable. In return for this view, Dolores wanted only to know about the boyfriend himself, his name, for example, and his occupation, and when Eilis intended to see him again. All of the other lodgers had scrutinized him carefully as well; they thought him handsome, they said, although Miss McAdam might have wished him taller, and Patty did not like his shoes. All of them presumed that he was Irish, or of Irish origin, and all of them begged Eilis to tell them about him, what he had said to her that made her dance the second set with him and if she was going to the dance the following Friday night and if she expected to see him there.

The following Thursday evening, when she went downstairs to make herself a cup of tea, she met Mrs. Kehoe in the kitchen.

"There's a lot of giddiness in the house at the moment," Mrs. Kehoe said. "That Diana has a terrible voice, God help her. If she squeals once more, I'll have to get the doctor or the vet to give her something to calm her down."

"It's the dancing is doing it to them," Eilis said drily.

"Well, I'm going to ask Father Flood to preach a sermon on the evils of giddiness," Mrs. Kehoe said. "And maybe he might mention a few more things in his sermon."

Mrs. Kehoe left the room.

On Friday evening at eight thirty Tony rang on the front door bell, and, before Eilis could escape from the basement door and alert him to the impending danger, the door was answered by Mrs. Kehoe. By the time Eilis reached the front door, as Tony told her later, Mrs. Kehoe had asked him several questions, including his full name, his address and his profession.

"That's what she called it," he said. "My profession."

He grinned as though nothing as amusing had ever occurred to him in his life.

"Is she your mom?" he asked.

"I told you that my mom, as you call her, is in Ireland."

"So you did, but that woman looked like she owned you."

"She's my landlady."

"She's a lady all right. A lady with loads of questions to ask."

"And, incidentally, what is your full name?"

"You want what I told your mom?"

"She's not my mom."

"You want my real name?"

"Yes, I want your real name."

"My real full name is Antonio Giuseppe Fiorello."

"What name did you give my landlady when she asked you?"

"I told her my name is Tony McGrath. Because there's a guy at work called Billo McGrath."

"Oh, for God's sake. And what did you tell her your profession was?"

"My real one?"

"If you don't answer me properly—"

"I told her I'm a plumber and that's because I am."

"Tony?"

"Yeah?"

"In future, if I ever allow you to call again, you will come quietly to the basement door."

"And say nothing to no one?"

"Correct."

"Suits me."

He took her to a diner where they had supper and then they walked together towards the dancehall. She told him about her fellow lodgers and her job at Bartocci's. He told her, in turn, that he was the oldest of four boys and that he still lived at home in Bensonhurst with his parents.

"And my mom made me promise not to laugh too much, or make jokes," he said. "She said Irish girls aren't like Italian girls. They're serious."

"You told your mom you were meeting me?"

"No, but my brother guessed that I was meeting a girl and he told her. I think they all guessed. I think I was smiling too much. And I had to tell them it was an Irish girl in case they thought it was some family they knew."

Eilis could not understand him. By the end of the night as he walked her home she knew only that she liked dancing close to him and that he was funny. But she would not have been surprised if everything he told her was untrue, instead just part of the joke he made out of most things or, in fact, she decided in the days that followed when she went over all he had said, out of everything.

In the house there was much discussion about her boyfriend the plumber. She told them, once Mrs. Kehoe had left the room, once Patty and Diana began to wonder why none of their friends had ever seen him before, that Tony was Italian and not Irish. She had made a point of not introducing him to any of them at the dance and now regretted, as the conversation began, that she had said anything at all about him.

"I hope that dancehall is not going to be inundated with Italians now," Miss McAdam said.

"What do you mean?" Eilis asked.

"Now they realize what is to be had."

The others were silent for a moment. It was after supper on the Friday night and Eilis wished that Mrs. Kehoe, who had left the room some time before, would return.

"And what is to be had?" she asked.

"That's all they have to do, it seems." Miss McAdam snapped her finger. "I don't have to say the rest."

"I think we have to be very careful about men we don't know coming into the hall," Sheila Heffernan said.

"Maybe if we got rid of some of the wallflowers, Sheila," Eilis said, "with the sour look on their faces."

Diana began to shriek with laughter as Sheila Heffernan quickly left the room.

Suddenly Mrs. Kehoe arrived back in the kitchen.

"Diana, if I hear you squeal again," she said, "I will call the Fire Brigade to douse you with water. Did someone say something rude to Miss Heffernan?"

"We were giving Eilis here advice, that's all," Miss McAdam said. "Just to beware of strangers."

"Well, I thought he was very nice, her caller," Mrs. Kehoe said. "With nice old-fashioned Irish manners. And we will have no further comment about him in this house. Do you hear, Miss McAdam?"

"I was only saying—"

"You were only refusing to mind your own business, Miss McAdam. It's a trait I notice in people from Northern Ireland."

As Diana shrieked again she put her hand over her mouth in mock shame.

"I'll have no more talk about men at this table," Mrs. Kehoe said, "except to say to you, Diana, that the man that gets you will be nicely hoped up with you. The hard knocks that life gives you will put a sorry end to that smirk on your face."

One by one they crept out of the kitchen, leaving Mrs. Kehoe with Dolores.

Tony asked Eilis if she would come to a movie with him some night in the middle of the week. In everything she had told him she had left out the fact that she had classes at Brooklyn College. He had not asked her what she did every evening, and she had kept it to herself almost deliberately as a way of holding him at a distance. She had enjoyed being collected by him on a Friday night at Mrs. Kehoe's up to now, and she looked forward to his company, especially in the diner before the dance. He was bright and funny as he spoke about baseball, his brothers, his work and life in Brooklyn. He had quickly learned the names of her fellow lodgers and of her bosses at work and he managed to allude to them regularly in a way that made her laugh.

"Why didn't you tell me about the college?" he asked her as they sat in the diner before the dance.

"You didn't ask."

"I don't have anything more to tell you." He shrugged, feigning depression.

"No secrets?"

"I could make up some, but they wouldn't sound true."

"Mrs. Kehoe believes that you're Irish. And you could be a native of Tipperary for all I know and just be putting on the rest. How come I met you at an Irish dance?"

"Okay. I do have a secret."

"I knew it. You come from Bray."

"What? Where's that?"

"What's your secret?"

"You want to know why I came to an Irish dance?"

"All right. I'll ask you: why did you come to an Irish dance?"

"Because I like Irish girls."

"Would any one do?"

"No, I like you."

"Yes, but if I wasn't there? Would you just pick another?"

"No, if you weren't there, I would walk home all sad looking at the ground."

She explained to him then that she had been homesick, and that Father Flood had inscribed her on the course as a way of making her busy, and how studying in the evening made her feel happy, or as happy as she had been since she had left home.

"Don't I make you feel happy?" He looked at her seriously.

"Yes, you do," she replied.

Before he could ask her any more questions that might, she thought, lead her to say that she did not know him well enough to make any further declarations about him, she told him about her classes, about the other students, about bookkeeping and keeping accounts and about the law lecturer Mr. Rosenblum. He knitted his brow and seemed worried when she told him how difficult and complicated the lectures were. Then when she recounted what the bookseller had said on the day when she went to Manhattan to buy law books, he became completely silent. When their coffee came he still did not speak but kept stirring the sugar, nodding his head sadly. She had not seen him like this before and found that she was looking closely at his face in this light, wondering how quickly he would return to his usual self and begin smiling and laughing again. But, when he asked the waiter for the bill, he remained grave and he did not speak as they left the restaurant.

Later, when the dance music became slow and they were dancing close to each other, she looked up and caught his gaze. He had the same serious expression on his face, which made him appear less clownish and boyish than before. Even when he smiled at her, he did not make it seem like a joke, or a way of having fun. It was a warm smile, sincere, and it suggested to her that he was stable, almost mature and that, whatever was happening now, he meant business. She smiled back at him but then looked down and closed her eyes. She was frightened.

He arranged that evening that he would collect her the following Thursday from college and walk her home. Nothing more, he promised. He did not want to disturb her, he said, from her studies. The following week, when he asked her to come to a movie with him on the Saturday, she agreed because all of her fellow lodgers, with the exception of Dolores, and some of the girls at work were going to go to *Singin' in the Rain,* which was opening. Even Mrs. Kehoe said that she intended to see the film with two of her friends and thus it became a subject of much discussion at the kitchen table.

Soon, then, a pattern developed. Every Thursday, Tony stood outside the college, or discreetly inside the hall if it were raining, and he accompanied her onto the trolley-car and then he walked her home. He was invariably cheerful, with news of the people he had worked for since he had seen her last, and the different tones they used, depending on their age or their country of origin, as they explained the problems they had with the plumbing. Some of them were, he said, so grateful for the service that they tipped him handsomely, often giving him too much; others, even those who had blocked their own drains with garbage, wanted to argue about the bill. All the managers of buildings in Brooklyn, he said, were mean, and when Italian managers discovered he was Italian too, they were even meaner. The Irish ones, he was sorry to tell her, were mean and stingy no matter what.

"They are real mean. They're stingy as hell, those Irish," he said, and grinned at her.

Each Saturday he took her to a movie; they often travelled on the subway into Manhattan to see something that had just opened. On the first such date, when they joined the queue for *Singin' in the Rain,* she discovered that she was dreading the moment when the cinema became dark and the film began. She liked dancing with Tony, how gradually they moved close to each other in the slow dances, and she liked walking home with him, how they waited until they were near Mrs. Kehoe's house but not too near, before he kissed her. And how he never, even once, made her feel that she should pull his hand away or draw back from him. Now, however, at their first film together, she believed that something would have to change between them. She was almost tempted to mention it as they stood in the queue, to avoid any unpleasantness inside in the dark. She wanted to say to him, as nonchalantly as she could, that she would prefer actually to see the film rather then spend two hours necking and kissing in the cinema.

Inside, having bought the tickets, he bought popcorn as well, and did not, to her surprise, usher her to the back seat of the cinema, but asked her where she wanted to sit and seemed happy to sit in the middle, where they would have the best view. Although he put his arm around her during the film and whispered to her a few times, he did nothing more. As they waited for the subway afterwards, he was in such good humour and had loved the film so much that she felt an immense tenderness for him and wondered if she would ever see a side of him that was disagreeable. Soon, as they went more regularly to movies, she saw that a sad film or a film with disturbing scenes could leave him silent and brooding afterwards, locked into some depressed dream of his own that it would take time to lift him out of. So too, if she told him anything that was sad, his face would change and he would stop making jokes and he would want to go over what she had told him. He was not like anyone else she had ever met.

She wrote to Rose about him, sending the letter to the office, but did not mention him in letters to her mother or to her brothers. She tried to describe him to Rose, how considerate he was. She added that because she was studying she did not have time to see him with his friends, or visit his family, even though he had invited her home for a meal with his parents and his brothers.

When Rose replied to her, she asked what he did for a living. Eilis had deliberately left this out of the letter because she knew that Rose would hope that she would go out with someone who had an office job, who worked in a bank or an insurance office. When she wrote back, she buried the information that he was a plumber in the middle of a paragraph, but she was aware that Rose would notice it and seize on it.

One Friday night soon afterwards, as they were coming into the dance together, both of them in good humour as the fierce cold had briefly lifted and Tony had talked about summer and how they might go to Coney Island, they were met by Father Flood, who seemed cheerful too. But there was something odd, Eilis thought, about the length of time he spoke to them and his insisting that they have a soda with him, which made her believe that Rose had written to Father Flood and that he was there to see what Tony was like for her.

Eilis was almost proud of Tony's casual good manners, of his easy way of responding to the priest, all of it underlined by a way of being respectful, of letting the priest talk, and not saying a single word out of place. Rose, she knew, would have an idea in her head of what a plumber looked like and how he spoke. She would imagine him to be somewhat rough and awkward and use bad grammar. Eilis decided that she would write to her to say that he was not like that and that in Brooklyn it was not always as easy to guess someone's character by their job as it was in Enniscorthy.

She watched now while Tony and Father Flood spoke about baseball and Tony forgot that he was talking to a priest as he became feverish in his enthusiasm for what he was saying and thus interrupted Father Flood in a mixture of amused friendliness and passionate disagreement about a game they had both seen and a player Tony said he would never forgive. For a while they appeared not to realize that she was even there and when they finally noticed they agreed that they would take her to a baseball game as long as she pledged in advance that she was a Dodgers fan.

Rose wrote to her, mentioning in her letter that she had heard from Father Flood that he liked Tony, who seemed very respectable and decent and polite, but she was still worried about Eilis seeing him and no one else during her first year in Brooklyn. Eilis had not even told her that she was seeing Tony three nights a week and, because of her lectures, she had time for nothing else. She never went out with her fellow lodgers, for example, and this was a huge relief to her. At the table, however, since she had seen every new movie she always had something to talk about. Once the others became used to the idea that she was dating Tony, they refrained from giving her further warnings or advice about him. She wished, having read Rose's letter a couple of times, that Rose would do the same. She was almost sorry now that she had told Rose about Tony in the first place. In her letters to her mother she still did not mention him.

At work she noticed that some of the girls were leaving and being quietly replaced until she and a few others were the most experienced and trusted on the shop floor. She found herself taking her lunch break two or three days a week with Miss Fortini, whom she thought intelligent and interesting. When Eilis told her about Tony, Miss Fortini sighed and said that she had an Italian boyfriend also and he was nothing but trouble and he would be worse soon when the baseball season was to begin, when he would want nothing more than to drink with his friends and talk about the games with no women around. When Eilis told her that Tony had invited her to come to a game with him, Miss Fortini sighed and then laughed.

"Yes, Giovanni did that with me too, but the only time he spoke to me at the game was to demand that I go and get him and his friends some hot dogs. He nearly bit off my nose when I asked him if they wanted mustard on them. I was disturbing his concentration."

When Eilis described Tony to Miss Fortini, she became very interested in him.

"Hold on. He doesn't take you drinking with his friends and leave you with all the girls?"

"No."

"He doesn't talk about himself all the time when he's not telling you how great his mother is?"

"No."

"Then you hold on to him, honey. There aren't two of him. Maybe in Ireland, but not here."

They both laughed.

"So what's the worst thing about him?" Miss Fortini asked.

Eilis thought for a moment. "I wish he was two inches taller."

"Anything else?"

Eilis thought again. "No."

Once the dates for the exams were posted up Eilis arranged to have all that week free from work and began to worry about her studies. Thus, in the six weeks before the exams started, she did not see Tony on the Saturday evenings for a movie; instead, she stayed in her room and went through her notes and waded through the law books, trying to memorize the names of the most important cases in commercial law and how these judgments mattered. In return, she promised that when the exams were finished she would accompany Tony to meet his parents and his brothers, to have a meal with them in the family apartment in Seventy-second Street in Bensonhurst. Tony also told her that he hoped to get tickets for the Dodgers and planned on taking her along with his brothers.

"You know what I really want?" he asked. "I want our kids to be Dodgers fans."

He was so pleased and excited at the idea, she thought, that he did not notice her face freezing. She could not wait to be alone, away from him, so she could contemplate what he had just said. Later, as she lay on the bed and thought about it, she realized that it fitted in with everything else, that recently he had been planning the summer and how much time they would spend together. Recently too he had begun to tell her after he kissed her that he loved her and she knew that he was waiting for a response, a response that, so far, she had not given.

Now, she realized, in his mind he was going to marry her and she was going to have children with him and they were going to be Dodgers fans. It was, she thought, too ridiculous, something that she could not tell anybody, certainly not Rose and probably not Miss Fortini. But it was not something he had begun to imagine suddenly; they had been seeing one another for almost five months and had not once had an argument or a misunderstanding, unless this, his aim to marry her, was a huge misunderstanding.

He was considerate and interesting and good-looking. She knew that he liked her, not only because he said that he did, but by the way he responded to her and listened to her when she spoke. Everything was right, and they had the long summer when the exams were over to look forward to. A few times in the dancehall, or even on the street, she had seen a man who had appealed to her in some way, but each time it was just a fleeting thought lasting not more than a few seconds. The idea of sitting by the wall again with her fellow lodgers filled her with horror. And yet she knew that in his mind Tony was moving faster than she was, and she knew that she would have to slow him down, but she had no idea how to do so in a way that did not involve being unpleasant to him.

The following Friday night, as they huddled together on the way home from the dancehall, he whispered to her once more that he loved her. When she did not respond he began to kiss her and then he whispered it to her again. Without warning, she found herself pulling away from him. When he asked her what was wrong she did not reply. His saying that he loved her and his expecting a reply frightened her, made her feel that she would have to accept that this was the only life she was going to have, a life spent away from home. When they reached Mrs. Kehoe's house, having walked in silence, she thanked him almost formally for the night and, avoiding eye contact with him, said goodnight and went inside.

She knew that what she had done was wrong, that he would suffer now until he saw her on Thursday. She wondered if he would call around to see her on Saturday, but he did not. She could think of no good reason to tell him that she wanted to see less of him. Maybe, she thought, she should say to him that she did not want to talk about their kids when they had known each other only a short time. But then he might ask her, she believed, if she was not serious about him and she would be forced to answer, to say something. And if it was not fully encouraging she might, she knew, lose him. He was not someone who would enjoy having a girlfriend who was not sure how much she liked him. She knew him well enough to know that.

On Thursday, as she came out of her class and was walking down the stairs, she spotted him but he did not see her; there were many students milling about. She stopped for a second and realized that she still did not know what she was going to say to him. Carefully, she went back up the stairs and found that if she moved along the first landing she would be able to see him from above. Somehow, she thought, if she could look at him, take him in clearly when he was not trying to amuse her or impress her, something would come to her, some knowledge, or some ability to make a decision.

She discovered a vantage point from where, unless he looked directly upwards and to the left, he would not see her. He was, she thought, unlikely to look in her direction as he seemed absorbed by the students coming and going in the lobby. When she directed her gaze down she saw that he was not smiling; he seemed nonetheless fully at ease and curious. There was something helpless about him as he stood there; his willingness to be happy, his eagerness, she saw, made him oddly vulnerable. The word that came to her as she looked down was the word "delighted." He was delighted by things, as he was delighted by her, and he had done nothing else ever but make that clear. Yet somehow that delight seemed to come with a shadow, and she wondered as she watched him if she herself, in all her uncertainty and distance from him, was the shadow and nothing else. It occurred to her that he was as he appeared to her; there was no other side to him. Suddenly, she shivered in fear and turned, making her way down the stairs and towards him in the lobby as quickly as she could.

He told her about his work, with a story of two Jewish sisters who wanted to feed him, who had a huge meal ready for him when he had restored their hot water, even though it was only three o'clock in the afternoon. He did an imitation of their accents. Even though he spoke as if nothing had happened between them on the previous Friday night, Eilis knew that this funny fast talk of his, as story followed story while they walked to the trolley-car, was unusual for a Thursday night and was partly a way of pretending that there had been no problem then and that there was none now.

As they came close to her street she turned to him. "There's something I need to say to you."

"I know that."

"You remember when you told me that you loved me?"

He nodded. The expression on his face was sad.

"Well, I didn't really know what to say. So maybe I should say that I have thought about you and I like you, I like seeing you, I care for you and maybe I love you too. And the next time if you tell me you love me, I'll—"

She stopped.

"You'll what?"

"I'll say I love you too."

"Are you sure?"

"Yes."

"Holy shit! Sorry for my language but I thought you were telling me that you didn't want to see me again."

She stood beside him looking at him. She was shaking.

"You don't look as though you mean it," he said.

"I mean it."

"Well, why aren't you smiling?"

She hesitated and then smiled weakly. "Can I go home now?"

"No. I want to just jump up and down. Can I do that?"

"Quietly," she said, and laughed.

He jumped into the air waving his hands.

"Let's get this straight," he said when he came towards her again. "You love me?"

"Yes. But don't ask me anything else and don't mention wanting kids who are Dodgers fans."

"What? You want kids who support the Yankees? Or the Giants?"

He was laughing.

"Tony?"

"What?"

"Don't push me."

He kissed her and whispered to her, and when they reached Mrs. Kehoe's house he kissed her again until she had to tell him to stop or they would have an audience. Even though she was studying the following night and would have to miss the dance, she agreed to see him and go for a walk with him, if only around the block.

The exams were easier than she had expected; even the law paper had easy questions, requiring only the most basic knowledge. When they were over she felt relief but knew also that she would have no excuse now when Tony wanted to make plans. He began by setting a date for her visit to his parents' house for supper. This worried her, since she already believed that he had told them too much about her; she now understood that she was going to be presented to them as something more than a girlfriend.

On the evening in question when he collected her he was in a relaxed mood. It was still bright and the air was warm and children were playing on the streets as older people sat on the stoops. It was something that had seemed unimaginable in the winter and it made Eilis feel light and happy as they walked along.

"I've got to warn you about something," Tony said. "I have a kid brother called Frank. He's eight going on eighteen. He's nice and he's smart but he's been talking of all the things he's going to say to my girlfriend when he meets her. He's got a real big mouth. I tried to pay him money to go and play ball with his friends and my dad has threatened him but he says none of us are going to stop him. Once he gets it off his chest, you'll like him."

"What will he say?"

"The thing is we don't know. He could say anything."

"He sounds very exciting," she said.

"Oh, yeah, and there's one more thing."

"Don't tell me. You have an old granny who sits in the corner and she wants to talk too."

"No, she's in Italy. The thing is that all of them are Italians and they look like Italians. They are real dark, all except me."

"And how did they get you?"

"My mom's dad was like me, at least that's the rumour, but I never saw him and my dad never saw him and my mom doesn't remember him because he was killed in the First World War."

"Does your dad think . . ." She began to laugh.

"It drives my mom crazy but he doesn't really think it, he just says it sometimes when I do something funny that I must be from some other family. It's a joke."

His family lived on the second storey of a three-storey building. Eilis was surprised at how young Tony's parents seemed. When his three brothers appeared, she saw, as he had told her, that each of them had black hair and eyes that were deep brown. The two older ones were much taller than Tony. Frank introduced himself as the youngest one. His hair, she thought, was astonishingly dark, as were his eyes. The other two were introduced to her as Laurence and Maurice.

She realized immediately that she should not comment on the difference between Tony and the rest of the family since she imagined that every single person who entered this apartment and saw them all together for the first time had a great deal to say on the subject. She pretended it was something that she had not even noticed. She presumed at the beginning that the kitchen was just the first room and that beyond it lay a parlour and a dining room, but slowly she understood that one door led to a bedroom where the boys slept and another door led to a bathroom. There was no other room. The small table in the kitchen, she saw, was set for seven. She imagined that there was another bedroom beyond the boys' room where the parents slept, but once Frank began to talk, he explained to her that each night their parents slept in a corner of the kitchen in a bed that he showed her was on its side against the wall, discreetly covered.

"Frank, if you don't stop talking you won't be fed," Tony said.

There was a smell of food and spices. The two middle brothers were studying her carefully, silently, awkwardly. They both, she thought, looked like film stars.

"We don't like Irish people," Frank suddenly said.

"Frank!" His mother moved from the stove towards him.

"Mom, we don't. We've got to be clear about it. A big gang of them beat up Maurizio and he had to have stitches. And the cops were all Irish too, so they did nothing about it."

"Francesco, shut your mouth," his mother said.

"Ask him," Frank said to Eilis, pointing to Maurice.

"They weren't all Irish," Maurice said.

"They had red hair and big legs," Frank said.

"Don't mind him," Maurice said. "Only some of them had."

Frank's father asked him to follow him into the hallway; when they returned after a few moments Frank was, to the amusement of his brothers, suitably chastened.

As Frank sat opposite her, quiet while food was brought to the table and wine poured, Eilis felt sorry for him and noticed how much he resembled Tony just now; feeling down seemed to have affected his entire being. Over the previous weekend, Eilis had received instructions from Diana about how to eat spaghetti properly using a fork only, but what was served was not as thin and slippery as the spaghetti Diana had made for her. The sauce was just as red, but was filled with flavours that she had never sampled before. It was, she thought, almost sweet. Every time she tasted it, she had to stop and hold it in her mouth, wondering what ingredients had gone into it. She wondered if the others, so used to this food, were being careful not to look at her too closely or make any comment as she attempted to eat it using only a fork as they did.

Tony's mother, who spoke at times with a strong Italian accent, asked her about the exams and if she intended to do another year at the college. She explained that it was a two-year course, and that, when she finished, she would be a bookkeeper and could work in an office rather than on the shop floor. As Eilis and Tony's mother discussed this, none of the boys spoke or looked up from their food. When Eilis tried to catch Frank's eye so she could smile at him, he did not respond. She glanced at Tony, but he too had his head down. She realized that she would love to run out of this room and down the stairs and through the streets to the subway to her own room and close the door on the world.

The main course was a flat piece of fried meat covered in a thin coating of batter. When Eilis tasted it, she found that there was cheese and then ham inside the batter. She could not identify the meat. And the batter itself was so crisp and full of flavour that, once more, each time she took a taste, she could not work out what had been used to make it. There were no vegetables or potatoes accompanying it, but as Diana had explained that this was normal for Italians, Eilis was not surprised. She was telling Tony's mother how delicious it was, trying not to imply that it was also strange, when a knock came to the door. Tony's father answered it and returned, shaking his head and laughing.

"Antonio, you are wanted. Number eighteen has a blocked drain."

"Dad, it's dinnertime," Tony said.

"It's Mrs. Bruno. We like her," his father said.

"I don't like her," Frank said.

"Francesco, shut your mouth," his father said.

Tony stood up and pushed his chair back.

"Take your overalls and your tools," his mother said. She pronounced the words as though with difficulty.

"I won't be long," he said to Eilis, "and if he says anything at all, report him to me." He pointed at Frank, who began to laugh.

"Tony is the street plumber," said Maurice and explained that since he worked as a mechanic they called him when cars and trucks and motorbikes needed repairing, while Laurence would soon be a qualified carpenter so that if people's chairs or tables broke they could call him.

"But Frankie here is the brains of the family. He's going to college."

"Only if he learns to keep his mouth shut," Laurence said.

"Those Irish guys who beat Maurizio up," Frank said as though he had not been listening to any of their conversation, "they moved out to Long Island."

"I'm glad to hear that," Eilis replied.

"And out there, they have these big houses and you have your own room and you don't get to sleep in the same room as your brothers."

"Would you not like that?" Eilis asked.

"No," he said, "or maybe just sometimes."

As he spoke, they all looked at him, Eilis noticed, and she had the impression that they thought the same thing as she did, that Frank was the most beautiful boy she had ever seen in her life. She had to stop herself looking at him too much as she waited for Tony to come back.

They decided to go ahead with dessert in Tony's absence. It was a sort of cake, Eilis thought, filled with cream and then soaked in some sort of alcohol. And, as she watched Tony's father unscrewing a machine and putting in water and spoonfuls of coffee, she realized that she would have plenty to tell her fellow lodgers. The coffee cups were tiny, and the coffee, when it came, was thick and bitter, despite the spoonful of sugar that she added. Although she did not like it, she attempted to drink it, as the rest of them seemed to think it was nothing special.

Slowly, the conversation became easier but still she found that she was on display and every word she said was being listened to carefully. When they asked her about home she tried to say as little as possible and then worried that they might think she had something to hide. Each time she spoke now she observed Frank staring at her, taking in everything as though he would need to memorize it. When the meal was over and Tony had still not returned, Laurence and Maurice said that they would go to get him away from the clutches of Mrs. Bruno and her daughter. Tony's parents refused Eilis's offer to help them clear off the table and appeared embarrassed now about Tony's absence.

"I thought it would just take him a second," his mother said. "It must have been serious. It's hard to say no to people."

When Tony's parents were away from the table, Frank signalled to her to come close.

"Has he taken you to Coney Island yet?" he whispered.

"No," she replied in a whisper.

"He took his last girlfriend there and they went on the big wheel and she puked hot dogs all over herself and she blamed him and wouldn't go out with him again. He didn't speak for a month."

"Is that right?"

"Francesco, get up and go out," his father said. "Or go and do homework. What was he saying?"

"He was telling me that Coney Island is nice in the summer," Eilis said.

"He's right. It is," his father said. "Has Tony not brought you?"

"No."

"I hope he will," he said. "You'll like it."

She detected a smile on his face.

Frank was watching her with wonder because, she thought, she had not told his father what he had really said. When his father turned away, she made a grimacing face at him and he stared at her in astonishment before he made a face back at her and left the room just as Tony, in his overalls, was returning with his two brothers. He dropped his tools and held his hands up: they were grimy.

"I'm a saint," he said, and grinned.

When Eilis told Miss Fortini that Tony was going to take her to the beach in Coney Island some Sunday now that the weather was becoming balmy, Miss Fortini expressed alarm. "I don't think you've been watching your figure," she said.

"Yes, I know," Eilis replied. "And I have no bathing costume."

"Italian men!" Miss Fortini said. "They don't care in the winter but in the summer on the beach you have to look your best. My guy won't go on the beach unless he already has a tan."

Miss Fortini said that she had a friend who worked in another store that sold good-quality bathing suits, much better than the ones on sale in Bartocci's, and she would get some on approval so that Eilis could try them. In the meantime, she advised her to begin watching her figure. Eilis attempted to say that she did not think Tony cared that much about suntans or how she might look on the beach, but Miss Fortini interrupted her to say that every Italian man cared about how his girlfriend looked on the beach, no matter how perfect she might be in other ways.

"In Ireland no one looks," Eilis said. "It would be bad manners."

"In Italy it would be bad manners not to look."

Later in the week Miss Fortini approached Eilis in the morning to say that the bathing suits were to be delivered in the afternoon and Eilis could try them on in the fitting room after work when the store had closed. Since the store was busy towards the end of the working day, Eilis had almost forgotten about it until she found Miss Fortini hovering around her with the package. They waited until everyone had left and then Miss Fortini informed the security that they would be there for a while longer, that she herself would turn the lights off and they would leave by a side door.

The first bathing suit was black and appeared the right size for her. Eilis pulled the curtains back and moved out of the changing cubicle so that Miss Fortini could see it. Miss Fortini seemed uncertain as she studied it carefully, putting one hand over her mouth as though this would help her to concentrate better and as though to emphasize that getting this right was a most serious matter. She walked around Eilis so that she could inspect how it fitted from behind and, moving closer, put her hand under the firm elastic that held the bathing suit in place at the top of Eilis's thighs. She pulled the elastic down a fraction and then patted Eilis twice on the bottom, letting her hand linger the second time.

"My, you are going to have to work on your figure," she said as she went to the package and took out a second bathing suit, which was green.

"I think the black might be too severe," she said. "If your skin was not so white, it might be fine. Now try this."

Eilis pulled back the curtain and changed into the green bathing suit. She could hear the humming of the harsh lights overhead but otherwise was aware only of the silence and the emptiness of the store and the intensity and sharpness of Miss Fortini's gaze as she appeared in front of her once more. Without speaking, Miss Fortini knelt down in front of her and once more put her fingers under the elastic.

"You'll have to shave down here," she said. "Otherwise, you'll spend your time on the beach pulling the elastic down. Do you have a good razor?"

"Just for my legs," Eilis said.

"Well, I'll get you one that will do the trick down here too."

Remaining on her knees, she turned Eilis around until Eilis could see herself in the mirror with Miss Fortini behind her, running her fingers under the elastic, her eyes fixed on what was in front of her. She was, Eilis thought, fully aware that she could be seen in the mirror; she could feel herself blushing as Miss Fortini stood up and faced her.

"I don't think these straps are right," she said and motioned to Eilis to put her arms through them and unloose them. When she did, the entire front of the bathing suit folded down and, for a moment, until she held the suit up with her two hands, her breasts were exposed.

"Is this one not all right?" she asked.

"No, try the others," Miss Fortini said. "Come here and try this one."

She seemed to be suggesting that Eilis not go behind the curtain again but change from one bathing suit to another beside the chair as she watched. Eilis hesitated.

"Quickly now," Miss Fortini said.

As Eilis lowered the suit she put one arm over her breast and bent over as she took it off, facing towards Miss Fortini so she did not feel so exposed. She put her hand out to take the suit, but Miss Fortini had lifted it and the other one that she had not tried, holding them up for perusal.

"Maybe I should go behind the curtain," Eilis said. "If one of the security men comes in."

She took both bathing suits and brought them into the cubicle and pulled the curtain. She was aware that Miss Fortini had been watching her carefully as she moved. She hoped that this would be over quickly and they would choose one of the suits and she hoped also that Miss Fortini would not say anything else about shaving.

Having put on the next suit, which was a bright pink, she opened the curtain and appeared again. Miss Fortini seemed immensely serious, and there was in the way she stood and gazed at her something clear that Eilis knew she would never be able to tell anyone about.

She stood still with her arms by her sides as Miss Fortini discussed the colour, wondering if it were too bright, and the cut of the suit, which she thought too old-fashioned. Once more, as she walked around, she touched the elastic at the top of Eilis's thighs and let her hand move over the rise of Eilis's bottom, patting her there, allowing her hand to linger.

"Now try the other," she said and stood where the curtain was, thus preventing Eilis from closing it. Eilis removed the bathing suit as quickly as she could and, in her haste to put on the last one, began to fumble, putting her leg in the wrong place. She had to bend to lift the suit and had to use both her hands to find the right way of putting it on. No one had ever seen her naked like this; she did not know how her breasts would seem, if the size of the nipples or the dark colour around them was unusual or not. She went from feeling hot with embarrassment to feeling almost cold. She was relieved when the suit was on and she was standing up once more being inspected by Miss Fortini.

Eilis did not think there was any difference between the suits; simply, she did not want the black one or the pink one, but, since the others fitted her and their colours were not extreme in any way, she felt happy to take either of them. Thus when Miss Fortini suggested that she try each of them on again before she finally decided, Eilis refused and said that she would take either and did not mind which. Miss Fortini said that she would send all of them back with a note in the morning to her friend in the nearby store and Eilis could go herself at lunchtime and collect the one she had chosen. Her friend would make sure, Miss Fortini said, that she got a good discount. When Eilis was dressed and ready, Miss Fortini turned off all the lights in the store and they left by a side entrance.

*   *   *

Eilis tried to eat less but it was hard, as she could not sleep if she was hungry. In the bathroom, when she looked at herself in the mirror, she did not think she was too fat, and when she tried on the bathing suit she had selected she was much more worried about how pale her skin was.

One evening when she came home from work she found an envelope for her on the side table in the kitchen. It was an official letter from Brooklyn College to say that she had passed her first-year exams in all subjects and if she needed to know her precise grades she could contact them. They hoped, the letter said, that she would be returning the following year, which would begin in September, and they provided dates by which she should register.

It was a beautiful evening. She thought she would miss supper and walk down to the parish house and show the letter to Father Flood. Once she had left a note for Mrs. Kehoe and made her way into the street, she began to observe how beautiful everything was, the trees in leaf, the people in the street, the children playing, the light on the buildings. She had never felt like this before in Brooklyn. The letter had lifted her spirits, given her a new freedom, she realized, and it was something she had not expected. She looked forward to showing it to Father Flood if he were at home and then, when she saw him the following night as arranged, to Tony, and then to writing home with the news. In one year she would be a qualified bookkeeper and she could start looking for a better job. In a year the weather would grow hotter and unbearable and then the heat would fade and the trees would lose their leaves and then the winter would return to Brooklyn. And that too would dissolve into spring and early summer with long sunny evenings after work until she would again, she hoped, get a letter from Brooklyn College.

And in all of her dreams, as she walked along, of how this year would be she imagined Tony's smiling presence, his attention, his funny stories, his holding her against him at one of the street corners, the sweet smell of his breath as he kissed her, the sense of his golden concentration on her, his arms around her, his tongue in her mouth. She had all of that, she thought, and now, with this letter, it was much more than she had imagined she would have when she arrived in Brooklyn first. She had to stop herself smiling as she moved along in case people thought that she was mad.

Father Flood came to the door with a sheaf of papers in his hand. He ushered her into the parlour at the front of his house. As he read the letter he looked worried and even when he handed it back to her he remained serious.

"You are marvellous," he said gravely. "That is all I have to say."

She smiled.

"Most people who come to this house without notice need something or have a problem," he said. "You hardly ever get pure good news."

"I have saved some money," Eilis said, "and will be able to pay my tuition the second year and then pay you back for last year when I get a job."

"One of my parishioners paid," Father Flood said. "He needed to do something for mankind so I made him pay your tuition for last year and I'll remind him soon that he needs to cough up for this year. I told him it's a good cause and it makes him feel noble."

"Did you tell him it was for me?" she asked.

"No. I gave him no details."

"Will you thank him for me?"

"Sure. How's Tony?"

She was surprised by the question, how casual and unworried

it seemed, how freely it suggested that Tony was a regular fixture rather than a problem or an interloper.

"He's great," she said.

"Has he taken you to a game yet?" the priest asked.

"No, but he threatens to all the time. I asked him if Wexford were playing but he didn't get the joke."

"Eilis, here's one piece of advice for you," Father Flood said as he opened the door to see her into the hallway. "Never make jokes about the game."

"That's what Tony said too."

"He's a solid man," Father Flood said.

As soon as she showed Tony the letter when they met the next evening he said that they would have to go to Coney Island the following Sunday to celebrate.

"Champagne?" she asked.

"Sea water," he replied. "And then a slap-up dinner in Nathan's afterwards."

She bought a beach towel at Bartocci's and a sun hat from Diana, who said that she did not want it any more. At supper, Diana and Patty produced their sunglasses for the season, which they had bought on the boardwalk at Atlantic City.

"I read somewhere," Mrs. Kehoe said, "that they could ruin your eyes."

"Oh, I don't care," Diana said. "I think they're gorgeous."

"And I read," Patty said, "that if you don't have them this year on the beach people will talk about you."

Miss McAdam and Sheila Heffernan fitted them on and, openly ignoring Dolores, passed them to Eilis to try.

"Well, they are very glamorous, I'll say that," Mrs. Kehoe said.

"I'll sell you that pair," Diana said to Eilis, "because I can get another pair on Sunday."

"Can you really?" Eilis asked.

When they discovered that Eilis had bought a new swimsuit, they insisted on seeing it. Eilis, when she came upstairs with it, deliberately handed it to Dolores first to hold up in front of her.

"You're lucky, Eilis, to have the figure for it," Mrs. Kehoe said.

"I can't go out in the sun at all," Dolores said. "I get all red."

Patty and Diana began to laugh.

On Sunday morning when Tony collected her he appeared surprised by the sunglasses.

"I'll have to tie a rope around you," he said. "All the guys at the beach will want to run away with you."

The subway station was packed with people going to the beach and there were cries of horror as the first two trains went through the station without stopping. The air was stifling as everyone crushed together. When finally a train stopped it seemed that there was no space for anyone and yet everyone began to crowd into the compartments, laughing and shouting and demanding that people move over and make room for them. By the time she and Tony, who was carrying a folded beach umbrella as well as a bag, found a door, there was no room at all in the train. She was amazed when Tony, holding her hand, began to push against the crowd in the compartment to make a space for both of them before the doors closed.

"How long is it going to take?" she asked.

"An hour, maybe more, it depends on how many stops it makes. But cheer up, think of the big waves."

The beach, when they finally arrived, was almost as packed as the train had been. She noticed that Tony had not lost his smile once during the journey, despite being deliberately squashed against a door by a man, encouraged by his wife. Now he seemed to feel, as he studied the crowd on the beach, where there was no place for newcomers, that they had been put there for his amusement. They moved along the boardwalk, but the only solution, Eilis saw, was to take a tiny spot that was empty and see if, by their very presence there, they could expand it so they both could unpack their belongings and lie in the sun.

Diana and Patty had warned her that no one changed on the beach in Italy. Italians had carried to America with them the custom of putting their bathing suits on under their clothes before they set out, thus avoiding the Irish habit of changing on the beach, which was, Diana said, ungraceful and undignified, to say the least. Eilis did not know if they were joking so she checked with Miss Fortini, who assured her that it was true. Miss Fortini also insisted that she should lose more weight and brought in a small pink-coloured razor for her and told her that she need not return it. Despite all this preparation, Eilis was nervous about taking off her clothes and appearing in her swimsuit in front of Tony; her efforts to pretend that it was nothing made her even more embarrassed. She wondered if he would notice that she had shaved and she felt she was too white and that her thighs and her bottom were too fat.

Tony stripped down to his bathing trunks instantly and, she was glad to see, nonchalantly looked at the crowds around them as she wriggled out of her clothes. As soon as she was ready, he wanted to go into the sea. He arranged with the family beside them that their things would be looked after and they made their way past the crowds down to the water's edge. Eilis laughed when she saw him recoiling from the cold; the water, compared to the water in the Irish Sea, seemed quite warm to her. She waded out while he struggled to follow her.

As she swam out, he stood helplessly up to his waist in the water, and when she motioned for him to follow her, shouting that he was not to be a baby, he shouted back that he could not swim. She did a gentle breaststroke in his direction and then slowly realized, by seeing what the couples around them were up to, what his plan was. He wanted, it seemed, the two of them to stand up to their necks in the water, holding each other as each wave crashed over them. When she embraced him, he held her so that she could not easily swim away from him. She could feel his erect penis hard against her, which made him smile even more than usual, and, when he wanted to put his hands on her bottom as he held her, she swam away from him. The thought had come into her mind of telling him who the last person to touch her bottom was. The idea of his reaction to this made her laugh so much that she did a vigorous backstroke, letting him presume, she hoped, that he was being too free under the water with his hands.

All day they moved between their place on the beach and the ocean. She put on her sun hat and he raised the umbrella to prevent sunburn and he also produced a picnic that his mother had prepared for him, including a thermos of ice-cold lemonade. In the water, the few times that she swam out on her own, she felt that the waves were stronger than at home, not so much in the way they broke but in the way they pulled out. She realized that she would have to be careful not to swim too far out of her depth in this unfamiliar sea. Tony, she saw, was afraid of the water, hated her swimming away from him. As soon as she returned to him each time, he made her put her arms around his neck and he lifted her from below so that her legs were wrapped around him. When he kissed her and then held her face back and looked at her, he seemed not to be embarrassed by his erection at all but proud of it. He was all boyish as he grinned at her; she, in turn, felt a great tenderness towards him and kissed him deeply as he held her. As the day waned, they were almost the last remaining in the water.

When Eilis complained of the heat at work they told her that it was only the beginning, but one day Miss Fortini told her that

Mr. Bartocci was about to turn on the air-conditioning and soon the place would be crowded with shoppers seeking relief from the heat. Her job, Miss Fortini said, was to make them all buy something.

Soon, Eilis looked forward to going to work, and longed, as she woke sweating in the night, for the air-conditioning in Bartocci's. In the evening Mrs. Kehoe put chairs out in front of the house and they sat there fanning themselves even in the shade, even after dark some nights. On Eilis's half-day Tony took a half-day too and they went to Coney Island and came back late. When she asked him if they could have a go on the huge wheel or one of the other amusements, he refused, managing each time to find an excuse why they could not. He gave her no hint that he had lost his previous girlfriend because he took her on the wheel. Eilis was fascinated by this, the easy, casual way he prevented them from going there, his sweet duplicity in giving no sign of what had happened before. She was almost glad to know that he had secrets and had ways of calmly keeping them.

As the summer wore on he could talk nothing except baseball. The names he told her about—names like Jackie Robinson and Pee Wee Reese and Preacher Roe—were the names she also heard about at work and saw mentioned in the newspapers. Even Mrs. Kehoe spoke about these players as though she knew them. She had gone the previous year to the house of her friend Miss Scanlan to watch a game on her television, and, since she was a Dodgers supporter, as she told everyone, she intended to do so again if Miss Scanlan, who was also a Dodgers supporter, would have her.

It seemed to Eilis for a while that no one spoke of anything else except the need to defeat the Giants. Tony told her with real excitement that he had secured tickets for Ebbets Field not only for himself and Eilis but for his three brothers and it was going to be the best day of their lives because they were going to get revenge for what Bobby Thomson had done to them the previous season. As he walked through the streets with her Tony was not alone in doing imitations of his favourite players and shouting about the hopes he had for them.

She tried to tell him about the Wexford hurling team and how they were beaten by Tipperary and how her brothers and her father used to sit glued to the old radiogram in the front room on summer Sundays even if Wexford were not playing. When he began to imitate the commentators, describing imaginary games of his own, she told him that Jack her brother had done the same.

"Hold on," he said. "You play baseball in Ireland?"

"No, it was hurling."

He seemed puzzled.

"So it wasn't baseball?" His face registered disappointment, then a sort of exasperation.

One night in the parish hall when the band, which had been playing swing tunes, began to play a tune that Tony seemed to recognize, he went crazy, as did many around him. "It's the Jackie Robinson song," he shouted. He began to swing an imaginary baseball bat. "They're playing 'Did You See Jackie Robinson Hit That Ball?'"

As soon as Eilis returned to her classes at Brooklyn College the baseball frenzy became worse. What surprised her was that she had noticed nothing of it the previous year although it must have been going on around her with the same intensity. Now she had returned to her routine of seeing Tony on Thursday nights after class, on Friday nights in the parish hall and on Saturday for a movie, and he talked of nothing except how this would be the perfect year for him if they could be together, Eilis and himself, and if Laurence and Maurice and Frankie could be with them too and if the Dodgers could win the World Series. To her great relief, he made no further mention of having kids who would be Dodgers supporters.

*   *   *

She walked with the four brothers through the crowds to Ebbets Field. They had left themselves plenty of time to stop and talk to anyone at all who had news of the players, or opinions about how the game would go, or to buy hot dogs and sodas, to linger outside, part of the crush. Slowly, the differences between the brothers became more apparent to her. While Maurice smiled and seemed easygoing, he did not speak to strangers and held himself back when the others did. Tony and Frank stayed close to each other all the time, Frank eager to know what Tony's latest opinion was. Laurence seemed to know most about the game and could easily contradict some of Tony's assertions. She laughed at Frank as he looked from Tony to Laurence when they argued about the merits of Ebbets Field itself, Laurence insisting it was too small and old-fashioned and would have to be moved, Tony answering that it would never be moved. Frank's eyes darted from one brother to the other; he appeared genuinely perplexed. Maurice never got involved in the arguments but managed to move them forward in the direction of the field, warning them that they were going too slowly.

When they found their seats, they put Eilis in the middle with Tony and Maurice on either side of her, Laurence on Tony's left and Frank to the right of Maurice.

"Mom told us we weren't to leave you at the edge," Frank said to her.

Both Tony and her fellow lodgers had explained the rules of the game to Eilis and made it seem like rounders, which she had played at home with her brothers and their friends; still she did not know what to expect because rounders, she thought, was fine in its way but it had never provoked the same excitement as hurling or football. At Mrs. Kehoe's the night before Miss McAdam had insisted that it was the best game in the world but all of the others thought that it was too slow, with too many breaks. Diana and Patty agreed that the best part was going off to get hot dogs and sodas and beers and finding that nothing important had happened while you were away, despite all the shouting and cheering.

"It was stolen from us the last time, that's all I have to say," Mrs. Kehoe said. "It was a very bitter moment."

Now, with half an hour to go before the game, everyone around them was behaving as though it was just about to begin. Tony, Eilis saw, had ceased to have any interest in her at all. Normally, he was attentive, smiling at her, asking her questions, listening to her, telling her stories. Now, in the heat of this excitement, he could no longer manage the role of caring, thoughtful boyfriend. He spoke at some length to the people behind him and conveyed what they had told him to Frank, ignoring her completely as he leaned over her to be heard. He could not stay quiet, standing up and sitting back down and craning his neck to see what was going on behind. All the while Maurice, who had bought a programme, perused it and regularly offered Eilis and his three brothers nuggets of information that he had gleaned. He seemed worried.

"If we lose this game Tony will go crazy," he said to her. "And if we win he'll go even more crazy and Frankie with him."

"So which would be better," she asked, "win or lose?"

"Win," he said.

Tony and Frank went to get more hot dogs and beers and sodas.

"Keep our seats," Tony said, and grinned.

"Yeah, keep our seats," Frank repeated.

When the players finally appeared, all four brothers jumped up and vied with one another to identify them, but quite soon, when something happened that seemed to displease Tony, he sat back in his seat, despondent. For a moment he held her hand.

"They're all against us," he said.

But when the game started Tony launched into a running commentary that rose to a climax every time there was any action. Sometimes, when Tony was quiet, Frank took over and drew their attention to something, only to be told to stop by Maurice, who watched each second with slow and deliberate intensity, hardly speaking at all. He was, nonetheless, she felt, even more involved and excited than Tony, despite all the shouting, cheering, cajoling and whooping that Tony did.

She simply could not follow the game, could make no sense of how you would score, or what constituted a good hit or a bad one. Nor could she work out which player was which. And it was as slow as Patty and Diana had said it would be. She knew, however, that she should not go to the bathroom because it was possible that the very moment she announced her departure would be the moment no one wanted her to miss.

As she sat quietly watching the game, trying to understand its intricate rituals, it struck Eilis that Tony, despite his constant movements and his screaming at Frank to pay attention to some score or other, and his cheering followed by statements of pure despair, did not manage to irritate her even once. She thought it was strange, and out of the side of her eye and sometimes directly she started to watch him, noticing how funny he was, how alive, how graceful, how alert to things. She began to appreciate also how much he was enjoying himself; he was doing so even more than his brothers, more openly, with greater humour and infectious ease. She did not mind, indeed she almost enjoyed the fact that he was paying her no attention, leaving it to Maurice to explain when he could what was happening.

Tony was so wrapped up in the game that it gave her a chance to let her thoughts linger on him, float towards him, noting how different from her he was in every way. The idea that he would never see her as she felt that she saw him now came to her as an infinite relief, as a satisfactory solution to things. His excitement and the excitement of the crowd began to lift her spirits until she even pretended that she could follow what was happening. She cheered for the Dodgers as much as anyone around her; and then she followed Tony's eyes, looking at what he was pointing to, and sat back silently with him when the team seemed to be losing.

Finally, after nearly two hours everyone stood up. She and Tony and Frank arranged to meet at the queue for the hot-dog stand closest to their seats after she had been to the bathroom. Since she was thirsty now and felt, when she had found them at the head of the line, that she wanted to be as much a part of everything as she could, she ordered a beer too, her first ever, and tried to run the mustard and ketchup along the hot dog with the same flourish as Tony and Frank.

By the time they got back to their seats, the game had resumed. She asked Maurice if it was really only half over and he explained that in baseball there is no half time, the break comes after the seventh inning near to the end and it's more of a pause— a stretch they call it. It struck her that he was the only one of the four brothers who had any sense of the depth of her ignorance of the game. She sat back and smiled to herself at the thought of this, its strangeness, how little it appeared to matter to her even in those moments when she found what was happening on the field most totally bewildering. All she knew was that luck and success were once more, for one reason or another, slowly evading the Brooklyn Dodgers.

Because she spent Thanksgiving with Tony's family, his mother thought that Eilis could come for Christmas too and seemed almost offended, asking if their food was not to her taste, when she refused. She explained that she could not let Father Flood down and was going to work in the parish hall for a second year. Tony and his mother told her several times that someone else could take her turn and do her work, but she was adamant. She felt slightly guilty at their assumption that she was performing an act of selfless charity when she would also, she knew, be happier in the parish hall working than spending a long day with a supper the night before in the small apartment with Tony and his family. She loved them, each of them, and found the differences between the four brothers intriguing, but sometimes she found the pleasure of being alone after a lunch or a supper with them greater than the pleasure of the meal itself.

In the days after Christmas she saw Tony every evening. On one of these evenings he outlined to her the plans they had, how he, Maurice and Laurence had bought at a bargain price a plot of land on Long Island that they were going to develop. It would take time, he said, maybe a year or two because it was a good distance from services and it looked like nothing except bare land. But soon, they knew, the services would reach there. What was empty now, he said, would within a few years have paved roads and water and electricity. On their plot there was enough space for five houses, each with its own garden. Maurice was going to evening classes in cost engineering and Tony and Laurence would be able to do the plumbing and the carpentry.

The first house, he explained, would be for the family; his mother longed for a garden and a proper house of her own. And then, he said, they would build three houses and sell them. But Maurice and Laurence had asked him if he wanted the fifth house and he had said that he did and he was asking her now if she would like to live in Long Island. It was near the ocean, he said, and not far from where the train stopped. But he did not want to take her there yet because it was winter and it was bare and bleak with nothing but waste ground and scrubland. The house would be theirs, he said, they could plan it themselves.

She watched him carefully because she knew that this was his way not only of asking her to marry him but of suggesting that marriage had been already tacitly agreed between them. It was the details of how they would live, the life he could offer her, that he was presenting now. Eventually, he said, he and his two brothers would set up a company and they would build houses. Now they were saving money and making plans, but with their skills and the first plot in their possession it would not be long and it would mean that they could soon, all of them, have a much better life. She said nothing in reply. She was almost in tears at what he was proposing and how practical he was as he spoke and how serious and sincere. She did not want to say she would think about it because she knew how that might sound. Instead, she nodded and smiled and reached out and held his two hands and pulled him towards her.

She wrote once more to Rose, using her sister's office address, and told her how far things had gone; she attempted to describe Tony, but it was difficult without making him sound too boyish or silly or giddy. She mentioned that he never used bad language or curse words because she thought it was important for Rose to know that he was not like anyone at home, that this was a different world and in this world Tony shone despite the fact that his family lived in two rooms or that he worked with his hands. She tore the letter up a few times; she had made it sound as though she were pleading for him, instead of merely trying to explain that he was special and that she was not staying with him simply because he was the first man she had met.

In her letters to her mother, however, Eilis had never once mentioned him; even though she had described Coney Island and the baseball game, she had said only that she had gone with friends. She wished now that she had made one or two casual references to him six months ago so that it might not come as such a surprise now, but when she made an attempt to put him into her letters to her mother she found that it was not possible without writing in a full paragraph about him and where she had met him and what he was like. She found that she postponed doing this every time she tried.

When Rose replied, the letter was brief. It was clear to her that Rose had heard once more from Father Flood. Rose said that Tony seemed very nice, and, since they were both young, they would not have to make any decisions, and that the best news was that Eilis would, by the summer, be a qualified bookkeeper and could start to look for experience. Rose imagined, she wrote, that Eilis must be really looking forward to getting off the shop floor and having a job in an office, which would not only pay more money but be easier on the legs.

At Bartocci's, everyone had become more relaxed about the coloured customers and Eilis was moved to different counters a number of times. Since Miss Fortini had told the Bartoccis about her passing her exams and being in her final year, Miss Bartocci had said that if any vacancy arose as a junior bookkeeper even before she was fully qualified then they would consider her.

The second-year course was simpler because Eilis was not as afraid of what might appear on the exam paper. And because she had read the law books and taken notes on them, she was able to follow most of what Mr. Rosenblum was talking about. But she was still careful to miss no lectures and not to see Tony except for each Thursday, when he walked her home, each Friday, when they went together to the dance at the parish hall, and each Saturday, when he took her to a diner and a movie. Even when the winter began to descend on Brooklyn, she liked her room and her routine, and as the spring came she began to study on the nights when she came home from her lectures and on Sundays as well so she could be sure to get through her exams.

*   *   *

She found work on the shop floor boring and tiring, and often, especially in the early days of the week when they were not busy, the time went slowly. But Miss Fortini was always watching and noticed if anyone took a break they were not due or were late or seemed not ready to serve the next customer. Eilis was careful how she stood, and she watched out in case a customer needed her. She learned that time passed more slowly if she heeded the clock or if she thought about it at all, so she learned to be patient, and then, once she finished work and walked out of the store each day, she managed to put it out of her mind completely and enjoy the freedom.

One afternoon when she saw Father Flood coming into the store she thought nothing of it. Although she had not seen him there since the day when he was called by the Bartoccis, she knew that he was a friend of Mr. Bartocci and might have business with him. She noticed him speaking to Miss Fortini first and saw him glancing over at her and making as though he was going to come over towards her, but instead after some discussion with Miss Fortini they both went in the direction of the office. She served a customer and then, seeing that someone had unfolded a number of blouses, she went over and put them neatly back in their place. When she turned, Miss Fortini was coming towards her and there was something in the expression on her face that made Eilis want to retreat from her, move away quickly pretending that she had not seen her.

"I wonder if you could come to the office for a moment," Miss Fortini said.

Eilis asked herself if she had done something, if someone had accused her of something.

"What is it about?" she asked.

"I can't tell you," Miss Fortini said. "It's just best if you follow me."

In the way Miss Fortini turned and walked briskly ahead Eilis felt even more that she had done something wrong that had only now been discovered. When they moved from the shop floor and she was following Miss Fortini down a corridor, she stopped.

"I'm sorry," she said, "but you will have to tell me what this is about."

"I can't tell you," Miss Fortini said.

"Can you give me some idea?"

"It's something in your family."

"Something or someone?"

"Someone."

Immediately, Eilis thought that her mother might have had a heart attack or fallen down the stairs or that one of her brothers had had an accident in Birmingham.

"Which of them?" she asked.

Miss Fortini did not reply but walked on ahead of her again until she came to a door at the end of a corridor, which she opened. She stood back and let Eilis enter. It was a small room and Father Flood was alone sitting on a chair. He stood up hesitantly and indicated to Miss Fortini that she should leave them.

"Eilis," he said. "Eilis."

"Yes. What is it?"

"It's Rose."

"What happened to her?"

"Your mother found her dead this morning."

Eilis said nothing.

"She must have died in her sleep," Father Flood said.

"Died in her sleep?" Eilis asked, going over in her mind when she had last heard from Rose or from her mother and if there was any hint of anything wrong.

"Yes," he said. "It was sudden. She was out playing golf yesterday and in the best of form. She died in her sleep, Eilis."

"And my mother found her?"

"Yes."

"Do the others know?"

"Yes, and they're heading home on the mail-boat. She's being waked tonight."

Eilis now wondered if there was any way she could go out into the street, find a way to stop this from having happened, or stop him from having told her. In the silence she almost asked Father Flood to go and not come into the store again like this, but she realized instantly how foolish that was. He was here. She had heard what he said. She could not push back time.

"I've arranged for your mother to come up to the Manse in Enniscorthy tonight and we'll call her from the presbytery here."

"Was it one of the priests who contacted you?"

"Father Quaid," he said.

"Are they sure?" she asked and then quickly put her hand out to stop him replying. "I mean, it all happened today?"

"This morning in Ireland."

"I can't believe it," she said. "No warning."

"I spoke to Franco Bartocci by telephone earlier and he said to take you home, and I spoke to Mrs. Kehoe and if you give me Tony's address I will send him word as well and let him know."

"What will happen?" she asked.

"The funeral will be the day after tomorrow," he said.

It was the softness in his voice, the guarded way he avoided her eyes, that made her start to cry. And when he produced a large and clean white handkerchief that he clearly had in his pocket prepared for this, she became almost hysterical as she pushed him away.

"Why did I ever come over here?" she asked, but she knew that he could not understand her because she was sobbing so much. She took the handkerchief from him and blew her nose.

"Why did I ever come over here?" she asked again.

"Rose wanted a better life for you," he replied. "She only did what was good."

"I won't ever see her again now."

"She loved how well you were doing."

"I'll never see her again. Isn't that right?"

"It's very sad, Eilis. But she's in heaven now. That's what we should think about. And she'll be watching over you. And we'll all have to pray for your mother and for Rose's soul, and you know, Eilis, we have to remember that God's ways are not our ways."

"I wish I had never come over here."

As she began to cry again, she kept repeating, "I wish I had never come over here."

"I have the car parked outside and we can go to the presbytery. You know it will do you good to have a talk with your mother."

"I haven't heard her voice since I left," Eilis said. "It's just been letters. It's awful that this is the first time I am going to phone her."

"I know that, Eilis, and she'll feel that too. Father Quaid said that he would collect her and drive her up to the Manse. I'd guess she's in shock."

"What will I say to her?"

Her mother's voice was faltering at first; she sounded as though she were talking to herself and Eilis had to interrupt to tell her that she could not hear.

"Can you hear me now?" her mother asked.

"Yes, Mammy, I can. It's much better now."

"It's like she's asleep and it was the same this morning," her mother said. "I went in to call her and she was fast asleep and I said I'd leave her. But I knew as I went down the stairs. It wasn't like her to sleep in like that. I looked at the clock in the kitchen and said I'd give her ten minutes more and then when I went up and touched her she was stone cold."

"Oh, God, that's terrible."

"I whispered an act of contrition into her ear. Then I ran next door."

The silence on the line was broken only by some faint crackling noises.

"She died in the night in her sleep," her mother eventually continued. "That's what Dr. Cudigan said. She had been seeing the doctor without telling anyone and she went for tests without telling anyone. Rose knew, Eily, she knew that it could happen any time because of her heart. She had a bad heart, Dr. Cudigan said, and there was nothing could be done. She went on as normal. She knew that she had a bad heart and she decided to carry on playing golf and doing everything. The doctor said that he told her to take it easy, but, even if she had, it might have been the same. I don't know what to think, Eily. Maybe she was very brave."

"She told no one?"

"No one, Eily, no one at all. And she looks very peaceful now. I looked at her before I came out and I thought for a second she was still with us, she's so like herself. But she's gone, Eily. Rose has gone and that is the last thing in the world I thought was going to happen."

"Who's in the house now?"

"The neighbours are all there and your uncle Michael and they came down from Clonegal, all the Doyles, and they're there too. And I said when your daddy died that I shouldn't cry too much because I had you and Rose and the boys and when the boys left I said the same and when you left I had Rose, but I have no one at all now, Eily, I have no one."

Eilis knew that she could not be understood as she tried to reply because she was crying so hard. Her mother was silent for a while on the other end of the phone.

"Tomorrow I'll say goodbye to her for you," her mother said when she began to speak again. "That's what I thought I'd do. I'll say goodbye to her from me and then I'll say goodbye to her from you. And she's with your father in heaven now. We'll bury her beside him. I often thought at night how lonely he might be on his own in the graveyard but he'll have Rose now. They're up in heaven, the two of them."

"They are, Mammy."

"I don't know why she was taken away so young, that's all I have to say."

"It's a terrible shock," Eilis replied.

"She was cold this morning when I touched her, as cold as anything."

"She must have died peacefully," Eilis said.

"I wish she had told me, or let me know something was wrong. She didn't want to worry me. That's what Father Quaid and the others said. Maybe I couldn't have done much but I would have watched out for her. I don't know what to think."

Eilis could hear her mother sighing.

"I'll go back now and we'll say the rosary and I'll tell her I was talking to you."

"I'd love if you would do that."

"Goodbye now, Eily."

"Goodbye, Mammy, and will you tell the lads I was on the phone to you?"

"I will. They'll arrive in the morning."

"Goodbye, Mammy."

"Goodbye, Eily."

When she had put the phone down she began to cry. She found a chair in the corner of the room and sat down trying to control herself. Father Flood and his housekeeper came and brought her tea and tried to calm her but she could not stop herself breaking into hysterical sobbing.

"I'm sorry," she said.

"Don't worry at all," the housekeeper said.

When she was calmer Father Flood drove her to Mrs. Kehoe's; Tony was already in the front room. She did not know how long he had been there and she looked at him and Mrs. Kehoe wondering what they had been talking about while they waited for her and if Mrs. Kehoe had finally found out that Tony was Italian and not Irish. Mrs. Kehoe was full of kindness and sympathy, but there was also, Eilis thought, a sense that the news and the visitors had caused excitement, distracted her pleasantly from the tedium of the day. She bustled in and out of the room addressing Tony by his first name and bringing a tray with tea and sandwiches for him and Father Flood.

"Your poor mother, that's all I have to say, your poor mother," she said.

For once, Eilis did not feel it necessary to be polite to Mrs. Kehoe. She looked away every time she spoke and did not respond to her at any point. This appeared to make Mrs. Kehoe even more solicitous, as she offered her tea at every moment or an aspirin and a glass of water, or insisted that she have something to eat. Eilis wished Tony would stop accepting further sandwiches and cakes from Mrs. Kehoe and thanking her for being so kind. She wanted him to leave and Mrs. Kehoe to stop talking and Father Flood to go as well, but she could not face her own room and the night ahead so she said nothing and soon Mrs. Kehoe and Tony and Father Flood spoke as though she were not there, going over the changes that had occurred in Brooklyn in the past few years and offering their opinions on what further changes might occur. Every so often they grew silent and asked her if she needed anything.

"The poor thing, she's in shock," Mrs. Kehoe said.

Eilis said that she needed nothing and closed her eyes as they continued to talk among themselves, Mrs. Kehoe wondering to the other two if she should buy a television for company in the evenings. She worried, she said, that it might not catch on and she'd be left with it. Both Tony and Father Flood advised her to buy a set, and this seemed only to cause further remarks about how there was no guarantee that they would go on making programmes and she did not think she would take the risk.

"When everyone gets one, I'll get one," she said.

Finally, when they had run out of subjects, it was arranged that Father Flood would say a mass for Rose at ten o'clock the following morning and that Mrs. Kehoe would attend, as would Tony and his mother. There would be the usual congregation as well, Father Flood said, and he would let them know before mass started that it was being said for the repose of the soul of someone very special and he would, before communion, say a few words about Rose and ask people to pray for her. He arranged to drive Tony home but waited tactfully in Mrs. Kehoe's front room with Mrs. Kehoe as Tony embraced Eilis in the hall.

"I'm sorry I can't talk," she said.

"I've been thinking about it," he said. "If one of my brothers had died, maybe that sounds selfish, but I was trying to imagine what you're feeling."

"I think about it," Eilis said, "and I can't bear it and then I forget about it for a minute and when it comes back it's as though I just heard the news. I can't get over it."

"I wish I could stay with you," he said.

"I'll see you in the morning, and tell your mother not to come if it's any trouble."

"She'll be there. Nothing is any trouble now," he said.

Eilis looked at the pile of letters Rose had sent her, wondering if between sending one of these and sending the next Rose had learned that she was sick. Or if she had known before Eilis had left. It changed everything Eilis thought about her time in Brooklyn, it made everything that had happened to her seem small. She looked at Rose's handwriting, its clarity and evenness, its sense of supreme self-possession and self-confidence, and she wondered whether, while writing some of these words, Rose had looked up and sighed and then, through sheer strength of will, steeled herself and carried on writing, not faltering for a single moment from her decision to let no one share her knowledge except the doctor who had told her.

It was strange, Eilis felt in the morning, how deeply she had slept and how instantaneously, on waking, she had known that she was not going to work but to a mass for Rose. Her sister, she knew, would still be in the house in Friary Street, they would take her to the cathedral later in the evening and she would be buried after mass in the morning. All of this seemed simple and clear and almost inevitable until she and Mrs. Kehoe set out together for the parish church. Walking the familiar street, passing people whom she did not know, Eilis realized that one of them could have died and not Rose, and this could be another spring morning, a hint of heat in the air, with her going to work as normal.

The idea of Rose dying in her sleep seemed unimaginable. Had she opened her eyes for a moment? Had she just lain still breathing the breath of sleep, and then, as though it were nothing, had her heart stopped and her breath? How could this happen? Had she cried out in the night and not been heard, or even murmured or whispered? Had she known something the previous evening? Something, anything, that might have given her a clue that this was her last day alive in the world?

She imagined Rose laid out now in the dark robes of the dead with candles flickering on the table. And later the coffin being closed, and the solemn faces of everyone in the hallway and outside in the street, her brothers wearing suits and black ties as they had at their father's funeral. All morning at mass and back in Father Flood's house, she went through each moment of Rose's death and her removal.

The others were surprised, almost alarmed, when she said that she wanted to go to work that afternoon. She saw Mrs. Kehoe whispering about it to Father Flood. Tony asked her if she was sure, and when she insisted he said that he would walk with her to Bartocci's and then meet her later back at Mrs. Kehoe's. Mrs. Kehoe had invited him and Father Flood to have supper with the other lodgers followed by a rosary to be said for Rose's soul.

Eilis went back to work the following day as well and was determined to go to her classes that evening. Since they could not go to a movie or a dance, she and Tony went to a diner nearby and he said he would not mind if she did not want to talk much or if she cried.

"I wish this hadn't happened," he said. "I keep wishing it hadn't happened."

"I think that too," Eilis said. "If only she'd let one of us know. Or if only nothing had happened and she was well at home. I wish I had a photograph of her so I could show you how beautiful she was."

"You are beautiful," he said.

"She was the most beautiful, everyone said that, and I can't get used to the idea of where she is now. I'll have to stop thinking about her dying and her coffin and all that and maybe start praying, but it's hard."

"I'll help you if you like," he said.

Eilis felt, despite the improving weather, that all of the colour had been washed out of her world. She was careful on the shop floor and proud that not once did she break down or have to go suddenly to the bathroom and cry. Miss Fortini told her that she was not to worry if she needed to go home earlier any day, or if she wanted to meet her outside working hours to talk about what had happened. Tony came every night to meet her after the classes and she liked how he allowed her to remain silent if she wanted. He simply held her hand, or put his arm around her and walked her home, where her fellow lodgers made clear to her one by one that if she needed anything, anything at all, she was to knock on their door or find them in the kitchen and they would do everything they could for her.

One night when she went up to the kitchen to make herself a cup of tea she saw that there was a letter for her on the side table that she had missed earlier. It was from Ireland and she recognized the handwriting as Jack's. She did not open it immediately but took it downstairs with her when the tea was made so she could read it without being disturbed.

Dear Eilis,

Mammy asked me to write to you because she isn't able. I am writing this in the front parlour at the table by the window. The house was full of people but now there isn't a sound. They have all gone home. We buried Rose today and Mammy asked me to tell you that it was a fine day and the rain kept off. Father Quaid said the mass for her. We came down on the train from Dublin and arrived yesterday morning after a bad night on the mail-boat. She was still being waked in the house when we arrived. She looked beautiful, her hair and everything. Everyone said she looked peaceful, just asleep, and maybe that was true before we came but when I saw her she looked different, not like herself at all, not bad or anything but when I knelt down and touched her I didn't think it was her at all for a minute. Maybe I shouldn't say this, but I thought it was best to let you know what it was like. Mammy asked me to tell you everything that happened, about all the people who came, the whole golf club and Davis's office shut for the morning. It wasn't like Daddy, when he died you would think he was alive one minute. Rose was like stone when I saw her, all pale like something from a picture. But she was beautiful and peaceful. I don't know what was wrong with me but I didn't think it was her at all until we had to carry the coffin, the boys and myself and Jem and Bill and Fonsey Doyle from Clonegal. It was the worst thing about it in that I couldn't believe we were doing that to her, closing her in there and burying her. I'll have to pray for her when I get back but I couldn't follow the prayers at all. Mammy asked me to say that she said a special goodbye to her from you but I couldn't stay in the room when Mammy was talking to her and I nearly couldn't carry the coffin I was crying so much. And I couldn't look at all in the graveyard. I covered my eyes for most of it. Maybe I shouldn't be telling you all this. The thing is that we have to go back to work and I don't think Mammy knows that yet. She thinks one of us might be able to stay but we can't, you know. Work beyond is not like that. I don't know what it's like over there but we have to be back and Mammy is going to be here on her own. The neighbours will all come in and the others but I think it hasn't hit her yet. I know she'd love to see you, she keeps saying that is the only thing she is hoping for but we don't know what to say about it. She didn't ask me to mention this but I'd say you'll be hearing from her when she's able to write. I think she wants you to come home. She's never slept a night on her own in the house and she keeps saying that she won't be able to. But we have to go back. She asked me if I had heard of any work in the town and I told her I'd ask around but the thing is I have to go back and so do Pat and Martin. I'm sorry for rambling on like this. The news must have come as a terrible shock to you. It did to us. We had trouble finding Martin for the whole day because he was out on a job. It's hard to think of Rose out in the graveyard, that's all I have to say. Mammy will want me to say that everyone was good and they were and she won't want me to say that she's crying all the time but she is, or most of the time anyway. I'm going to stop writing now and

*put this in an envelope. I'm not going to read it over because I
started a few times and when I read it over I tore it up and had to
start again. I'll seal the envelope and I'll post it in the morning.
Martin, I think, is telling her that we have to go tomorrow. I hope
this letter isn't all terrible but, as I said, I didn't know what to
put into it. Mammy will be glad I sent it and I'll go and tell her
now that it's written. You'll have to say a prayer for her. I'll go
now.*

Your loving brother, Jack

Eilis read the letter a few times and then she realized that she
could not stay on her own now, she could hear Jack's voice in the
words he wrote, she could feel him in the room with her and it
was as though he had come in from a hurling match and his team
had lost and he was breathless with the news. If she had been at
home she could have spent time talking to Jack, listening to him,
sitting with her mother and Martin and Pat, going over what had
happened. She could not imagine Rose lying dead; she had
thought of her as asleep and being laid out like someone who was
sleeping but now she had to think of her like stone, all the life
gone out of her, and her closed in the coffin, all changed and
changing and gone from them. She almost wished Jack had not
written but she knew that someone had to write and he was the
best at writing.

She moved around the room, wondering what she should do.
It struck her for a second that she could get a subway to the harbour and find the next boat going across the Atlantic and simply
pay the fare and wait and get on the boat. But she realized quickly
that she could not do this, they might not have an empty place and
her money was in the savings bank. She thought of going upstairs,
and in her mind she went through each of her fellow lodgers but
none of them could be any use to her now. The only person who
could be any use to her was Tony. She looked at the clock; it was

ten thirty. If she could get there quickly on the subway, then she could be at his house in less than an hour, maybe a bit longer if the late trains did not come so often. She found her coat and went quickly into the corridor. She opened and closed the basement door and went up the steps trying not to make a sound.

His mother answered the door in her dressing gown and took her upstairs to the door of the apartment. It was clear that the family had retired for the night and Eilis knew that she did not seem now in a deep enough distress to justify her intruding at this hour. She saw through the door that Tony's parents' bed was already folded out and she came close to telling Tony's mother that it was fine, she was sorry for disturbing them and would go home. But that, she realized, would make no sense. Tony, his mother said, was getting dressed and he was going to go out with her; he shouted from the bedroom that they could go to the diner around the corner.

Suddenly, Frank appeared in his pyjamas. He had moved so quietly that she did not notice him until he was standing nearly in front of her. He seemed immensely curious and stealthy, almost comically so, like a figure in a movie who has just witnessed a robbery or a murder on a dark street. And then he looked at her openly and smiled at her and she had no choice but to smile in return just as Tony appeared and then Frank had to go back to his bedroom, having been told to mind his own business and leave Eilis alone.

From Tony's appearance, she knew that he had been asleep. He checked in his pockets for his keys and then he slipped back into the kitchen, where she could not see him, and whispered something to his mother or his father and then came out again, the expression on his face grave and responsible and concerned.

As they walked down the street towards the diner Tony held her close to him. They moved slowly and did not speak. For a second, as they had made their way down the stairs of his building, she had felt that he was angry with her for calling so late, but now she understood that he was not. He had a way of snuggling in close to her when they walked together that made her know that he loved her. He was doing this now even more intensely than usual. She also knew it would matter to him that if she needed help like this she would feel secure coming to him rather than Father Flood or Mrs. Kehoe, that he would come first for her. More than anything else she had ever done, she thought, this was the most direct and emphatic way she had ever made clear to him that she would stay with him.

In the diner, once they had ordered, he read Jack's letter slowly, almost too slowly, she thought, letting his lips move with some of the words. It struck her that she should not have shown it to him and should not have come to his house like this. It would be impossible for him to read the parts about her mother wanting to see her, her mother unable to be alone, without his feeling that she might go and that this was her way of breaking the news to him. As she watched him reading, his face pale, his expression deadly serious, as he seemed to be fiercely concentrating, she guessed that he was going over those parts of the letter that seemed to suggest she was needed by her mother in Enniscorthy. She was sorry now that she had not managed to contain herself earlier, that she had not foreseen this. And she felt stupid because she knew that no matter what she said it would be impossible to convince Tony that she wasn't going to go back to Ireland.

When he handed her the letter there were tears in his eyes.

"Your brother must be a very nice man," he said. "I wish . . ." He hesitated for a moment and then reached across the table and held her hand. "I don't mean I wish, but it would have been right if you and me had been there at the funeral, if I could have been there with you."

"I know," she said.

"And soon your mother will write," he said, "and you must come to my house before you even open her letter."

She could not tell if he meant it when he suggested that she should not be alone when she opened her mother's letter because he should be close by to comfort her. Or if he really meant, in fact, that, since he could not read her mind or guess precisely what her intentions were, he would like to see what her mother had to say about her going or her staying.

All this was a mistake, she thought again, as she set about apologizing for having disturbed him. When she realized how cold this sounded and how it seemed to set her at a distance from him, she told him how grateful she was for him coming out with her now when she needed him. He nodded, but she knew that he was disturbed by the letter, or maybe he was just as upset by it as she had been, or maybe he was a puzzling mixture of both.

He insisted on taking her home, even though she protested that he could easily miss the very last subway back. Once more, they did not speak, but as he walked her from the subway station through the dark cold empty streets to Mrs. Kehoe's, she felt that she was being held by someone wounded, that the letter had somehow, in its tone, made clear to him what had really happened and made plain to him also that she belonged somewhere else, a place that he could never know. She thought that he was going to cry; she felt almost guilty that she had handed some of her grief to him, and then she felt close to him for his willingness to take it and hold it, in all its rawness, all its dark confusion. She was almost more upset now than she had been when she had ventured out in search of him.

When they reached the house he held her but did not kiss her. She moved as close to him as she could until she felt the warmth of him and they both began to sob. She wished that she could tell him, in a way that would make him believe her, that she would not go, but then it struck her that Tony might feel she should go, that the letter had made him see where her duty lay, that he was crying now for everything, for Rose who was dead, for her mother who was lonely, for Eilis who would have to go, and for himself who would be left. She wished she could say something clear, or even wished that she could tell what he was thinking or why he was crying now harder than she was.

She knew that she could not walk alone down the steps into the basement and turn on the light in her room and be on her own there. And she knew also that he could not turn from her and walk away. As she produced the door key from the pocket of her coat, she pointed to Mrs. Kehoe's window and put her finger to her lips. They tiptoed down the steps to the basement and she opened the door and turned on the light in the hall and closed the door without making a sound and opened the door of her room for him before turning off the light in the hall.

The room was warm and they both took off their coats. Tony's face was puffed and raw from crying. When he tried to smile she moved towards him and held him.

"Is this where you live?" he whispered.

"Yes, and if you make one sound, I'll be evicted," she said.

He kissed her gently and responded with his tongue only when she opened her mouth for him. His body was warm and seemed strangely vulnerable to her now as she pulled him against her. She ran her hands down his back and under his shirt until she was touching his skin. They moved towards the bed without speaking. As they lay beside each other, he lifted her skirt and opened his trousers enough for her to feel his penis against her. She knew that he was waiting for a sign from her, that he would do nothing more as they continued to kiss. She opened her eyes and saw that his were closed. Quietly, she moved away from him and took off her panties and by the time she lay beside him again he had pulled his trousers down further and his underwear too so that she could touch him. He tried to put his hands on her breasts but could not easily unloose her brassiere; he put his hand on her back and concentrated on kissing her fiercely.

When he moved on top of her and entered her she tried not to gasp as she began to panic. It was not only the pain and the shock but the idea that she could not control him, that his penis was pushing into her deeper than she wanted it to go. With each thrust it seemed to move further into her until she was sure it was going to injure something inside her. She felt a relief as it pulled back but only to find it worse each time as it pushed up into her. She tightened as much as she could to stop it and she wished she could call out or indicate that he should not push in so hard, that he was going to break something.

That she could not shout made her panic even greater; she put her energy into tightening her whole body with all the force she could gather. And as she did so he gasped, he made noises that she did not imagine anyone could make, a sort of muffled whining that did not let up. As he stopped moving she tightened more, hoping that he would now take his penis out, but instead he lay on top of her, gasping. It seemed to her that he was unaware of anything except his own breathing, that in these minutes as she lay with him quietly on top of her he did not know or care that she existed. She had no idea how they were going to face each other now. She did not move as she waited for him to do something.

What he did once he moved away from her surprised her. He stood up without saying anything, looked at her, smiled and took his shoes and socks off and then removed his trousers and underpants. He knelt on the bed and slowly undressed her, and when she was naked, with her arms covering her breasts, he took off his shirt so that he was naked too. He approached gently, almost shyly, and lifted the bed covers and they both moved in between the sheets and lay together for some time quietly. She realized when she touched him once more, his penis erect again, how smooth and beautiful he was, and how much stronger he seemed naked than when he was with her in the street or in the dancehall, where, compared to men who were taller or bigger, he had often appeared almost frail. When she understood that he wanted to enter her again she whispered to him that he had pushed in too far the first time.

"I thought you would go up into my neck." She laughed under her breath.

"I wish I could," he said.

She pinched him hard.

"No, you don't wish you could."

"Hey, that hurt," he whispered and kissed her, moving slowly on top of her.

This time the pain was almost worse than before, as though he were hitting against something inside her that was bruised or cut.

"Is that better?" he asked.

She tightened as much as she could.

"Hey, that's beautiful," he said. "Can you do that more?"

Once again, as he pushed in further, he seemed to become unaware that she was with him. He seemed lost to the world. And this sense of him as beyond her made her want him more than she had ever done, made her feel that this now and the memory of it later would be enough for her and had made a difference to her beyond anything she had ever imagined.

The next day he was waiting for her after work and they walked from Fulton Street to the subway station without speaking. Once there, they arranged to meet again outside the college when the classes had finished. He appeared grave, almost angry with her, as they parted. Later, when he had walked her home, she turned before going down the basement steps and saw he was still standing there. He gave her a grin that reminded her so much of his brother Frank's way of grinning, so full of mischief and innocence, that she laughed and pointed at him in mock accusation.

It was clear, once she arrived in the kitchen and was waiting for the kettle to boil, that Mrs. Kehoe, who was alone at the table, was not speaking to her. She felt a lightness that almost caused her to ask Mrs. Kehoe what the problem was, but instead she moved around the kitchen pretending that she noticed nothing strange.

It struck her then that Mrs. Kehoe, who generally, Eilis believed, heard every sound and missed nothing, had heard Tony either entering or leaving the basement or, perhaps worse indeed, heard him during the night. In all the outrages that could be committed by the lodgers, this had never even been mentioned as a possibility by the lodgers themselves or by Mrs. Kehoe. It was in the realm of the unthinkable. While Patty and Diana often talked freely about boyfriends, the idea that one of them would spend an entire night in the company of her boyfriend, or allow him access to her bedroom, was out of the question. As Eilis sat in the chilly silence created by Mrs. Kehoe, she determined to deny emphatically and brazenly that Tony had been near her room and declare that such an idea shocked her as much as it did her landlady.

She made poached eggs and toast and was relieved when Patty and Diana came in with news about a coat that Patty had seen and was going to buy if it was still there on Friday when she got paid. Mrs. Kehoe stood up without speaking and left the kitchen banging the door.

"What's biting her?" Patty asked.

"I think I know," Diana said, looking at Eilis, "but as God is my witness I heard nothing."

"Heard what?" Patty asked.

"Nothing," Diana said. "But it sounded lovely."

*   *   *

Eilis slept deeply and woke in the morning exhausted and sore. It was as though Rose's death had happened long ago, and her night with Tony remained with her as something powerful, still present. She wondered how she would know if she was pregnant, how early the signs would come. She touched her stomach, asking herself if at this very moment something could be happening there, some tiny connection like a small knot, or smaller even, smaller than a drop of water but with everything in it that was needed for it to grow. She wondered if there was anything she could do to stop it, if there was something she could wash herself with, but as soon as she thought of that she knew that even the idea was wrong and that she would have to go to confession and make Tony go too.

She hoped that he would not grin at her again as he had done the previous evening and that he would realize the trouble she was in if she was pregnant. But if she was not pregnant, she hoped he would understand, as she did now, that what they had done was wrong, and more wrong because it had been done when Rose was barely in her grave. Even when she went to confession, Eilis realized, and told the priest what they had done, she would never be able to tell anyone that just half an hour before they had been crying. It would seem too strange.

As soon as she saw Tony that evening she told him that they would both have to go to confession the following evening, which was Friday, and that she presumed he understood this.

"I couldn't go to Father Flood," she said, "or any priest who might recognize me. I know it shouldn't matter, but I couldn't."

Tony suggested that they should go to his local church, where most of the priests were Italians.

"Some of them don't understand a word you're saying if you speak in English," he said.

"That's not a real confession, then."

"But I think they recognize some key words."

"Don't make jokes. You are going to confession too."

"I know that," he said. "And will you promise me something?" He moved close to her. "Will you promise to be kind to me after the confession? I mean to hold my hand and talk to me and smile?"

"And will you promise me to make a good confession?"

"Yes, I will," he said, "and my mom wants you to come to lunch on Sunday. She's worried about you."

The following evening they met outside his church. Tony insisted that they go to separate priests; hers, he said, a priest called Anthony with a long Italian surname, was young and nice and spoke English. He himself, he said, was going to go to one of the older Italian ones.

"Make sure he understands what you say," she whispered.

When she told the priest she had had sexual intercourse twice with her boyfriend three nights earlier, he left silence for a long time.

"Was this the first time?" he asked when he spoke eventually.

"Yes, Father."

"Do you love one another?"

"Yes, Father."

"What will you do if you are pregnant?"

"He will want to marry me, Father."

"Do you want to marry him?"

She could not answer. After a while, he asked her again, his tone sympathetic.

"I would like to marry him," she said hesitantly, "but I am not ready to marry him now."

"But you say you love him?"

"He is a good man."

"Is that enough?"

"I love him."

"But you are not sure?"

She sighed and said nothing.

"Are you sorry for what you did with him?"

"Yes, Father."

"For your penance I want you to say just one Hail Mary, but say it slowly and think about the words, and you must promise to come back in one month. If you are pregnant, we will have to talk again, and we will help you in every way we can."

When she got back to Mrs. Kehoe's she discovered that a lock had been put on the basement gate and she had to let herself in by the main door. Mrs. Kehoe was in the kitchen with Miss McAdam, who had decided that she was not going to the dance.

"I'm going to keep the basement locked in future," Mrs. Kehoe said as though speaking to Miss McAdam alone. "You wouldn't know who would be going down there."

"You are very wise," Miss McAdam said.

As Eilis made her supper, Mrs. Kehoe and Miss McAdam treated her as though she were a ghost.

Eilis's mother wrote and mentioned how lonely she was and how long the day was and how hard the night. She said that neighbours looked in on her all the time and people called after tea but she had run out of things to say to them. Eilis wrote to her a number of times; she told her mother all the news about the summer styles in Bartocci's and other stores on Fulton Street and about preparing for her exams, which would come in May, saying she was studying hard because if she passed she would be a qualified bookkeeper.

She never mentioned Tony in any of her letters home and she wondered if, by now, her mother, in clearing out Rose's room or in receiving what was in her desk at the office, had found and read her letters to Rose. She saw Tony every day, sometimes merely meeting him outside the college and travelling with him on the trolley-car and letting him walk her as far as Mrs. Kehoe's. Since the night he had spent in her room everything was different between them. She felt that he was more relaxed, more willing to be silent and not trying to impress her so much or make jokes. And every time she saw him waiting for her, she felt that they had become closer. Every time they kissed, or even brushed against each other as they walked along the street, she was reminded of that night they had been together.

Once she discovered that she was not pregnant, she thought of the night with pleasure, especially after she had returned to the priest, who somehow managed to imply that what had happened between her and Tony was not hard to understand, despite the fact that it was wrong, and was maybe a sign from God that they should consider getting married and raising a family. He seemed so easy to talk to the second time that she was tempted to tell him the whole story and ask him what she should do about her mother, whose letters to her were increasingly sad, the handwriting at times wandering strangely across the page, almost illegible, but she left the confession box without saying anything more.

One Sunday after mass, as she was walking out of the church with Sheila Heffernan, Eilis noticed that Father Flood, who often stood in front of the church after mass greeting his parishioners, had averted his eyes and moved into the shadows when they approached and was soon speaking to a number of women with immense concentration. She waited behind only to find that the priest, having spotted her, turned his back and walked away from her quickly. It occurred to her immediately that Mrs. Kehoe had spoken to him and that she should go to see him as soon as possible before he did something unthinkable such as write to her mother about her, although she had no idea what she would say to him.

Thus after lunch with Tony and his family, she made an arrangement to see Tony later, but said that she had to go now and study. She refused to allow him to come on the subway with her. She went straight from the subway station to Father Flood's house.

It was only when she was sitting in the front parlour waiting for him that it struck her that she could not easily mention Mrs. Kehoe, she would have to wait for him to do so. If he did not raise the subject, she thought, she could talk about her mother and maybe even discuss the possibility of moving into the office at Bartocci's were a vacancy to arise after she passed her bookkeeping exams. As she heard footsteps approaching in the hallway, she knew she had a choice. She could appear humble before him and imply an abject apology even if she did not admit everything, or she could model herself on Rose, stand up now as Rose might have and speak to Father Flood as though she were entirely incapable of any wrongdoing.

Father Flood seemed uneasy when he came into the room and did not immediately catch her eye.

"I hope I am not disturbing you now, Father," she said.

"Oh, no, not at all. I was just reading the paper."

She knew that it was important to speak now before he did.

"I don't know if you've heard from my mother but I have had letters and she seems not to be well at all."

"I'm sorry to hear that," Father Flood said. "You know I did think it must be hard for her."

Whatever way he looked at her, he managed to let her know that he meant more than he said, that he was suggesting it might be hard for her mother not only losing Rose but having a daughter who would take a man home to her room for the night.

Eilis now held his gaze and left enough silence for him to know that she had understood the implications of his words but had no intention of giving them any further consideration.

"As you know, I hope to get my exams next month and this would mean that I would be a qualified bookkeeper. I have some money saved and I thought I might go home, just to see my mother, for as long as Bartocci's would let me have unpaid leave. Also, like many of the other lodgers, I have been having difficulty with Mrs. Kehoe and when I come back from Ireland I might consider changing my lodgings."

"She's very nice, Mrs. Kehoe," Father Flood said. "There aren't many Irish places like that now. In the old days there used to be more."

Eilis did not reply.

"So you want me to talk to Bartocci?" he asked. "How long would you like to go for?"

"A month," Eilis said.

"And you would come back and work on the shop floor until a job in the office came up?"

"Yes."

He nodded his head and seemed to be thinking about something.

"Would you like me to talk to Mrs. Kehoe as well?" he asked.

"I thought you already had."

"Not since Rose died," Father Flood said. "I'm not sure I have seen her since then."

Eilis studied his face but she could not tell whether it was true or not.

"Would you not make it up with her?" Father Flood asked.

"How would I do that?"

"She's very fond of you."

Eilis said nothing.

"I'll tell you what," Father Flood said. "I'll square Bartocci if you make it up with Ma Kehoe."

"How would I do that?" she repeated.

"Be nice to her."

* * *

Before she had seen Father Flood, it had not occurred to Eilis that she might go home for a brief stay. But once it had been said and did not sound ridiculous and had met with Father Flood's approval, then it became a plan, something that she was determined to do. At lunchtime the following day she went to a travel agent and found prices for liners crossing the Atlantic. She would wait until her exam results came out, but once she knew them she would go home for a month; it would take five or six days each way, so she would have two and half weeks with her mother.

Although she wrote to her mother later that week she did not mention anything about her plans to go home. When she saw Father Flood in the department store one day she knew that he was there on her behalf because he winked at her as he passed and she hoped he would have news for her soon.

On Friday, when Tony had walked her home after the dance, she found a letter from Father Flood that had been delivered by hand. Mrs. Kehoe soon arrived into the kitchen to announce that she was about to make tea and that she hoped Eilis would join her. Eilis smiled warmly at Mrs. Kehoe and said that she would love that and then went to her room and opened the letter. The Bartoccis, Father Flood said, could offer her one month's unpaid leave, the date to be arranged with Miss Fortini, and, if she passed her exams, they hoped they could offer her a job in the office over the next six months. She left the letter on the bed and went upstairs to find her tea almost poured.

"Would you feel safe if I took the lock off the basement gate?" Mrs. Kehoe asked her. "I didn't know what to do so I asked that nice Sergeant Mulhall whose wife plays poker with me and he said that he would have his officers keep a special watch on it and report on any untoward activity down there."

"Oh, that's a great idea, Mrs. Kehoe," Eilis said. "You should thank him on behalf of all of us the next time you see him."

Colm Tóibín

*   *   *

She hoped that the law exam would be as easy as the last time. And she was happy with the work she had done in all the other subjects. As part of the final exam, however, every student would be given all the details of the annual life of a company, rent and heat and light, wages, the fact that machinery and other assets might devalue each year, debt, capital investment and tax. On the other side, there would be sales, money coming in from a number of sources, be they wholesale or retail. And all of this would have to be entered into ledgers in the correct column, it would have to be done neatly so that at an annual general meeting when the board and shareholders of a company wanted to see clearly how profit or loss had been made, they could do so from these ledgers. Anyone who failed this part of the exam, they were told, would not get a passing mark even if they did well in other papers. They would have to repeat the entire exam.

One evening close to the exams, when Tony was walking her home, Eilis told him about her plan to go home for a month once the results came. She had already written to her mother telling her the news. Tony said nothing to her, but, when they arrived at Mrs. Kehoe's, he asked her to walk with him around the block. His face was pale and he seemed serious and did not look at her directly as he spoke.

When they were away from Mrs. Kehoe's he sat on a stoop where there was no one, leaving her standing against the railings. She knew that he would be upset about her going like this but was ready to explain to him that he had family in Brooklyn and he did not know what it was like to be away from home. She was prepared to tell him that he would go home too for a visit under similar circumstances.

"Marry me before you go back," he said almost under his breath.

"What did you say?" She went to the stoop and sat beside him.

"If you go, you won't come back."

"I'm just going for a month, I told you."

"Marry me before you go back."

"You don't trust me to come back."

"I read the letter your brother wrote. I know how hard it would be for you to go home and then leave again. I know it would be hard for me. I know what a good person you are. I would live in fear of getting a letter from you explaining that your mother could not be left alone."

"I promise you I will come back."

Each time he said "marry me" he looked away from her, mumbling the words as though he were talking to himself. Now he turned and looked at her clearly.

"I don't mean in a church and I don't mean we live together as man and wife and we don't have to tell anybody. It can be just between the two of us and we can get married in a church when we decide after you come back."

"Can you get married just like that?" she asked.

"Sure you can. You have to give them notice and I'll get a list of things we need to do."

"Why do you want me to do it?"

"It will just be something between us."

"But why do you want it?"

When he spoke now he had tears in his eyes. "Because if we don't do it, I'm going to go crazy."

"And we'll tell no one?"

"No one. We'll take a half-day off work, that's all."

"And will I wear a ring?"

"You can if you want, but if you don't that's fine. All this could, if you wanted, be just something private between the two of us."

"Would a promise not be the same?"

"If you can promise, then you can easily do this," he said.

205

*   *   *

He arranged a date soon after her exams and they set about making all the preparations and filling out the forms that were required. The Sunday before the date she went as usual to his family for lunch. As she sat down she felt that Tony had told his mother, or that his mother had guessed something. There was a new tablecloth on the table, and the way his mother was dressed suggested an important occasion. Then when Tony's father came in with his three brothers she saw that they were all wearing jackets and ties, which they did not normally do. Once they sat down to eat, she noticed that Frank was unusually quiet at the beginning and then every time he tried to speak the others interrupted him before he could start.

Several times more, in the course of the meal, when he opened his mouth to say something he was stopped.

Eventually, Eilis insisted that she needed to hear what he had to say.

"When we're all in Long Island," he said, "and when you have your house there, will you make them build me a room so I can come and stay with you when they're all making me miserable?"

Tony, Eilis saw, had his head down.

"Of course, Frank. And you will be able to come any time you like."

"That's all I wanted to say."

"Grow up, Frank," Tony said.

"Grow up, Frank," Laurence repeated.

"Yeah, Frank," Maurice added.

"See?" Frank motioned to Eilis and pointed at his three brothers. "That is what I have to tolerate."

"Don't worry," Eilis said. "I'll deal with them."

At the end of the meal, as the dessert was served, Tony's father produced special glasses and opened a bottle of Prosecco. He proposed that they drink for a safe journey and a safe return for Eilis. She wondered if it was still possible that Tony had told them nothing about the wedding, just about her plans to go home for a month; it struck her as unlikely that he would have let Frank know, unless Frank had overheard. Maybe they were just having a special lunch because she was going home, she thought.

In the good cheer that followed the dessert she almost began to hope that he had told them that he and she were getting married.

He arranged the ceremony for two o'clock in the afternoon a week before she was to leave. The exams had gone well and she was almost certain that she would qualify. Because other couples to be married came with family and friends, their ceremony seemed brisk and over quickly and caused much curiosity among those waiting because they had come alone.

On their journey to Coney Island on the train that afternoon Tony raised the question for the first time of when they might marry in church and live together.

"I have money saved," he said, "so we could get an apartment and then move to the house when it's ready."

"I don't mind," she said. "I wish we were going home together now."

He touched her hand.

"So do I," he said. "And the ring looks great on your finger."

She looked down at the ring.

"I'd better remember to take it off before Mrs. Kehoe sees it."

The ocean was rough and grey and the wind blew white billowing clouds quickly across the sky. They moved slowly along the boardwalk and down the pier, where they stood watching the fishermen. As they walked back and sat eating hot dogs at Nathan's, Eilis spotted someone at the next table checking out her wedding ring. She smiled to herself.

"Will we ever tell our children that we did this?" she asked.

"When we are old maybe and have run out of other stories," Tony said. "Or maybe we'll save it up for some anniversary."

"I wonder what they'll think of it."

"The movie I'm taking you to is called *The Belle of New York*. They'll believe that bit. But the idea that, when the movie was over, we took the subway home and I dropped you off at Mrs. Kehoe's. They won't believe that."

When they finished eating, they walked together towards the subway and waited for the train to take them into the city.

Part Four

Her mother showed Eilis Rose's bedroom, which was filled with light from the morning sun. She had left everything, she said, exactly as it was, including all of Rose's clothes in the wardrobe and in the chest of drawers.

"I had the windows cleaned and the curtains washed and I dusted the room myself and swept it out, but other than that it's exactly the same," her mother said.

The house itself did not seem strange; Eilis noted only its solid, familiar aura, the lingering smell of cooked food, the shadows, the sense of her mother's vivid presence. But nothing had prepared her for the quietness of Rose's bedroom and she felt almost nothing as she stood looking at it. She wondered if her mother wanted her to cry now, or had left the room as it was so she could feel even more deeply Rose's death. She did not know what to say.

"And some day now," her mother said, "we can go through the clothes. Rose had just bought a new winter coat and we'll see if it suits you. She had lovely things."

Eilis suddenly felt immensely tired and thought that she should go to bed once they had eaten breakfast but she knew that her mother had been planning this moment when they would both stand in this doorway together and contemplate the room.

"You know, I sometimes think she's still alive," her mother said. "If I hear the slightest sound upstairs, I often think it must be Rose."

As they ate breakfast Eilis wished she could think of something more to say but it was hard to speak since her mother seemed to have prepared in advance every word that she said.

"I have arranged a wreath to be made specially for you to leave on her grave and we can go out in a few days if the weather keeps up and then we can let them know it's time to put Rose's name and her dates below your father's."

Eilis wondered for a moment what might happen were she to interrupt her mother and say: "I am married." She thought her mother would have a way of not hearing her, or of pretending that she had not spoken. Or else, she imagined, the glass in the window might break.

By the time she managed to say that she was tired and would need to lie down for a while, her mother had not asked her one question about her time in America, or even her trip home. Just as her mother seemed to have prepared things to say and show to her, Eilis had been planning how this first day would go. She had planned to give an account of how much more smooth the crossing from New York to Cobh had been than her first voyage from Liverpool, and how much she had enjoyed sitting up on deck taking in the sun. She had planned also to show her mother the letter from Brooklyn College telling her that she had passed her exams and would, in time, be sent a certificate to say that she was a qualified bookkeeper. She had also bought her mother a cardigan and scarf and some stockings, but her mother had almost absentmindedly left them aside, saying that she would open them later.

Eilis loved closing the door of her old room and drawing the curtains. All she wanted to do was sleep, even though she had slept well in the hotel in Rosslare Harbour the night before. She had sent Tony a postcard from Cobh saying that she had arrived safely, and had written him a letter from Rosslare describing the journey. She was glad she did not have to write now from her bedroom, which seemed empty of life, which almost frightened her in how little it meant to her. She had put no thought into what it would be like to come home because she had expected that it would be easy; she had longed so much for the familiarity of these rooms that she had presumed she would be happy and relieved to step back into them, but, instead, on this first morning, all she could do was count the days before she went back. This made her feel strange and guilty; she curled up in the bed and closed her eyes in the hope that she might sleep.

Her mother woke her saying it was almost teatime. She had slept, she guessed, for almost six hours and wanted nothing more than to go back to sleep. Her mother told her that there was hot water in case she wanted a bath. She opened her suitcases and began to hang clothes in the wardrobe and store other things in the chest of drawers. She found a summer dress that did not seem to be too wrinkled and a cardigan and clean underwear and a pair of flat shoes.

When she came back into the kitchen, having had her bath and put on the fresh clothes, her mother looked her up and down in vague disapproval. It struck Eilis that maybe the colours she was wearing were too bright, but she did not have any darker colours.

"Now the whole town has been asking for you," her mother said. "God, even Nelly Kelly was asking for you. I saw her standing at the door of the shop and she let a big roar at me. And all your friends want you to call round, but I told them that it would be better to wait until you are settled."

Eilis wondered if her mother had always had this way of speaking that seemed to welcome no reply, and suddenly realized that she had seldom been alone with her before, she had always had Rose to stand between her and her mother, Rose who would have plenty to say to both of them, questions to ask, comments to make and opinions to offer. It must be hard for her mother too, she thought, and it would be best to wait a few days and see if her mother might become interested in her life in America, enough for her slowly to introduce the subject of Tony, enough for her to tell her mother that she was going to marry him when she went back.

They sat at the dining-room table going through all the letters of condolence and mass cards they had received in the weeks after Rose died. Eilis's mother had had a memorial card printed with a photograph of Rose at her most glamorous and happy, giving her name and her age and the date of her death, with short prayers below and on the other side of the card. These had to be sent out. But also, to those who had written letters or those who had visited the house, special notes or longer letters had to be included. Eilis's mother had divided the memorial cards into three piles: one that needed just a name and address on the envelope and a card enclosed, the second requiring a note or a letter from her, and the last needing Eilis to write a note or a letter. Eilis remembered vaguely that this had happened too after her father died, but Rose, she recalled, had taken care of everything and she had not been actively involved.

Her mother knew some of the letters of condolence she had received almost by heart and had also a list of everyone who had called to the house, which she went through slowly for Eilis, remarking on some who had come too often or stayed too long, or others who had gossiped too much or given offence by something they had said. And there were cousins of her mother from out beyond Bree who had brought neighbours of theirs, rough people from out the country, to the house, and she hoped never to lay eyes on either the cousins or their neighbours again.

Then, she said, Dora Devereux from Cush Gap and her sister Statia had come one night and they had never stopped talking, the two of them, with news about people no one else in the room had ever heard of. They had left a mass card each, her mother said, and she would write them a short note thanking them for their visit but trying not to encourage them to call again in a hurry. But Nora Webster had come, she said, with Michael who had taught the boys in school, and they were the nicest people in the whole town. She wouldn't mind, she said, if they came again, but as they had young children she didn't think they would.

As her mother read out lists of other people, Eilis was almost inclined to giggle at names she had not heard of, or thought of, during her time in America. When her mother mentioned an old woman who lived down near the Folly, Eilis could not resist speaking. "God, is she still going?"

Her mother looked sorrowful and put on her glasses again as she began to search for a letter she had mislaid from the captain of the golf club saying what a treasured lady-member Rose had been and how much she would be missed. When she found it, she looked at Eilis severely.

Every letter or note Eilis wrote had to be inspected by her mother, who often wanted it done again or a paragraph added at the end. And in her own letters, as in Eilis's, she wanted it emphasized that, since Eilis was home, she had plenty of company and needed no more visitors.

Eilis marvelled at the different ways each person had expressed condolences once they had gone beyond the first one or two sentences. Her mother tried too, in how she replied, to vary the tone and the content, to write something suitable in response to each person. But it was slow and by the end of the first day Eilis had still not gone out into the street or had any time alone. And less than half the work was done.

The following day she worked hard, saying to her mother a number of times that if they continued talking or going over each letter received they would never complete the task in front of them. Yet not only did her mother work slowly, insisting that she and not Eilis would have to write most of the letters, but wanting Eilis to look at each one she completed, but also she could not resist making regular comments on those who had written, including people Eilis had never met.

Eilis tried to change the subject a few times, wondering to her mother if they might go to Dublin together some day, or even go to Wexford on the train some afternoon. But her mother said that they would wait and see, the thing was to get these letters written and sent and then they would go through Rose's room and sort out her clothes.

As they had their tea on the second day, Eilis told her mother that if she did not contact some of her friends soon, they would be insulted. Now that she had begun, she was determined to win a free day, not to have to go straight from writing letters and addressing envelopes under her mother's sharp and increasingly cranky supervision to sorting out Rose's clothes.

"I arranged for the wreath to be delivered tomorrow," her mother said, "so that's our day for the graveyard."

"Yes, well, I'll see Annette and Nancy tomorrow evening, then," Eilis said.

"You know, they called around asking when you were coming back. I put them off, but if you want to see them, then you should invite them here."

"Maybe I'll do that now," Eilis said. "If I leave a note for Nancy, then she can get in touch with Annette. Is Nancy still going out with George? She said they were getting engaged."

"I'll let her give you all the news," her mother said, and smiled.

"George would be a great catch," Eilis said. "And he's good-looking as well."

"Oh, I don't know," her mother said. "They could make a slave out of her in that shop. And that old Mrs. Sheridan is very noble. I wouldn't have any time for her at all."

Walking out into the street brought Eilis instant relief, and, as it was a beautiful warm evening, she could happily have walked for miles. She noticed a woman studying her dress and her stockings and her shoes and then her tanned skin, and she realized with amusement as she moved towards Nancy's house that she must look glamorous in these streets. She touched her finger where the wedding ring had been and promised herself that she would write to Tony that evening when her mother had gone to bed and work out a way of posting her letter in the morning without her mother knowing. Or maybe, she thought, it would be a good way of letting her mother gently into the secret, in case she had not seen the letters that Eilis had written to Rose, that there was someone special for her in America.

The next day, as they walked out to the graveyard with the wreath, anyone they met whom they knew stopped to talk. They complimented Eilis on how well she looked but did not do so too effusively or in too frivolous a tone because they could see that she was on her way with her mother to her sister's grave.

It was only as they walked up through the main avenue of the graveyard towards the family plot that Eilis understood fully the extent to which she had been dreading this. She felt sorry for how much she had been irritated by her mother over the previous days and now walked slowly, linking her arm while carrying the wreath. A few people in the graveyard stood and watched as they approached the grave.

There was another wreath almost withered that her mother removed, and then she stood back beside Eilis, facing the headstone.

"So, Rose," her mother said quietly, "here's Eilis, she's home now and we've brought fresh flowers out to you."

Eilis did not know if her mother expected her to say something too, but, since she was crying now, she was not sure she could make herself clear. She held her mother's hand.

"I'm praying for you, Rose, and thinking about you," Eilis whispered, "and I hope you're praying for me."

"She's praying for all of us," her mother said. "Rose is up in heaven praying for all of us."

As they stood there silently at the grave, Eilis found the idea that Rose was below the earth surrounded by darkness almost impossible to bear. She tried to think about her sister when she was alive, the light in her eyes, her voice, her way of putting a cardigan over her shoulders if she felt a draught, her way of handling their mother, making her interested in even the smallest detail of Rose's and Eilis's lives, as though she too had the same friends, the same interests, the same experiences. Eilis concentrated on Rose's spirit and tried to keep her mind from dwelling on what was happening to Rose's body just beneath them in the damp clay.

They walked home by Summerhill and then past the Fair Green to the Back Road because her mother said that she did not want to meet anybody else that day, but it occurred to Eilis that she did not want anyone to see Eilis who might invite her out or cause her to leave her mother's side at any point.

That evening, when Nancy and Annette called Eilis noticed Nancy's engagement ring immediately. Nancy explained that she had been engaged to George for two months now, but she hadn't wanted to write to Eilis about it because of Rose.

"But it's great you'll be here for the wedding. Your mother is delighted."

"When is the wedding?"

"On Saturday, the twenty-seventh of June."

"But I'll be gone back," Eilis said.

"Your mother said you'll still be here. She wrote and accepted the invitation on behalf of the two of you."

Her mother came into the room with a tray and cups and saucers and a teapot and some cakes.

"There you are now," she said. "It's lovely to see you both, a bit of life in the house again. Poor Eilis was fed up with her old mother. And we're looking forward to the wedding, Nancy. We'll have to get the best of style for it. That's what Rose would want."

She left the room before any of them could speak. Nancy looked at Eilis and shrugged. "You'll have to come now."

Eilis worked out in her head that the wedding was four days after the planned date of her departure; she also remembered that the travel agent in Brooklyn had said she could change the date as long as she notified the shipping company in advance. She decided there and then that she would stay an extra week and hoped that no one in Bartocci's would object too strongly. It would be easy to explain to Tony that her mother had misunderstood her date of departure, even though Eilis did not believe that her mother had misunderstood anything.

"Or maybe you have someone waiting impatiently for you in New York?" Annette suggested.

"Such as Mrs. Kehoe, my landlady," Eilis replied.

She knew that she could not trust herself to begin to confide in either of her friends, especially when they were together like this, without letting them know too much. And if she told them, she would soon find that one of their mothers would mention to her mother that Eilis had a boyfriend in New York. It was best, she thought, to say nothing, to talk instead about clothes and her studies and tell them about the other lodgers and Mrs. Kehoe.

They, in turn, told her the news from the town—who was going out with whom, or who was planning to get engaged, adding that the freshest news was that Nancy's sister, who had been going out with Jim Farrell on and off since Christmas, had finally broken it off with him and had a new boyfriend who was from Ferns.

"She only got off with Jim Farrell as a dare," Nancy said. "He was being as rude to her as he was to you that night, do you remember how rude he was? And we all bet money that she wouldn't get off with him. And then she did. But she couldn't bear him in the end, she said he was a terrible pain in the neck, even though George says he's really a nice fellow if you get to know him, and George was in school with him."

"George is very charitable," Annette said.

Jim Farrell, Nancy said, was coming to the wedding as a friend of George, but her sister was demanding that her new boyfriend from Ferns also be invited. In all this talk of boyfriends and plans for the wedding, Eilis realized that if she were to tell Nancy or Annette about her own secret wedding, attended by no one except her and Tony, they would respond with silence and bewilderment. It would seem too strange.

For the next few days as she moved around the town, and on Sunday, when she went to eleven o'clock mass with her mother, people commented on Eilis's beautiful clothes, her sophisticated hairstyle and her suntan. She tried to make plans to see Annette or Nancy either together or separately every day, telling her mother in advance what she intended to do. On the following Wednesday, when she told her mother that, if it was fine, she was going the next day in the early afternoon to Curracloe with George Sheridan and Nancy and Annette, her mother demanded that she cancel her outing that evening and begin the task of going through Rose's belongings, deciding what to keep and what to give away.

They took out the clothes hanging in the wardrobe and put them on the bed. Eilis wanted to make clear that she did not need any of her sister's clothes and that it would be best to give away everything to a charity. But her mother was already setting aside Rose's winter coat, so recently acquired, and a number of frocks that she said could easily be altered to fit Eilis.

"I won't have much room in my suitcase," Eilis said, "and the coat is lovely but the colour is too dark for me."

Her mother, still busy sorting the clothes, pretended that she had not heard her.

"What we'll do is we'll take the frocks and the coat to the

dressmaker's in the morning and they'll look different when they are the proper size, when they match your new American figure."

Eilis, in turn, began to ignore her mother as she opened the bottom drawer of the chest and poured its contents on to the floor. She wanted to make sure that she found her letters to Rose, if they were here, before her mother did. There were old medals and brochures, even hairnets and hairpins, which had not been used for years, and folded handkerchiefs and some photographs that Eilis put aside, as well as a large number of score cards for golf. But there was no sign in this drawer, or in any of the others, of the letters.

"Most of this is rubbish, Mammy," she said. "It'll be best just to keep the photographs and throw the rest away."

"Oh, I'll need to look at all that, but come over here now and help me fold these scarves."

Eilis refused to go to the dressmaker's the following morning, telling her mother finally and emphatically that she did not want to wear any of Rose's frocks or coats, no matter how elegant they were or how much they cost.

"Do you want me to dump them, then?"

"There are a lot of people would love them."

"But they are not good enough for you?"

"I have my own clothes."

"Well, I'll leave them in the wardrobe in case you change your mind. You could give them away and then find someone you didn't know at mass on Sunday wearing them. That'd be nice now."

In the post office Eilis had bought enough stamps and special envelopes for letters to America. She wrote to Tony explaining that she was staying a few weeks extra and to the shipping company at the office in Cobh cancelling the return passage she had booked and asking them to let her know how to arrange a later date for her return. She thought that she would wait until closer to the date to alert Miss Fortini and Mrs. Kehoe to her late arrival. She wondered if it would be wise to use illness as an excuse. She told Tony about the visit to Rose's grave and about Nancy's engagement, assuring him that she kept his ring close to her so that she could think about him when she was alone.

At lunchtime she put a towel and her bathing costume and a pair of sandals into a bag and walked to Nancy's house, where George Sheridan was going to collect them. It had been a beautiful morning, the air sweet and still, and it was hot, almost stifling in the house as they waited for George to arrive. When they heard the sound of the horn beeping in the station wagon he used to make deliveries they went outside. Eilis was surprised to see Jim Farrell as he held the door open for her and then got in beside her, allowing Nancy to sit beside George in the front passenger seat.

Eilis nodded coldly at Jim and sat as far away from him as she could. She had spotted him at mass the previous Sunday but had been careful to avoid him. As they moved out of the town, she realized that he, and not Annette, was coming with them; she was angry with Nancy for not having told her. She would have cancelled had she known. She was further infuriated when George and Jim began a discussion about some rugby game as the car made its way along the Osbourne Road towards Vinegar Hill and then turned right towards Curracloe. She thought for a moment of interrupting the two men to tell them that in Brooklyn there was a Vinegar Hill too but that it was nothing like the Vinegar Hill that overlooked Enniscorthy, even though it was called after it. Anything, she thought, to shut them up. Instead, she decided that she would not speak once to Jim Farrell, not even acknowledge his presence, and that as soon as there was a gap in the conversation she would introduce a topic on which he could not contribute.

When George had parked the car and George and Nancy

moved ahead towards the boardwalk that led over the sand dunes to the beach, Jim Farrell spoke to her very quietly, asking her how her mother was, saying that he and his mother and father had been to Rose's funeral mass. His mother, he said, had been very fond of her in the golf club. "All in all," he said, "it was the saddest thing that has happened in the town for a long time."

She nodded. If he wanted her to think well of him, she thought, then she should let him know as soon as possible that she had no intention of doing so, but this was hardly the moment.

"It must be difficult being home," he said. "Although it must be nice for your mother."

She turned and smiled sadly at him. They did not speak again until they reached the strand and caught up with George and Nancy.

Jim, it turned out, had not brought a towel or his togs and said that the water was, in any case, probably too cold. Eilis looked at Nancy and then shot a withering glance at Jim for Nancy to witness. As Jim removed his shoes and socks and rolled up the bottoms of his trousers and went down to the water, the other three began to change. If this had been years ago, Eilis thought, she would have worried during the entire journey from Enniscorthy about her swimsuit and its style, about whether she was too unshapely or awkward on the beach, or what George and Jim would think of her. But now, however, that she was still suntanned from the boat and from her trips to Coney Island with Tony, she felt oddly confident as she walked down the strand, passing Jim Farrell paddling at the edge of the water without saying a word to him, wading out and then, as the first high wave approached, swimming into it as it broke and then out beyond it.

She knew he was watching her and the idea that she should really have splashed him as she passed him made her smile. For a second it came into her mind as something she could tell Rose and that Rose would love, but then she realized with a sense of regret close to an actual pain that Rose was dead and there were things like this, ordinary things, that she would never know, that would not matter to her now.

Later, Nancy and George walked together towards Ballyconnigar, leaving Eilis and Jim to follow. Jim began to ask her questions about America. He said he had two uncles in New York and he used to imagine them among the skyscrapers of Manhattan until he found out that they were two hundred miles from New York City. It was in New York State, he said, and the village one of them was in was smaller than Bunclody. When she told him that a priest, who had been a friend of her sister, had encouraged her to go and helped her there, he asked her the name of the priest. When she said Father Flood, she was taken aback for a moment when Jim Farrell said that his parents knew him well; his father, he thought, had been in St. Peter's College with him.

Later, they drove to Wexford and had their tea in the Talbot Hotel, where the wedding party was going to be held. When they got back to Enniscorthy, Jim invited them to have a drink in his father's pub before going home. His mother, who was serving behind the bar, knew all about their outing and greeted Eilis with an effusive warmth that Eilis found almost unsettling. Before they parted, they agreed that they would repeat the outing the following Sunday. George mentioned the possibility of going from Curracloe to the dance in Courtown.

Eilis had no key to the front door of the house in Friary Street so she had to knock; she hoped that her mother was not asleep. She could hear her coming slowly to answer the door and thought she must have been in the kitchen. Her mother spent some time opening locks and pulling back bolts.

"Well, here you are," her mother said, and smiled. "I'll have to get you a key."

"I hope I didn't wake you."

"No, when I saw you going off I thought to myself that you'd be back late, but it isn't that late because there's still a bit of light in the sky."

Her mother closed the door and led her towards the kitchen.

"Now, tell me something," she said, "did you have a great outing?"

"It was nice, Mammy, and we went to Wexford for our tea."

"And I hope that Jim Farrell wasn't too ignorant?"

"He was fine. Minding his manners."

"Well, the big news is that Davis's offices sent up for you and they have a crisis because all the lorry drivers have to be paid tomorrow and so do all the men working in the mill and one girl is on her holidays and Alice Roche is sick and they were at their wits' end when someone thought of you. And they want you to be there at half past nine in the morning, and I said you would be. It was better to say yes than no."

"How did they know I was here?"

"Sure the whole town knows you're here. So I'll have your breakfast on the table at half past eight and you'd better wear sensible clothes. Nothing too American now."

Her mother had a smile of satisfaction on her face and this came as a relief to Eilis, who had, over the previous days, begun to dread the silences between them and resent her mother's lack of interest in discussing anything, any single detail, about her time in America. They spoke now in the kitchen about Nancy and George and the wedding and arranged to go to Dublin the following Tuesday to buy an outfit for the day. They discussed what they should buy Nancy as a wedding present.

When Eilis went upstairs she felt, for the first time, less uneasy about being home and found that she was almost looking forward to the day dealing with wages at Davis's and then the weekend. As she was undressing, however, she noticed a letter on the bed and instantly saw that it was from Tony, who had put his name and address on the envelope. Her mother must have left it there, having decided not to mention it. She opened it with a feeling close to alarm, wondering for a second if there was anything wrong with him, relieved when she read the opening sentences that declared his love for her and emphasized how much he missed her.

As she read the letter she wished that she could take it downstairs and read it to her mother. The tone was stiff, formal, old-fashioned; the letter was clearly by someone not used to writing letters. Yet Tony managed to put something of himself into it, his warmth, his kindness and his enthusiasm for things. And there was also something there all the time in him, she thought, that was in this letter too. It was a feeling that were he to turn his head, she might be gone. That afternoon, as she had enjoyed the sea and warm weather and the company of Nancy and George and even, towards the end, Jim, she had been away from Tony, far away, basking in the ease of what had suddenly become familiarity.

She wished now that she had not married him, not because she did not love him and intend to return to him, but because not telling her mother or her friends made every day she had spent in America a sort of fantasy, something she could not match with the time she was spending at home. It made her feel strangely as though she were two people, one who had battled against two cold winters and many hard days in Brooklyn and fallen in love there, and the other who was her mother's daughter, the Eilis whom everyone knew, or thought they knew.

She wished she could go downstairs now and tell her mother what she had done, but she knew she would not. It would be simpler to claim that work called her back to Brooklyn and write then, when she had returned, to say that she was seeing a man whom she loved and hoped to get engaged to and married to. She would only be home for less than two more weeks. As she lay in bed she thought it would be wise to make the best of it, take no big decisions in what would be an interlude. A chance to be at home like this would be unlikely to come her way again ever. In the morning, she thought, she would get up early and write to Tony and post the letter on her way to work.

In the morning it was hard not to think that she was Rose's ghost, being fed and spoken to in the same way at the same time by her mother, having her clothes admired using the same words as were used with Rose, and then setting out briskly for work. As she took the same route Eilis had to stop herself walking with Rose's elegant, determined walk, and move more slowly.

In the office Maria Gethings, about whom Rose used to talk, was waiting for her and brought her into the inner sanctum where the cash was kept. The problem was, Maria said, that this was the busy season and all the lorry drivers and the men working in the mill had done overtime the previous week. They had filled out their hours but no one had worked out the money they were due, which was set out on a special form and added to their usual wages, which came with another form, a wage slip. They were not even in alphabetical order, Maria said.

Eilis said that if Maria left her alone for about two hours with all the information about the rates at which overtime was paid, she would work out a system, as long as she could ask Maria questions whenever she needed. She said that she would function best on her own but she would let Maria know if she had even the smallest query. Maria said that she would close the door and leave her undisturbed in this office, mentioning on her way out that the men usually came for their wage packets at around five and the money was in cash in the safe to pay them with.

Eilis found a stapler and began to attach the overtime form for each man to his normal wage sheet. She put them in alphabetical order. When she had all of them done, she went through each overtime form, calculating from the list of rates, which varied considerably depending on years of service and levels of responsibility, how much each man was owed and then adding this to his wages on the wage sheet, so that there was a single figure for each man. She wrote this figure on a separate list, which she then had to tot up to find out how much money was needed to pay the men everything they were owed. The work was straightforward because the terms were clear, and, so long as she concentrated on making no mistakes in the addition, she thought she would be able to complete the task, provided there were enough loose notes and coins in the safe.

She took a short lunch break, insisting to Maria that she would not need any help, just a pile of envelopes and someone to open the safe and run to the bank or the post office for loose change if there was not enough. By four o'clock she had everything done and the amount of cash used up equalled the amount in her original tot. She had given each man a slip in his envelope that included details of the money due, and had also kept a copy of each for the office files.

This was the work she had been dreaming about as she had stood on the shop floor in Bartocci's, seeing the office workers walking in and out as she was telling customers that the Sepia- and Coffee-coloured stockings were for lighter skin and the Red Fox for darker, or as she had sat listening to the lectures and preparing for the exams in Brooklyn College. She knew that once she and Tony were married she would stay at home, cleaning the house and preparing food and shopping and then having children and looking after them as well. She had never mentioned to Tony that she would like to keep working, even if just part time, maybe doing the accounts from home for someone who needed a bookkeeper. In Bartocci's she did not think any of the women in the office were married. She wondered, as she came to the end of her day's work at Davis's, if maybe she could do the bookkeeping for the company that Tony was going to set up with his brothers. As she thought about this, she realized that she had forgotten to write to him that morning and resolved that she would make time that evening and write to him then.

On Sunday, just after lunch, with the weather still warm, George and Nancy and Jim pulled up in front of her house on Friary Street. Jim held the back door of the car open for her while she got in. He had a white shirt on with the sleeves rolled up; she noticed the black hair on his arms and the whiteness of his skin. He was wearing hair oil; she thought that he had made a real effort in how he dressed. As they left the town, he spoke to her quietly about how the pub had been the previous night and how lucky he was that, even though his parents had made it over to him, they were still willing to work there when he wanted to go out.

George said that Curracloe might be too crowded and he thought they should go to Cush Gap instead and make their way down the cliff. This was where Eilis had come with Rose and her brothers and her parents when they were children, but she had not been there for years nor thought about it. As they drove through Blackwater village she almost pointed out the places she knew, such as Mrs. Davis's pub where her father had gone in the evenings, or Jim O'Neill's shop. But she stopped herself. She did not want to sound like someone who had come back home after a long time away. And, she thought, this was something that she might never see again on a summer Sunday like this, but for the others it was nothing, just a decision George had made to go to a quieter place.

She was sure that if she began to talk about her memories of this place, they would notice the difference. Instead, she took in each building as they drove up the hill before the turn to Ballyconnigar, remembering things that had happened, small outings to the village with Jack, or a day when their cousins the Doyles had come to visit. This made her silent and made her feel withdrawn from the ease and the quiet sense of comfort and cheer in the car as it turned left and made its way along the narrow sandy lane to Cush.

Once they had parked the car, George and Nancy walked ahead towards the cliff, leaving Jim and Eilis walking behind. Jim was carrying his own togs and towel as well as her bag with her swimsuit and towel. When they came halfway down the lane, they stopped for a moment at Cullens' house, in front of which Jim's old teacher Mr. Redmond was sitting wearing a straw hat. He was clearly on his holidays.

"This might be the only summer we'll get, sir," Jim said.

"Best take full advantage of it so," Mr. Redmond replied. Eilis noticed that his speech was slurred.

As they moved on, Jim said in a low voice that Mr. Redmond was the only teacher he had ever liked and it was a pity he had had the stroke.

"Where's his son?" Eilis asked.

"Eamon? He's studying, I'd say. That's what he usually does."

When they came to the bottom of the lane and peered over the edge of the cliff, they saw that the sea below them was calm, almost smooth. The sand close to the water's edge was a dark yellow. There was a line of sea birds flying low over the waves, which seemed barely to swell before they broke quietly, almost noiselessly. There was a vague mist that masked the line between the horizon and the sky but otherwise the sky was a pure blue.

George had to run down the last stretch of sand at the gap in the cliff; he waited for Nancy to follow and held her in his arms. Jim did the same, and Eilis found that, when he caught her, he held her in an embrace that was almost too close and he did this as though it was something they were used to doing. She shivered for a second at the thought of Tony seeing her now.

They spread two rugs out on the sand as Jim took off his shoes and socks and went down to test the water, returning to say that it was almost warm, much better than the previous day, and he was going to change and go in for a swim. George said he would go with him. The last to get down in the water, they agreed, would have to buy dinner. Nancy and Eilis put on their swimsuits but stayed sitting on the rugs.

"They're like a pair of children sometimes," Nancy said as they watched George and Jim involved in horseplay in the sea. "If they had a ball, they'd spend an hour playing with it."

"Whatever happened to Annette?" Eilis asked.

"I knew you wouldn't come on Thursday if I told you Jim was coming, and I knew you wouldn't come with just me and George, so I told you Annette was coming; it was a white lie," Nancy said.

"And whatever happened to Jim's manners?"

"He's only bad-mannered when he's nervous," Nancy said. "He doesn't mean it. He's a big softie. Also, he likes you."

"When did that start?"

"When he saw you at eleven o'clock mass with your mother last Sunday."

"Will you do me a favour, Nancy?"

"What is it?"

"Will you run down to the sea and tell Jim to go and take a running jump at himself? Or, better still, go down and tell him that you know someone who lives beside a marl pond, and ask him why he doesn't drop in sometime."

They both fell over laughing on the rug.

"Have you everything ready for the wedding?" Eilis asked. She wanted to hear no more about Jim Farrell.

"Everything except my future mother-in-law, who makes a new statement every day about something she wants or doesn't want. My mother thinks she's an awful old snob."

"Well, she is, isn't she?"

"I'll knock that out of her," Nancy said, "but I'll wait until after the wedding."

When George and Jim returned, all four of them set out walking along the strand, the two men running at first to dry themselves. Eilis was amused at how tight and flimsy their swimming togs were. No American man would be seen on a beach in anything like that, she thought. Nor would two men in Coney Island move as unself-consciously as these two did, seeming not to be alert at all to the two women watching them as they ran awkwardly ahead, keeping close to the hard sand at the water's edge.

No one else was on this stretch of strand. Eilis understood now why George had chosen this lonely place. He and Jim, and perhaps Nancy too, had planned a perfect day in which she and Jim would be just as much a couple as Nancy and George. She realized, as they turned back and Jim began talking to her again, letting the other two go ahead, that she liked his bulky, easygoing presence and the tone in his voice, which came so naturally from the streets of the town. He had clear blue eyes, she thought, that saw no harm in anything. And she was fully aware that these blue eyes of his lingered on her now with an interest that was unmistakable.

She smiled at the thought that she would go along with most of it. She was on her holidays and it was harmless, but she would not go into the sea with him as though she were his girlfriend. She would, she reasoned, like to be able to face Tony knowing that she had not done that. She and Jim stood and watched George and Nancy playing in the shallow water and moving together towards the waves. When Jim suggested that they follow, she shook her head and walked on ahead of him. She wondered for a second, as he caught up with her, how she would feel if she learned that Tony had gone to Coney Island on a day like today with a friend and two young women, one of whom he spent time alone with walking by the sea. It was impossible, she thought, something he would never do. And he would suffer at even the slightest hint of what she was doing now as they arrived back at where they had left their belongings and Jim smoothed out the rug for her and, still wearing only his togs, smiled and settled himself down beside her under the warm sun.

"My father says that this part of the coast is being badly eroded," he said as though they were in the middle of a conversation.

"We used to stay here years ago for a week or two in the hut that Michael Webster and Nora bought. I can't remember who owned it when we rented it. You would notice the change every summer when you came down," she said.

"My father says that he remembers your father here years ago."

"They all used to come on bicycles from the town."

"Are there beaches near Brooklyn?"

"Oh, yes," she said, "and in the summer they're always crowded at the weekend."

"I'd say you'd get every type of person there," he said as though he approved of the idea.

"Every type," she said.

They did not speak for a while as Eilis sat up and watched Nancy floating on the water with George swimming close to her. Jim sat up and watched them too.

Quietly, he spoke: "Will we go and try the water?"

Eilis was waiting for this and had already planned to say no. If he had insisted too much she had even planned to say that she had someone special in Brooklyn, a man to whom she would be returning soon. But his tone, when he spoke, was unexpected in its humility. Jim spoke like someone who could be easily hurt. She wondered if it was an act, but he was looking at her with an expression so vulnerable that she, for a second, could not make her mind up what to do. She realized that, if she refused, he might walk alone down to the water like someone defeated; somehow she did not want to have to witness that.

"Okay," she said.

For a second as they waded into the water he caught her hand. But as a wave approached she moved away from him and without hesitating any further swam directly out. She did not turn to see if he was following her but kept swimming, alert to where Nancy and George were kissing and holding each other in a firm embrace and trying to avoid them as much as Jim Farrell.

She appreciated how Jim, despite being a strong swimmer himself, did not seek to follow her at first; instead he did a back-stroke parallel to the beach and left her alone. She was enjoying the water, having forgotten its purity and calmness. And as she wallowed there, staring at the blue sky, kicking her feet to keep herself afloat, Jim approached her but was careful not to touch her or come too close. When he caught her eye, he smiled. Everything he did now, every word he said and every move he made, seemed deliberate, restrained and well thought out, done so as not to irritate her or appear to be moving too fast. And almost as an aspect of this care, he made his interest in her totally clear.

She understood that she should not have let things move so quickly, that she should have told Nancy after their first outing that her duty lay in being at home with her mother, or accompanying her mother on outings, and that she could not go out again with Nancy and George and Jim Farrell. She thought for a second of confiding in Nancy, not telling her the whole truth but telling her that she would soon be engaged when she returned to Brooklyn. But she realized that it was best to do nothing. She would, in any case, be going back soon.

When she got out of the water with Jim, George had a camera ready. As Nancy watched, Jim stood behind Eilis with his arms around her; she could feel the heat from him, his torso pressing against her as George took several more pictures of them before Jim took shots of George and Nancy in the same pose. Soon, as they saw a lone walker coming north from Keating's, they waited and George, having shown the outsider how the camera worked, asked him to take shots of all four of them. Jim moved as though casually, but nothing he did was casual, Eilis thought, as she felt the weight of his body once more behind her. He was careful, however, not to move as close to her as George moved to Nancy. Not once did she feel his crotch pushing against her. It would be too much and she believed he had decided not to risk it. When the photographs were taken she went back to the rug and changed and lay in the sunshine until the others were ready to go.

On the way back to Enniscorthy it was decided that they would have tea in the grill of the Courtown Hotel, which George thought was open until nine, and they would go to the dance afterwards. George teased Nancy about how long she would take to get ready, Nancy insisting that both she and Eilis would have to wash their hair after the sea water.

"Quick wash, then," George said.

"It can't be quick," Nancy replied.

Jim looked at Eilis and smiled. "God, they're not even married yet and they are bickering."

"It's for a good cause," Nancy said.

"She's right," Eilis said.

Jim reached over affectionately and squeezed her hand. "I'm sure you're both right," he said with enough sarcasm and self-mockery to prevent himself sounding as though he were trying to win favour with her.

They agreed to be ready by seven thirty. Eilis's mother went through all her dresses and shoes while she washed her hair. She had the iron and the ironing board prepared in case there were creases in the dress they chose. When Eilis appeared with a towel over her head, she saw that her mother had selected a blue dress with a floral pattern, one that was Tony's favourite, and a pair of blue shoes. Eilis was almost going to tell her that she could not wear this, but she realized that any explanation she invented would cause unnecessary tension so she went ahead and put it on.

Her mother, who seemed not to resent being left alone for the rest of the evening but rather excited by Eilis's dressing up to go out again, set about ironing it while Eilis put curlers in her hair, and turned on the electric drier that had belonged to Rose.

George and Jim both knew the owner of the Courtown Hotel from rugby and they had arranged a special table with candles and wine and a special menu with champagne afterwards. Eilis observed other diners glancing over at them as though they were the most important people in the restaurant. George and Jim were both wearing sports jackets and ties and flannel trousers. As Eilis watched Nancy perusing the menu and ordering her food, she noticed something new about her: she was more refined than before, taking the solemnity of the waiter's manners seriously, whereas a few years earlier she would have raised her eyes to heaven at his pomposity, or said something casual and friendly to him. Soon, Eilis thought, she would be Mrs. George Sheridan and that would count for something in the town. She was beginning to play the role with relish.

Later in the bar of the hotel George and Jim and the owner of the hotel looked handsome and smooth as they spoke about the rugby season that had ended. It was strange, Eilis thought, that George and Jim were not in Courtown with the sisters of their friends. Everyone in the town, she knew, had been surprised when George began going out with Nancy, whose brothers would never have played rugby in their lives, and presumed it was because Nancy was so good-looking and had such good manners. And two years ago, Eilis remembered, when Jim Farrell had been openly rude to her, she thought it was because she came from a family that did not own anything in the town. Now that she was back from America, she believed, she carried something with her, something close to glamour, which made all the difference to her as she sat with Nancy watching the men talk.

She did not expect to see so many people from Enniscorthy in the dancehall. Many of the dancers seemed to know that Nancy and George were soon to be married and they were congratulated as they moved around the hall. Jim, Eilis noticed, had a way of nodding at people, acknowledging simply that he recognized them. It was not unfriendly, nor was it an invitation to approach him. He seemed to her more severe than George, who was all smiles, and she wondered if that came from running a pub, knowing who many people were and managing at the same time to stand apart from them.

She danced with Jim all night except when George and Jim switched partners and then only briefly. She knew that she was being watched and commented on by people from the town, especially when the tempo of the music was fast and it was clear that she and Jim were good dancers, but also later, when the lights went down and the music was slow and they danced close to each other.

Outside, when the dance was over, the night was still warm. Jim and she let George and Nancy walk ahead of them towards the car and told them they would join them soon. All day Jim had behaved impeccably: he had not bored or irritated her, or pressed himself too much on her; he seemed immensely considerate, funny at times, willing to be silent, polite as well. He also stood out in the dancehall, where some were drunk or others were too old or looked as though they had travelled to Courtown on tractors. He was handsome, graceful, smart, and, as the night wore on, she was proud to be with him. Now, they found a space in between a guest house and a new bungalow and began to kiss. Jim moved slowly; at intervals he held her head in his hands so that he could look at her eyes in the semi-darkness and kiss her passionately. The feel of his tongue in her mouth made her respond to him with ease at first and then with something close to real excitement.

In the car on the way back to Enniscorthy, as they sat together in the back seat, they tried to disguise what they were doing but eventually gave up, causing much laughter on the part of Nancy and George.

On Monday morning, when there was a message for Eilis to come down to Davis's, she presumed that it meant they wanted to pay her. When she turned up, she found Maria Gethings waiting for her once more.

"Mr. Brown wants to see you," Maria said. "I'll check if he has anyone with him now."

Mr. Brown had been Rose's boss and was one of the owners of the mill. Eilis knew he came from Scotland and had often seen him driving in a very large and shiny car. She had noticed the awe in Maria's voice when she mentioned his name. After a short time, Maria returned and said that he would see Eilis immediately. She ushered Eilis down a corridor and into a room at the end. Mr. Brown was sitting in a high leather chair behind a long desk.

"Miss Lacey," he said, standing up and leaning across the desk to shake Eilis's hand. "I wrote to your mother when poor Rose died and we were very cut up and I wondered if I should have called as well. And I am told you are home from America and Maria tells me that you have a certificate in bookkeeping. Is it American bookkeeping?"

Eilis explained that she did not think there was any great difference between the two systems.

"I don't suppose there is," Mr. Brown said. "Anyway, Maria was very happy with how you did the wages last week, but we were not surprised, of course, you being Rose's sister. Rose was the essence of efficiency and is much missed."

"Rose was a great example to me," Eilis said.

"Until the busy season is over," Mr. Brown went on, "it will be hard for us to know how we are fixed in the office, but we may certainly need a bookkeeper and someone familiar with how the wages are paid in the long term. But we would like you to continue with the wages on a part-time basis and then we can speak to you in a while."

"I will be going back to the United States," Eilis said.

"Well, yes, of course," Mr. Brown said. "But you and I will speak again before you make any firm decisions."

Eilis was about to say that she had already made a firm decision, but since Mr. Brown's tone suggested that he did not need just now to have any further discussion on the matter, she realized that she was not expected to reply. Instead, she stood up, and Mr. Brown did too, accompanying her to the door and sending his regards to her mother before he saw her out to the care of Maria Gethings, who had an envelope for her ready with cash inside.

That evening Eilis had promised to go to Nancy's house to look at the list of people invited to the wedding breakfast and work out with her where they should be seated. She recounted her interview with Mr. Brown with puzzlement.

"Two years ago," she said, "he wouldn't even see me. I know that Rose asked him if there was any possibility of a job for me and he just said no. Just no."

"Well, things have changed."

"And two years ago Jim Farrell seemed to think it was his duty to ignore me in the Athenaeum even though George had practically asked him to dance with me."

"You have changed," Nancy said. "You look different. Everything about you is different, not for those who know you, but for people in the town who only know you to see."

"What's changed?"

"You seem more grown up and serious. And in your American clothes you look different. You have an air about you. Jim can't stop trying to get us to find more excuses to go out together."

Later, as Eilis had a cup of tea with her mother before they went to bed, her mother reminded her that she knew the Farrells, although she had not been in the house, which was over the pub, for years.

"You don't notice it much from outside," she said, "but it is one of the nicest houses in the town. The two rooms upstairs have double doors between them and I remember even years ago people used to comment on how large it was. And I hear that the parents are moving out to Glenbrien where she's from, to a house that her aunt left her. The father loves horses, he's a great man for the races, and he is going to have horses out there, or so I heard. And Jim is getting the whole place."

"He'll miss them so," Eilis said. "Because they run the pub when he wants to go out."

"Oh, it'll be all very gradual, I'd say," her mother replied.

Upstairs on the bed Eilis found two letters from Tony and she realized, almost with a start, that she had not written to him as she had intended. She looked at the two envelopes, at his handwriting, and she stood in the room with the door closed wondering how strange it was that everything about him seemed remote. And not only that, but everything else that had happened in Brooklyn seemed as though it had almost dissolved and was no longer richly present for her—her room in Mrs. Kehoe's, for example, or her exams, or the trolley-car from Brooklyn College back home, or the dancehall, or the apartment where Tony lived with his parents and his three brothers, or the shop floor at Bartocci's. She went through all of it as though she were trying to recover what had seemed so filled with detail, so solid, just a few weeks before.

She put the letters on the chest of drawers and decided that she would reply when she returned from Dublin the following evening. She would tell Tony about all the preparations for Nancy's wedding, the outfits that she and her mother had bought. She might even tell him about her interview with Mr. Brown and how she had informed him that she would be returning to Brooklyn. She would write as though she had not yet received these two letters and she would not open them now, she thought, but wait until she had written her own letter.

The idea that she would leave all of this—the rooms of the house once more familiar and warm and comforting—and go back to Brooklyn and not return for a long time again frightened her now. She knew as she sat on the edge of the bed and took her shoes off and then lay back with her arms behind her head that she had spent every day putting off all thought of her departure and what she would meet on her arrival.

Sometimes it came as sharp reminder, but much of the time it did not come at all. She had to make an effort now to remember that she really was married to Tony, that she would face into the sweltering heat of Brooklyn and the daily boredom of the shop floor at Bartocci's and her room at Mrs. Kehoe's. She would face into a life that seemed now an ordeal, with strange people, strange accents, strange streets. She tried to think of Tony now as a loving and comforting presence, but she saw instead someone she was allied with whether she liked it or not, someone who was, she thought, unlikely to allow her to forget the nature of the alliance and his need for her to return.

A few days before the wedding, when Eilis had been working a half-day at Davis's office and Jim Farrell had collected her there and they had gone for a meal in Wexford and then to the pictures and were now on the way home, he asked her when she planned to go back to Brooklyn. She had received a letter from the shipping company suggesting that she contact them by telephone when she wished to arrange her return passage, but she had not been in touch with them.

"I still have to phone the shipping company, but it will probably be the week after next."

"You are going to be missed here," he said.

"It's very hard leaving my mother on her own," she replied.

He said nothing for a while until they were passing through Oylegate.

"My parents are going to move out to the country soon. My mother's people came from Glenbrien and her aunt left her a place out there and they're doing work on it at the moment."

Eilis did not say that her mother had already told her this. She did not want Jim to know that they were discussing his living arrangements.

"So I'll be on my own in the house over the pub."

She was going to ask him in jest if he could cook but realized that it might sound like a leading question.

"You must come for your tea some evening," he said. "My parents would love to meet you."

"Thank you," she said.

"We'll arrange it after the wedding."

It was decided that Jim would drive Eilis and her mother and Annette O'Brien and her younger sister Carmel to the wedding reception in Wexford after the ceremony in Enniscorthy Cathedral. That morning they were awake early in Friary Street, her mother coming into her bedroom with a cup of tea, telling her that it was a cloudy day and she was hoping now that the rain would keep off. The night before, both of them had left their clothes out carefully for the morning. Eilis's costume, which she had bought in Arnotts in Dublin, had had to be altered, as the skirt and the sleeves were too long. It was bright red and with it she was wearing a white cotton blouse with accessories she had brought from America— stockings with a tinge of red, red shoes, a red hat and a white handbag. Her mother was going to wear a grey tweed suit that she had bought in Switzers. She was sad that she had to wear plain flat shoes, as her feet hurt her now and swelled up if there was any heat or if she had to walk too far. She was going to wear a grey silk blouse that had belonged to Rose not only, she said, because she liked it but because Rose had loved it and it would be nice at Nancy's wedding to wear something that Rose had loved.

It had been arranged that if it were raining Jim would collect them and drive them to the cathedral but if it were fine he would meet them there. Eilis had written several letters to Tony and had opened one that had told her about a trip to Long Island with Maurice and Laurence to look at the site they had bought and to divide it into five plots. There were strong rumours now, he said, that services like water and electricity would soon be coming very cheaply in their direction. Eilis folded this letter and put it in the drawer with Tony's other letters and the photographs from the day at the strand in Cush, which Nancy had given her. She stood now looking at the picture of herself and Jim, how happy they seemed: he with his arms around her neck, grinning at the camera, and she leaning her head back, smiling as though she had not a care in the world. She did not know what she was going to do with these photographs.

As her mother watched the weather, Eilis knew she was hoping for rain, that it would please her more than anything for Jim Farrell to come in his car to collect her and Eilis and take them the short distance to the cathedral. It was one of those days when the neighbours, because of the wedding, would feel free to come openly to their doors to inspect Eilis and her mother in all their style and wish them a nice day out. And there would be neighbours, Eilis thought, who already were aware that she had been seeing Jim Farrell and would view him in the same way as her mother did, as a great catch, a young man in the town with his own business. Being collected by Jim Farrell, she thought, would be for her mother the highlight of everything that had happened since Eilis came home.

When the first drops of rain hit against the glass of the window, a look of undisguised satisfaction appeared on her mother's face. "We won't risk it," she said. "I'd be afraid we'd get as far as the Market Square and then it would spill. I'd worry about the red running into that white blouse of yours."

Her mother then spent the next half-hour at the front window watching in case the rain eased off or in case Jim Farrell came early. Eilis stayed in the kitchen but she made sure she had everything ready were Jim to come. Her mother came to the kitchen at one point to say that they would usher him into the parlour, but Eilis insisted that they should both be ready to leave once Jim came in his car. Eventually, she went to the window with her mother to look out.

When Jim came, he opened the driver's door and emerged briskly with an umbrella. Both Eilis and her mother moved fussily into the hall. Her mother answered the door.

"Don't worry about the time," Jim said. "I'll drop the two of you straight in front of the cathedral and then I'll park. I think we have plenty of time."

"I was going to offer you a cup of tea," her mother said.

"No time for that, though," Jim said, and smiled. He was wearing a light suit, a blue shirt with a striped blue tie and tan-coloured shoes.

"You know I think this is just a shower," her mother said as she made her way out to the car. Eilis saw that Mags Lawton next door had appeared and was waving. She stood at the door waiting for Jim to come back with the umbrella but did not return Mags's wave or encourage her to make any comment. Just as she closed the door and went towards the car, Eilis saw two other doors opening and knew that, much to her mother's delight, news would spread that Eilis and her mother in all their style had been collected by Jim Farrell.

"Jim is a perfect gentleman," her mother said as they walked into the cathedral. Her mother, Eilis noticed, moved slowly, with an air of pride and dignity, not looking to her left or her right, fully aware that she was being watched and fully enjoying the spectacle that she and Eilis, soon to be joined by Jim Farrell, were making in the church.

This was nothing, however, to the spectacle of Nancy in a white veil and a long white dress walking slowly up the aisle with her father while George waited for her at the altar. As the mass began and the church had settled down, Eilis, with Jim beside her, found herself entertaining a thought that had come to her in the early mornings when she lay awake in her bed. She asked herself what she would do if Jim proposed marriage to her. The idea, most of the time, was absurd; they did not know one another well enough and so it was unlikely. Also, she thought that she should do everything possible not to encourage him to ask, since she would not be able to say anything in reply except refuse him.

She could not stop herself from wondering, however, what would happen if she were to write to Tony to say that their marriage was a mistake. How easy would it be to divorce someone? Could she possibly tell Jim what she had done such a short while earlier in Brooklyn? The only divorced people anyone in the town knew were Elizabeth Taylor and perhaps some other film stars. It might be possible to explain to Jim how she had come to be married, but he was someone who had never lived outside the town. His innocence and his politeness, both of which made him nice to be with, would actually be, she thought, limitations, especially if something as unheard of and out of the question, as far from his experience as divorce, were raised. The best thing to do, she thought, was to put the whole thing out of her mind, but it was hard now, as the ceremony went on, not to dream about herself being there at the altar and her brothers home for the wedding and her mother knowing that Eilis would be living in a nice house just a few streets from her.

When she came back from receiving communion, Eilis tried

to pray and found herself actually answering the question that she was about to ask in her prayers. The answer was that there was no answer, that nothing she could do would be right. She pictured Tony and Jim opposite each other, or meeting each other, each of them smiling, warm, friendly, easygoing, Jim less eager than Tony, less funny, less curious, but more self-contained and more sure of his own place in the world. And she thought of her mother now beside her in the church, the devastation and shock of Rose's death having been softened somewhat by Eilis's return. And she saw all three of them—Tony, Jim, her mother—as figures whom she could only damage, as innocent people surrounded by light and clarity, and circling around them was herself, dark, uncertain.

She would have done anything then, as Nancy and George walked down the aisle together, to join the side of sweetness, certainty and innocence, knowing she could begin her life without feeling that she had done something foolish and hurtful. No matter what she decided, she thought, there would not be a way to avoid the consequences of what she had done, or what she might do now. It occurred to her, as she walked down the aisle with Jim and her mother and joined the well-wishers outside the church, where the weather had brightened, that she was sure that she did not love Tony now. He seemed part of a dream from which she had woken with considerable force some time before, and in this waking time his presence, once so solid, lacked any substance or form; it was merely a shadow at the edge of every moment of the day and night.

As they posed for photographs outside the cathedral, the sun came out fully and many onlookers came to view the bride and bridegroom getting ready to travel to Wexford in a large hired car decorated with ribbons.

*   *   *

At the wedding breakfast, Eilis spoke to Jim Farrell on one side and on the other a brother of George's who had come home from England for the wedding. She was watched fondly and carefully by her mother. It struck her as almost funny that every time her mother put a morsel of food into her mouth she looked over to check that Eilis was still there and Jim Farrell firmly to her right and that they seemed to be having an agreeable time. George Sheridan's mother, she saw, looked like an elderly duchess who had been left with nothing except a large hat, some old jewellery and her immense dignity.

Later, after the speeches, when photographs were being taken of the bride and bridegroom, and then the bride with her family and the bridegroom with his, Eilis's mother sought her out and whispered to her that she had found a lift to Enniscorthy for herself and the two O'Brien girls. Her mother's tone was nearly too pleased and conspiratorial. Eilis realized that Jim Farrell would believe that her mother had engineered this and she realized also that there was nothing she could do to let him know that she had not been involved. As she and Jim were watching the car going off, and cheering the newly married couple, they were approached by Nancy's mother, who was in a state of happiness, aided, Eilis thought, by many glasses of sherry and some wine and champagne.

"So, Jim," she said, "I'm not the only one who says that the next outing we'll all have will be your big day. Nancy will have plenty of advice to give you when she comes home, Eilis."

She began to laugh in a cackling way that Eilis thought was unseemly. Eilis looked around to make sure that no one was paying them any attention. Jim Farrell, she saw, was staring coldly at Mrs. Byrne.

"Little did we think," Mrs. Byrne went on, "that we'd have Nancy in Sheridan's, and I hear the Farrells are moving out to Glenbrien, Eilis."

The expression on Mrs. Byrne's face was one of sweet insinuation; Eilis wondered if she might make an excuse and simply run towards the ladies' so that she would not have to listen to her any more. But then, she thought, she would be leaving Jim on his own with her.

"Jim and I promised my mother we'd make sure she knows where the car is," Eilis said quickly, pulling Jim by the sleeve of his jacket towards her.

"Oh, Jim and I!" exclaimed Mrs. Byrne, who sounded like a woman from the outskirts of the town making her way home on a Saturday night. "Do you hear her? Jim and I! Oh, it won't be long now and we'll all have a great day out and your mother'll be delighted, Eilis. When she came down with the wedding present the other day she told us she'd be delighted and why wouldn't she be delighted?"

"We have to go, Mrs. Byrne," Eilis said. "Can you excuse us?"

As they walked away Eilis turned towards Jim and narrowed her eyes and shook her head. "Imagine having her as a mother-in-law!" she said.

It was, she thought, merely a small act of disloyalty, but it would prevent Jim from thinking that she had anything to do with Mrs. Byrne in her present state.

Jim managed a wintry smile. "Can we go?" he asked.

"Yes," she said, "my mother knows exactly where the lift to Enniscorthy is. There is no need for us to stay here any longer." She tried to sound imperious and in control.

They drove out of the car park of the Talbot Hotel and along the quays and then crossed the bridge. Eilis decided that she would put no further thought into what her mother might have said to Mrs. Byrne or, indeed, what Mrs. Byrne herself had said. And if Jim wanted to, and if it helped to explain his silence and the rigid set of his jaw, then he could do so all he pleased. She was determined not to speak until he did and not to do anything to distract him or cheer him up.

As they turned towards Curracloe, he finally spoke. "My mother asked me to let you know that the golf club is going to inaugurate a prize in memory of Rose. It will be given by the lady captain as a special trophy on Lady Captain's Day for the best score by a lady newcomer to the club. Rose, she says, was always really nice to people who were new to the town."

"Yes," Eilis said, "she was always good with new people, that's true."

"Well, they're having a reception to announce the prize next week and my mother thought that you could come to tea with us and then we'd go out to the golf club for the reception."

"That would be very nice," Eilis said. She was about to say that her mother would be pleased when she told her the news but she thought that they had heard enough about her mother for one day.

He parked the car and they walked down towards the strand. Although it was still warm, there was a strong haze, almost a mist, over the sea. They began to walk north towards Ballyconnigar. She felt relaxed with Jim now that they were away from the wedding and happy that he had not mentioned what Mrs. Byrne had said and did not seem to be thinking about it.

Once they had passed Ballyvaloo, they found a place in the dunes where they could sit comfortably. Jim sat down first and then made space for her so that she was resting against him with her back to him. He put his arms around her.

There was no one else on the strand. They looked at the waves crashing gently on the soft sand, remaining for some time without speaking.

"Did you enjoy the wedding?" he asked eventually.

"Yes, I did," she replied.

"So did I," he said. "It's always funny for me seeing everyone's brothers and sisters because I'm an only child. I think it must have been hard for you losing your sister. Today, watching George with his brothers and Nancy with her sisters made me feel strange."

"Was it difficult being an only child?"

"It matters more now, I think," Jim said, "when my parents are getting older and there's just me. But maybe it mattered in other ways. I was never really good at getting on with people. I could talk to customers in the pub and all that, I knew how to do that. But I mean friends. I was never good at making friends. I always felt that people didn't like me, or didn't know what to make of me."

"But surely you have a lot of friends."

"Not really," he said, "and then it was harder when they started having girlfriends. I always found it difficult to talk to girls. Do you remember that night when I met you first?"

"You mean in the Athenaeum."

"Yes," he said. "On the way into the hall that night Alison Prendergast, who I was sort of going out with, broke it off with me. I knew it was coming but she actually did it on the way into the dance. And then George, I knew, really fancied Nancy and she was there. So he could be with her. And then he brought you over and I had seen you in the town and I liked you and you were on your own and you were so nice and friendly. I thought—here we go again. If I ask her to dance I'll be tongue-tied, but I still thought I should. I hated standing there on my own, but I couldn't bring myself to ask you."

"You should have," she said.

"And then when I heard you were gone I thought it was just my luck."

"I remember you that night," she said. "I had the impression you didn't like us, both me and Nancy."

"And then when I heard you were home," he said as though he had not been listening, "and I saw you and you looked so fantastic and I was so down after the whole episode with Nancy's sister, I thought that I'd do anything to meet you again."

He pulled her closer to him and put his hands on her breasts. She could hear him breathing heavily.

"Can we talk about what you are going to do?" he asked.

"Of course," she replied.

"I mean if you have to go back, then maybe we could get engaged before you go."

"Maybe we can talk about it soon," she said.

"I mean, if I lost you this time, well, I don't know how to put it, but . . ."

She turned around towards him and they began to kiss and they stayed there until the mist became heavier and the first hints of the night coming down, then they walked back towards the car and drove to Enniscorthy.

A few days later a note came from Jim's mother formally inviting Eilis to tea the following Thursday and telling her about the reception in the golf club to honour Rose, which they could attend afterwards. Eilis showed the letter to her mother and asked her if she would like to go to the reception as well, but her mother said no, it would be too sad for her, and she was happy for Eilis to go with the Farrells and thus represent the family.

It rained all the following weekend. Jim called on the Saturday and they went to Rosslare and had dinner in the evening in the Strand Hotel. As they were lingering over the dessert, she was tempted to tell him everything, to ask him for his help, even his advice. He was, she thought, good, and he was also wise and clever in certain ways, but he was conservative. He liked his position in the town, and it mattered to him that he ran a respectable pub and came from a respectable family. He had never done anything unusual in his life, and, she thought, he never would. His version of himself and the world did not include the possibility of spending time with a married woman and, even worse, a woman who had not told him or anybody else that she was married.

She looked at his kind face in the soft light of the hotel restaurant and decided that she would tell him nothing now. They drove to Enniscorthy. At home as she looked at the letters from Tony stored in the chest of drawers in her bedroom, some of them still unopened, she realized that there would never be a time to tell him. It could not be said; his response to her deception could not be imagined. She would have to go back.

Once the event in the golf club was over, she decided, she would pick a date. For some time now, she had postponed writing to Father Flood, or Miss Fortini, or Mrs. Kehoe, explaining her extended absence. She would write, she determined, over the next few days. She would try not to postpone any further what she had to do. But the prospect of telling her mother the date of her departure and the prospect of saying goodbye to Jim Farrell still filled her with fear, enough for her once more to put both ideas out of her mind. She would think about them soon, she thought, but not now.

On the day before the event at the golf club she had gone alone in the early afternoon to the graveyard to visit Rose's grave again. It had been drizzling and she carried an umbrella. Once she arrived in the graveyard, she noticed that the wind was almost cold, even though it was early July. In this grey, blustery light the graveyard where Rose lay seemed a bare and forlorn place, no trees, nothing much growing, just rows of headstones and paths and underneath all the silence of the dead. Eilis saw names on headstones that she recognized, the parents or grandparents of her friends from school, men and women whom she remembered well, all gone now, held here on the edge of the town. For the moment, most of them were remembered by the living, but it was a memory slowly fading as each season passed.

She stood at Rose's grave and tried to pray or whisper something. She felt sad, she thought, and maybe that was enough—to come here and let Rose's spirit know how much she was missed. But she could not cry or say anything. She stood at the grave for as long as she could and then walked away, feeling the sharpest grief as she was actually leaving the graveyard itself and walking towards Summerhill and the Presentation Convent.

When she reached the corner of Main Street, she decided that she would walk through the town rather than go along the Back Road. Seeing faces, people moving, shops doing business, she thought, might cure her of the gnawing sadness, almost guilt, that she felt about Rose, about not being able to speak properly to her or pray for her.

She passed the cathedral on the opposite side and was making her way towards the Market Square when she heard someone calling her name. When she looked, she saw that Mary, who worked for Miss Kelly, was shouting at her and beckoning to her to cross the road.

"Is there something wrong?" Eilis asked.

"Miss Kelly wants to see you," Mary said. She was almost out of breath and looked frightened. "She says I'm to make sure and bring you back with me now."

"Now?" Eilis asked, laughing.

"Now," Mary repeated.

Miss Kelly was waiting at the door.

"Mary," she said, "we are going upstairs for a minute and if anyone is looking for me, then tell them I'll be down in my own good time."

"Yes, miss."

Miss Kelly opened the entrance to the part of the building

where she lived and ushered Eilis in. As Eilis closed the door
behind her, Miss Kelly led her up a dark stairway to the living
room, which looked onto the street but seemed almost as dark as
the stairwell and had, Eilis thought, too much furniture in it.
Miss Kelly pointed to a chair covered in newspapers.

"Put those on the floor and sit down," she said.

Miss Kelly sat opposite her on a faded-looking leather armchair.

"So how are you getting on?" she asked.

"Very well, thanks, Miss Kelly."

"So I hear. And I was just thinking about you yesterday and
wondering if I would ever see you because I heard from Madge
Kehoe in America just yesterday."

"Madge Kehoe?" Eilis asked.

"She'd be Mrs. Kehoe to you but she's a cousin of mine. She
was, before she married, a Considine, and my mother, God rest
her, was a Considine, and so we are first cousins."

"She never mentioned that," Eilis said.

"Oh, the Considines were always very close," Miss Kelly said.
"My mother was the same."

Miss Kelly's tone was almost skittish; it was, Eilis thought, as
though she were doing an imitation of herself. Eilis asked herself
if it could possibly be true that Miss Kelly was a cousin of Mrs.
Kehoe.

"Is that right?" Eilis asked coldly.

"And of course she told me all about you when you arrived
first. But then there was no news here and Madge has a policy that
she only keeps in touch with you if you keep in touch with her. So
what I do is I telephone her about twice a year. I never stay long
on the line because of the cost. But it keeps her happy, especially
if there is news. And then when you came home, well, that was
news and I heard you were never out of Curracloe, and in Courtown with your finery, and then a little bird who happens to be a

customer of mine told me that he took a photograph of you all in Cush Gap. He said you made a lovely group."

Miss Kelly seemed to be enjoying herself; Eilis could think of no way of stopping her.

"And so I telephoned Madge with all the news, and about you paying out the wages down in Davis's."

"Did you, Miss Kelly?"

It was clear to Eilis that Miss Kelly had prepared every word of what she was saying. The idea that the man who had taken the photograph in Cush, a figure Eilis barely remembered and had never seen before, had been in Miss Kelly's shop talking about her and that this news was conveyed to Mrs. Kehoe in Brooklyn suddenly made her afraid.

"And once she had news of her own, then she telephoned back," Miss Kelly said. "So, now."

"And what did she say, Miss Kelly?"

"Oh, I think you know what she said."

"Was it interesting?"

In her tone, Eilis tried to equal Miss Kelly's air of disdain.

"Oh, don't try and fool me!" Miss Kelly said. "You can fool most people, but you can't fool me."

"I am sure I would not like to fool anyone," Eilis said.

"Is that right, Miss Lacey? If that's what your name is now."

"What do you mean?"

"She told me the whole thing. The world, as the man says, is a very small place."

Eilis knew from the gloating expression on Miss Kelly's face that she herself had not been able to disguise her alarm. A shiver went through her as she wondered if Tony had come to see Mrs. Kehoe and told her of their wedding. Instantly, she thought this unlikely. More likely, she reasoned, was that someone in the queue that day in City Hall had recognized her or Tony, or seen their names, and passed the news on to Mrs. Kehoe or one of her cronies.

She stood up. "Is that all you have to say, Miss Kelly?"

"It is, but I'll be phoning Madge again and I'll tell her I met you. How is your mother?"

"She's very well, Miss Kelly."

Eilis was shaking.

"I saw you after that Byrne one's wedding getting into the car with Jim Farrell. Your mother looked well. I hadn't seen her for a while but I thought she looked well."

"She'll be glad to hear that," Eilis said.

"Oh, now, I'm sure," Miss Kelly replied.

"So is that all, Miss Kelly?"

"It is," Miss Kelly said and smiled grimly at her as she stood up. "Except don't forget your umbrella."

On the street, Eilis searched in her handbag and found she had the letter from the shipping company with the number to call to reserve a place on the liner. In the Market Square she stopped at Godfrey's and bought some notepaper and envelopes. She walked along Castle Street and down Castle Hill to the post office. At the desk, she gave them the number she wished to phone and they told her to wait in the kiosk in the corner of the office. When the phone rang, she lifted the receiver and gave her name and details to the shipping company clerk, who found her file and told her that the earliest possible sailing from Cobh to New York was Friday, the day after tomorrow, and he could, if that suited her, reserve a place for her in third class at no extra charge. Once she agreed, he gave her the time of the sailing and the planned date of arrival and she hung up.

Having paid for the phone call, she asked for airmail envelopes. When the clerk found some, she asked for four and went to the small writing booth near the window and wrote four letters. To Father Flood, Mrs. Kehoe and Miss Fortini she simply apologized for her late departure and told them when she would be arriving. To Tony, she said that she loved him and missed him and would be with him, she hoped, by the end of the following week. She gave him the name of the liner and the details she had about the possible time of arrival. She signed her name. And then, having closed the other three envelopes, she read over what she had written to Tony and thought to tear it up and ask for another but decided instead to seal it and hand it in at the desk with the rest.

On the way up Friary Hill she discovered that she had left her umbrella in the post office but did not go back to collect it.

Her mother was in the kitchen, washing up. She turned as Eilis came in.

"I thought after you had left that I should have gone with you. It's a lonely old place, out there."

"The graveyard?" Eilis asked as she sat down at the kitchen table.

"Isn't that where you were?"

"It is, Mammy."

She thought she was going to be able to speak now, but she found that she could not; the words would not come, just a few heavy heaves of breath. Her mother turned around again and looked at her. "Are you all right? Are you upset?"

"Mammy, there's something I should have told you when I came back first but I have to tell you now. I got married in Brooklyn before I came home. I am married. I should have told you the minute I got back."

Her mother reached for a towel and began to wipe her hands. Then she folded the towel carefully and deliberately and moved slowly towards the table.

"Is he American?"

"He is, Mammy. He's from Brooklyn."

257

Her mother sighed and put her hand out, holding the table as though she needed support. She nodded her head slowly.

"Eily, if you are married, you should be with your husband."

"I know."

Eilis started to cry and put her head down on her arms. As she looked up after a while, still sobbing, she found that her mother had not moved.

"Is he nice, Eily?"

She nodded. "He is," she said.

"If you married him, he'd have to be nice, that's what I think," she said.

Her mother's voice was soft and low and reassuring, but Eilis could see from the look in her eyes how much effort she was putting into saying as little as possible of what she felt.

"I have to go back," Eilis said. "I have to go in the morning."

"And you kept this from me all the time?" her mother said.

"I am sorry, Mammy."

She began to cry again.

"You didn't have to marry him? You weren't in trouble?" her mother asked.

"No."

"And tell me something: if you hadn't married him, would you still be going back?"

"I don't know," Eilis said.

"But you are getting the train in the morning?" her mother said.

"I am, the train to Rosslare and then to Cork."

"I'll go down and get Joe Dempsey to collect you in the morning. I'll ask him to come at eight so you'll be in plenty of time for the train." She stopped for a moment and Eilis noticed a look of great weariness come over her. "And then I'm going to bed because I'm tired and so I won't see you in the morning. So I'll say goodbye now."

"It's still early," Eilis said.

"I'd rather say goodbye now and only once." Her voice had grown determined.

Her mother came towards her, and, as Eilis stood up, she embraced her.

"Eily, you're not to cry. If you made a decision to marry someone, then he'd have to be very nice and kind and very special. I'd say he's all that, is he?"

"He is, Mammy."

"Well, that's a match, then, because you're all of those things as well. And I'll miss you. But he must be missing you too."

Eilis was waiting for her mother to say something else as her mother moved and stood in the doorway. Her mother simply looked at her, however, without saying anything.

"And you'll write to me about him when you get back?" she asked eventually. "You'll tell me all the news?"

"I'll write to you about him as soon as I get back," Eilis said.

"If I say any more, I'll only cry. So I'll go down to Dempsey's and arrange the car for you," her mother said as she walked out of the room in a way that was slow and dignified and deliberate.

Eilis sat quietly in the kitchen. She wondered if her mother had known all along that she had a boyfriend in Brooklyn. The letters Eilis had written to Rose had never been mentioned and yet they must have turned up somewhere. Her mother had gone through Rose's things with such care. She asked herself if her mother had long before prepared what she would say if Eilis announced that she was going back because she had a boyfriend. She almost wished her mother had been angry with her, or had even expressed disappointment. Her response had made Eilis feel that the very last thing in the world she wanted to do now was spend the evening alone packing her suitcases in silence with her mother listening from her bedroom.

At first she thought that she should go to see Jim Farrell

now, but then realized that he would be working behind the bar. She tried to imagine going into the pub and finding him there and trying to talk to him, or waiting while he found his father or his mother to take over the bar as she went out with him and told him that she was leaving. She could imagine his hurt, but she was unsure what exactly he would do, whether he would tell her that he would wait while she got a divorce and attempt to convince her to stay, or whether he would demand an explanation from her as to why she had led him on. Seeing him, she thought, would achieve nothing.

She thought of writing a note to say that she had to go back and posting it in the door of his house for him to find either late that night or in the morning. But if he found it that night, he would instantly seek her out. Instead, she decided, she would drop the note in the door the following morning on her way to the railway station. She would simply say that she had to go back and she was sorry and she would write when she arrived in Brooklyn and would explain her reasons.

She heard her mother coming back and walking slowly up the stairs to her room and she thought of following her, of asking her to stay with her while she packed, and talk to her. But there had been something, she thought, so steely and implacable about her mother's insistence that she wanted to say goodbye only once that Eilis knew it would be pointless now to ask for her blessing or whatever it was she wanted from her before she left this house.

In her room, she wrote the note to Jim Farrell, then left it aside; she pulled her suitcase out from under the bed and placed it on the bed and began to fill it with her clothes. She could imagine her mother listening as the wardrobe door was opened and hangers with clothes on them were pulled off the rail. She imagined her mother tensely following her as her footsteps crossed the room. The suitcase was almost full by the time she opened the drawer where she had kept Tony's letters. She took them and slipped them in at the side of the case. She would read the ones she had not opened on her journey across the Atlantic. For a moment, as she held the photographs taken that day in Cush, the one with her and Jim and George and Nancy, and the one of her alone with Jim as they smiled so innocently at the camera, she thought she would tear them up and put them in the bin downstairs. But then she thought better of it and slowly took all her clothes out of the case and placed the two photographs face down safely at the bottom of the case and then covered them over again. Some time in the future, she thought, she would look at them and remember what would soon, she knew now, seem like a strange, hazy dream to her.

She closed the case, carried it downstairs and left it in the hallway. It was still bright outside, and, as she sat at the kitchen table having something to eat, the last rays of the sun came through the window.

A few times over the hours that followed she was tempted to carry up a tray with tea and biscuits or sandwiches to her mother; her mother's door remained closed and there was not a sound from the room. She knew that if she knocked on the door, or opened it, her mother would firmly tell her that she did not want to be disturbed. Later, when she decided to go to bed, Eilis passed the door of Rose's room and thought to enter, to look for the last time at the place where her sister had died, but, although she stopped outside for a second and lowered her eyes in a sort of reverence, she did not open the door.

As she had not drawn the curtains she was woken by the morning light. It was early and there was no sound except for birdsong. She knew that her mother would be awake too, listening for every sound. She moved quietly, carefully, putting on the fresh clothes she had left out for herself, going downstairs to stuff the old clothes with her toiletries into the suitcase. She checked that she had everything—money, her passport, the letter from the shipping company and the note for Jim Farrell. Quietly, she sat in the front parlour to watch out for Joe Dempsey's car.

When it arrived, she made sure she was at the door before he knocked. She put her finger to her lips to indicate that they should not speak. He put the suitcase in the boot of the car as she left her key to the house on the hallstand. As they drove away, she asked him to stop for a moment at Farrell's in Rafter Street, and, when he did so, she dropped the note through the letter box of the hall door.

As the train moved south, following the line of the Slaney, she imagined Jim Farrell's mother coming upstairs with the morning post. Jim would find her note among bills and business letters. She imagined him opening it and wondering what he should do. And at some stage that morning, she thought, he would come to the house in Friary Street and her mother would answer the door and she would stand watching Jim Farrell with her shoulders back bravely and her jaw set hard and a look in her eyes that suggested both an inexpressible sorrow and whatever pride she could muster.

"She has gone back to Brooklyn," her mother would say. And, as the train rolled past Macmine Bridge on its way towards Wexford, Eilis imagined the years ahead, when these words would come to mean less and less to the man who heard them and would come to mean more and more to herself. She almost smiled at the thought of it, then closed her eyes and tried to imagine nothing more.

Colm Tóibín is the author of six internationally acclaimed novels: *The South,* winner of the *Irish Times*/Aer Lingus Literature Prize; *The Heather Blazing,* winner of the Encore Award for best second novel; *The Story of the Night; The Blackwater Lightship,* a finalist for the Booker Prize and the International IMPAC Dublin Literary Award; *The Master,* a *New York Times Book Review* "10 Best Books of the Year" title, a finalist for the Man Booker Prize, and winner of the International IMPAC Dublin Literary Award, Le prix du meilleur livre étranger, and the *Los Angeles Times* Book Prize for Fiction; and, most recently, *Brooklyn,* winner of the Costa Novel Award. Tóibín is also the author of a book of short fiction, *Mothers and Sons.*

His non-fiction includes *Bad Blood: A Walk Along the Irish Border; Homage to Barcelona; The Sign of the Cross: Travels in Catholic Europe;* and *Love in a Dark Time.* He is also the co-author, with Carmen Callil, of *The Modern Library: The 200 Best Novels in English Since 1950.*

Colm Tóibín lives in Dublin, Ireland.